The Park House

The Park House

A Novel

WRITTEN BY

KACIE FOOS

Library of Congress Cataloging- in Publication Data
Title: The Park House / Kacie Foos
LCCN 2024903281

First American Edition: 2024
Editors: Sarah De Souza and Jennifer Mann
Cover Design: Caterina Baldi
Interior Book Design: Alison Cnockaert

Hard Cover ISBN: 979-8-9900997-0-8
Soft Cover ISBN: 979-8-9900997-2-2

For my Father who read to me,

For my Mother who believed in me,

For my Husband who loves me,

And for my daughter Frankie, never stop chasing

mysterious white rabbits...

Imagine yourself as a living house. God comes in to rebuild that house. At first, perhaps, you can understand what He is doing. He is getting the drains right and stopping the leaks in the roof and so on: you knew that those jobs needed doing and so you are not surprised. But presently He starts knocking the house about in a way that hurts abominably and does not seem to make sense. What on earth is He up to? The explanation is that He is building quite a different house from the one you thought of—throwing out a new wing here, putting on an extra floor there, running up towers, making courtyards. You thought you were going to be made into a decent little cottage: but He is building a palace. He intends to come and live in it Himself.

A QUOTE FROM 'MERE CHRISTIANITY' BY AUTHOR C.S. LEWIS

1

Time

EVERY CLOCK AMELIA passed seemed to demand her attention. She noticed, this particular Thursday at her salon, a diamond- encrusted Rolex a client was wearing—really *stared* at it. Not so much at its beauty, but at the ticking of the seconds. Those ticks were more important now. A shift had happened, and each day she felt as if she was counting down to something important.

"Good morning, Roma Salon, this is Amelia. Yes, we have you down at ten thirty today Mrs. Rochester. Yes, you are confirmed. We look forward to seeing you too. Have a lovely day." She spoke with ease as she answered the phone at her desk, just another well-rehearsed role in the ebb and flow of her workdays.

Amelia was elegant and poised, and what every salon owner in Beverly Hills dreamed of for a receptionist.

Firstly: a natural beauty. It wasn't a shallow thing to want a stunning receptionist to welcome your elite clientele. It was expected.

Secondly: funny. When she needed to be.

Third: she was on a first name basis with all their regulars.

Beverly Hills was and is considered a small town to those who have worked there for a long time, and Amelia had been a staple of the salon for six years. To her, the salon was her Los Angeles family. Her home away from home. She was never nervous around clients—whether it was a Prince from Abu Dhabi, a Washington politician, or the current Oscar winner. She had worked with them all, and carried herself with grace and trustworthiness as she handled thousands of dollars each day.

This particular Thursday, she had put together a cream-colored pant suit she had recently found at a thrift store. Her long dark hair lay elegantly past her shoulders.

Not even the wealthiest of clientele could tell that her hair was actually a wig.

The salon owner, a short, impeccably dressed Italian man named Dante, appeared over Amelia's shoulder to look at her computer screen while holding his scissors in his left hand. Dryers were blowing, the smell of ammonia and hairspray filled the air, and lively Italian music cut through the hubbub.

"Ciao Amelia. Remind me, what time are you leaving today?" he asked in his thick accent.

"I'm leaving at two today, Dante," she whispered, as Oliver, who also manned the reception desk, averted his eyes respectfully and began tapping at his keyboard.

"Okay, perfect." He touched a strand of her wig and forced a smile.

He never knows what to say, Amelia thought.

Health questions weren't legally permitted in the work environment. After all, everyone sues everyone in California for absolutely everything! She remembered a neighbor in her aunt's crappy apartment building who had lost all her money to a man who sued her for accidentally running over his beloved family cat. It had fallen asleep behind her car's tire in the parking lot.

"I will be back tomorrow morning to open." Amelia comforted him.

"Oh no. I have a client that's not on the books coming in at eight. I will be here to open the salon." Dante fumbled telling his lie.

Oliver agreed, "Yes, and I'll arrive a little early to help out."

Amelia didn't have the courage to argue. "Alright, then I'll plan to see you at ten and I can close."

"Take the day off. Come back Saturday. Oliver and I have everything handled."

Oliver was Amelia's confidant as well as co-worker. Like Amelia, his passion was in architecture, restoration, and interior design. They ran the front desk in perfect harmony, a well-paired team.

"Absolutely." Oliver smiled pleasantly. "Closing suits me—I have a date at Crustacean at seven thirty."

"A date you say?" Dante asked, leaning into the desk, "Who with? Who is this man?"

Oliver scoffed and replied, "It was set up through a close friend."

Amelia and Dante exchanged a private glance, knowing that was all he was going to share with them. Oliver was a very private man. Which Amelia highly respected, especially in the environment they worked in, which was consistently filled with gossip about co-workers' love lives or divorces, as well as lengthy post-mortems on the latest customer drama.

"Well, I'm very happy for you," Amelia encouraged him. The phone began to ring and

Dante scurried back into the whirlwind of the salon.

Amelia knew Dante didn't have a client the following morning. That was a lie he had created to cover her. Oliver would be heroically managing the salon by himself tomorrow. They both knew that she would need the day, if not days to recover.

The salon ran like the dress rehearsal for a ballet. Clients and employees entering and exiting the wings, dancing around each other, raising a judgmental eyebrow or praising one another's hard work. The steady noise of hair dryers, laughter, and curse words made for a rather chaotic orchestra.

As business went on as usual, Amelia and her coworker Oliver answered phones and checked clients in with nimble ease. They were masters of the art of transaction. Pay a compliment, take the card or cash, gratuity envelopes, scheduling next appointments, another compliment and goodbye. It was exhausting, and no one knew how much Amelia secretly hated it.

Their desk faced onto the Rodeo Collection's courtyard via a large glass window. The Santa Ana winds were picking up at this time of year, and beautiful pink Bougainvillea petals had started to drift down and sprinkle the white tiles outside. Through the window, Amelia would watch an assortment of handsomely-dressed men and women with shopping bags slink into the courtyard. As they filtered inside, eager tourists would peek through the salon windows, hoping to catch a celebrity sighting. The courtyard was a constant blend of travelers on their vacations and locals living their best lives. Amelia had never personally experienced either.

Yes, she was grateful she had a job that made decent money to pay her bills. Being able to afford insurance was huge for her. Her daily bus route to and from work was manageable, and she was able to meet some of the most remarkable and well-known people in the world. She had been blessed in so many ways, but what she had been facing the last year had taken a toll on her health. She hid it perfectly.

No one would possibly know that she had been battling cancer for the past three months.

It was during a mammogram she had done as part of a workplace health initiative that a doctor had discovered a small tumor in Amelia's right breast. After leaving the medical offices, she took the long bus route back to her Aunt Rita's apartment.

How was this even possible? I'm twenty-seven, she had thought. *Am I going to die before I reach twenty-eight? How long do I have to live?*

"No!" She immediately said aloud on the bus, attracting more than one confused glance from her fellow passengers. That was her immediate response. *No.*

That night she read the leaflet provided by the clinic: Just Been Diagnosed? 6 Next Steps. As it advised, she followed up with her Oncologist—a word which was still unfamiliar, yet would soon become part of her daily vocabulary—and faced her unavoidable scheduled surgery. A biopsy revealed cancerous cells. Her doctor recommended six months of preventative chemotherapy post-surgery to make sure they removed everything. After he left the examination room, she tried to process his instructions. Thinking about chemo, she scratched her head absent-mindedly and thought: *I'm going to lose my hair.*

Then her thoughts turned to Dante. What would he say? What would this mean for her job? Getting through the biopsy had been awful enough, but facing Dante was going to make her tremble at the knees. Her sprightly five-foot-five Italian boss did not look threatening in any way, but it was *how* he would respond that terrified her. He had a secret Napoleon complex which always kept her on her toes.

Trying to calm her nerves as she walked into the salon that day, she reminded herself

that he couldn't fire her for having cancer. That would be unthinkable, as well as illegal. Yet she knew she would be asking a great deal—an unreliable schedule, the unknown factor of what was actually going to happen when she had chemicals rushing through her body.

When she finally found the courage to mutter the words, "Dante, I have cancer."

To her surprise, Dante let out a huge sigh, "Thank God! I thought you were going to quit on me!" He suddenly realized his error, but it was too late and they burst out laughing together. It was the moment they both realized they needed each other.

Dante was first and foremost her employer, and had a temper like a rabid dog, but nonetheless he and Amelia were like family. After all, they spent countless hours together at work. Each year, Dante would travel back to Italy to spend time with his parents and *nonno*, but when he was at home in Los Angeles he lived at the Salon. Dante would open the shop every day, just as Amelia was arriving, and they were often the last people to leave.

Amelia grew up and was living presently with her Aunt Rita's apartment with her cousin Tessa, who had a similar disposition to her mother in that they were equally miserable about everything. They had a similar ability to suck the joy out of any room they entered with their negative outlooks and victim complexes. These two unpleasant women were her only living relatives and they couldn't be more different from herself. Both shorter, clumpy women, with black hair and dark eyes. Tessa always dressed like a Kardashian sister, and Aunt Rita was rarely seen without ill-fitting jeans and a Miami neon brightly colored blouse. They were bitter, jealous, and resentful toward Amelia in every way.

One evening, Amelia had sat down and watched *Pretty Woman* with her Aunt Rita. Her aunt had paused it and pointed to the screen and said, "That's where you need to work!"

Amelia had almost spat out her water she was drinking. "On Hollywood Boulevard? As a prostitute?"

"No, you idiot," Rita replied, delivering one of her signature withering glares. "In Beverly Hills. If you want to be taken seriously, you have to become a part of your client's world. All your clients live in Beverly Hills."

Amelia, who didn't know what she meant, stared blankly at her aunt.

"Listen to me, Amelia. If you get a job there, you can surround yourself with all the right people. Then maybe you can schmooze your way to the top. Work on someone's penthouse. Something like that. Either way, you can't keep living under my roof without paying rent anymore. I took care of you long enough. If you want to stay you have to pay bills."

Rita was right. Amelia needed a job and fast. She knew her aunt would be more than happy to kick her out. So she made the hard choice, deciding to halt her applications for the interior design jobs she dreamt of, and instead consolidated her energy into finding a job on the most famous street in the world. Rodeo Drive.

As luck would have it, she did.

2

The Man With The Lion Head Cane

AMELIA REALIZED WHAT time it was and told Oliver she was heading out for lunch. She grabbed her purse and walked to Ruby's Coffee Shop. As she entered the busy café, she was flirtatiously greeted with a familiar wave from across the counter.

"Hi Amelia."

She greeted him. "Hey Tom."

"What are we having today beautiful?" the barista asked with a smile. Amelia had come to know Tom well over the years and was used to his playful manner. She studied the specials on the menu board.

"I'd love your soup of the day."

"That's it?"

"That's all for me today. I'm on a very tight budget." This was only half the truth.

Really, she could barely stomach anything these days. Broccoli and cheddar soup would be just enough to push her through till evening.

"In that case it's on me today," Tom said with a mock-courteous bow.

"No, Tom, it's not." Amelia insisted. She had become accustomed to

Tom always attempting to treat her to a free meal. She slid the money across the counter. "Thanks, Tom."

"Someday, Amelia," Tom said with a wistful gaze at the ceiling. "Someday!"

In that moment, Amelia suddenly realized the film character Tom had always reminded her of. Ducky from *Pretty in Pink*. She giggled to herself with the image of the character's pointy-toed white shoes in her head as she scoped out a quiet corner table. Reaching inside her purse, she pulled out her book. Lovingly, she touched the familiar pages. The binding was starting to weather away, she noticed. Flipping to the bookmark that held her place, she began to read *Mansfield Park*. Just as she was getting to the bit about Mr Bertram and Maria's triumphant day, the glass door of the café swung open.

She glanced up to see who was entering and found herself completely awestruck by the man who stood proudly in the entryway, a loud *CLACK* at his heels.

After working in Beverly Hills for many years, during her lunch hour she tended to only see people she knew, with the cafes and streets full of familiar faces—aside from the odd tourists that would barge in asking for the nearest restroom or directions.

The man who walked through the door was someone Amelia certainly had never seen before. He reminded her of a dark, twisted character from a Tim Burton film. This tall, lean man stood dressed in black from head to toe. He had very pale skin with a confident and curious smile and sported a black bowler hat. He was undoubtedly younger, then how he dressed. What caught her eye the most was that he was leaning on a long cane. It was no ordinary cane by any means. A large brass Lion Head was fixed as the handle, and a brass fitting at the bottom end made a *CLACK* as it hit the tile floor as if to announce his arrival. Smoke drifted up from his fingers as he lifted a cigarette to his mouth to inhale deeply.

Amelia noticed quickly that she was not the only one who had looked in his direction. She could feel other patrons picking up on his distinct appearance as they traded curious glances from their seats. So she was surprised when she suddenly felt his eyes dart in her direction. Embarrassed by how unguardedly she had been staring at him, she quickly returned her attention to *Mansfield Park*. She could feel the blood rise from her feet up to her face. Flushed, she tried to focus on the words in front of her, but Jane Austen's long, elegant sentences distorted into a blur.

Tom, who was carrying Amelia's soup on a tray, approached the man. "I'm sorry sir, there is no smoking allowed."

Looking down at the broccoli and cheddar soup and back to Tom, the man slowly said—in a thick English accent, "Dear Boy, this cigarette is far less threatening than whatever that is you're carrying,"—then lifted the cigarette to his lips and inhaled.

Tom insisted. "I'm sorry, sir, but you will have to put that out."

The man opened his fingers and dropped his cigarette on the tiled floor, then extinguished it with the brass tip of his cane. Tom watched him, mouth slightly open in shock. "I meant outside, but whatever," he said, collecting himself. "If you'd like to have a seat, I'll bring you a menu shortly."

The man stared back down at the soup Tom was carrying and slightly gagged. He produced a fresh cigarette from his jacket pocket and placed it in his mouth. "I've changed my mind." He tipped his hat in Amelia's direction, who had been listening to their conversation. "Good day."

Amelia's eyes shot back down to her book. Tom arrived at her table, "Here is your soup." he said, placing the large bowl of broccoli and cheddar soup in front of her. It smelled mildly of rotten eggs and had a thick, gloopy texture. She looked away from the soup and back to Tom.

"Who was that strange man?"

Tom glanced back over his shoulder at the curious man standing outside the front glass door, smoking his cigarette, then taking a pocket watch out and checking the time.

"I've never seen him before," Tom said.

They both watched the man staring at his watch for a moment, until a chef in the kitchen yelled: "Tom, we got orders up!"

"I'll be back to check on you." Tom flirted and quickly ran off to the kitchen.

Amelia nodded her head. When she glanced back over her shoulder, she noticed that the man had disappeared. She searched up and down the street through the restaurant's window, but he had vanished just as mysteriously as he had arrived. She sighed, looking down at her bowl and picking up the spoon, she blew on the hot thick liquid and took a slurp. Her stomach turned in protest and she put down the spoon. Her body couldn't handle lunch today.

∽◌◌◌∾

IT WAS TWO o'clock. Amelia had been dreading each passing minute. It was now time. After clocking out on her computer, she began to collect her things in secret distress. She gave a quick goodbye to Oliver and waved at Dante, who was busy blow-drying his client, and Dante returned an encouraging wave goodbye.

As the glass door closed behind her, she imagined herself as one of the fabulous women leaving the salon for the day in head-to-toe Dior—or Vivian Ward, strolling down Rodeo Drive with her shopping bags, smiling because she could finally buy whatever she wanted... everyone admiring her beauty. She dreamed of taking a phone call from a client who would rave that her interior design was going to be featured in the next *Architectural Digest*. She dreamed. She dreamed of anything and everything other than what she was about to do.

But she wasn't Vivian Ward. She was Amelia, and she was walking down Rodeo Drive to the medical offices where she would receive the dreaded word. Chemotherapy.

3

Chemo

THERE IS NOTHING therapeutic about Chemo*therapy*. Just the thought of it made her sick, knowing that she would be running back and forth to a bathroom for the rest of the week, pretending to everyone that she was fine. One round of chemo each month doesn't sound so bad on paper, but it is a horrible reality when played out on someone's body—especially if they are entirely alone.

Her oncologist had recommended six months of preventative chemo just in case there was a cell or two that was missed. The idea made her angry and sad. But here she was, returning for a second round.

As she turned the corner away from her work, she pulled some flats out of her purse and exchanged them for her high heels. The walk was just a mere few blocks away but today it felt like miles. Her long wig was feeling hotter against her scalp by the time that she arrived at the door of the medical offices.

Pulling a medical mask out of her purse, she reluctantly placed it on her face. As if chemotherapy wasn't bad enough, she was forced to wear a mask for the entire procedure. After adjusting the mask strings on her ears and gently straightening her wig, she walked inside.

Despite this being the hottest September LA had seen in years, the hospital seemed to exist in its own climate thanks to a robust HVAC system which emitted icy blasts of air through invisible vents into the corridors, causing Amelia to shiver— *appropriate*, she thought.

She pulled her sweater out of her purse and put it on before she had even reached the elevator. *I'm just stalling. No matter how much time I kill, I still have to go though with this.* She pushed the elevator button going up.

To her unexpected surprise, a very handsome man in scrubs entered the elevator at the second floor. Freckles, broad shoulders and a cheerfully efficient way about him. *In another life*, Amelia thought, *he would be the perfect husband.* He turned around to face her and asked, "How are you today?"

He spoke through his mask and she imagined his perfect white teeth and Ken-like smile. "I'm wonderful, thank you," she lied. "How are you?"

"Can't complain. It's such a beautiful day."

She nodded her head in agreement, "Yes it is."

The elevator stopped for Amelia and the man's demeanor changed subtly. "Have a nice day," he offered. His voice was friendly still, but there was a professional distance which wasn't there before. He knew this was the chemotherapy floor.

"Thank you," she muttered.

Amelia made her way to the reception desk where Elaine, the regular receptionist, was diligently working while an elderly woman stood nearby wearing a Volunteer badge. With a warm smile, Elaine greeted Amelia. "How can I assist you today?"

"I'm Amelia Levingston, and I have an appointment," Amelia replied.

Elaine extended her hand politely. "I'll need your insurance card and your ID, please."

Amelia retrieved her wallet and started searching for her ID and insurance card. She couldn't help but ask, "Don't you folks keep these on record?"

Elaine met her gaze and explained, "Yes, we do. We just need to verify your identity."

At that moment, self-pity got the better of Amelia. "Oh, right. Because of all the different wigs I wear." She regretted this almost immediately. The volunteer standing near Elaine became uncomfortable and wandered away from the desk. Amelia bit her tongue.

"No ma'am." Elaine replied dryly.

"Sorry. Bad joke."

Elaine ignored her. "Take a seat Miss Levingston. Someone will be with you shortly."

"Thank you, Elaine," Amelia said, not meeting her eyes.

She located a nearby chair and turned her attention toward the lobby's television, which showed a colorful reel of scenic landscapes from around the world. Just as Amelia began to daydream about standing high above the savage coastline of Ireland, her thoughts were interrupted by an approaching nurse. "Amelia Levingston?"

Startled, Amelia replied "That's me."

"Is there anyone that will be joining you today?"

"No. Not today."

"Please, follow me," the nurse instructed, leading her around the corner into a smaller room with a solitary chair. "I'll need to collect some lab samples from you first before we proceed."

Amelia complied, settling into the chair and rolling up her sleeve. As she did, she couldn't help but notice the tiny scars on her arm, the telltale marks of the recurring blood work she'd undergone in recent months. The nurse proceeded to attach a blood pressure monitor to her arm and said, "Let's start by checking your temperature and blood pressure."

"Okay," Amelia responded, bracing herself for the usual discomfort. Suddenly, a thick English accent echoed loudly from the chemo lounge down the hallway, shrill with frustration. "Ouch! Be more careful for heaven's sake!"

The nurse rolled her eyes, and Amelia's jaw dropped in surprise. The nurse leaned in and whispered with a hint of amusement, "He's one of our more colorful patients."

Amelia couldn't help but respond with a touch of sarcasm, "Ah, yes, he sounds positively like a modern-day Mary Poppins."

The nurse removed the blood pressure monitor and took a seat next to Amelia, ready to collect her blood samples. Amelia observed the nurse as she began filling vials with blood, a process that seemed all too familiar by now.

As the nurse worked, she maintained a positive demeanor. "Almost finished. Are you feeling alright?" she inquired in a bright voice.

Amelia replied bluntly, "I'll just be happy when this is all over with." Cancer made you less polite, she was beginning to realize.

Once the nurse had entered all of Amelia's information into her computer, she guided her into the chemo lounge. Eight large, tan reclining chairs were arranged in a circle, each facing the center. In one of the chairs, a frail woman was peacefully slumbering under a cozy blanket, while her friend sat nearby, quietly knitting. Then her eyes widened in surprise.

There, seated was the same man who had entered Ruby's Coffee Shop earlier that day. He reclined in his chair with his cane leaning nearby, and a sour expression on his face. She noted the absence of his hat, which lay on the chair to his right, revealing his shiny bald head. His dark blue eyes locked onto Amelia's as she followed her nurse, the sense of unease churning within.

The nurse pointed to the chair on the man's left and said, "You will be sitting here today."

Amelia gently grasped the nurse's arm and implored, "Shouldn't I sit more in the middle so we can give them their privacy?"

The man, seemingly amused, interjected with a snicker, "So she doesn't have to sit near Ebenezer Scrooge himself?"

Sheepishly, Amelia responded. "Oh no, I don't mean that...sir. I just wanted to respect your privacy."

The nurse chimed in, reassuring her. "I'm sorry, but we have a full house today. Every chair in the room is scheduled."

The man's tone turned cold as he remarked, "The cancer business is thriving these days, isn't it?"

From across the room, the woman knitting let out an audible huff in the man's direction. Reluctantly, Amelia settled into the large recliner. The nurse reached for her purse, but Amelia stopped her, saying, "I just need to take my book out." She retrieved her worn copy of Mansfield Park. She noticed the man glance at it, followed by an eye roll and a snort. Irritated, she did her best to ignore him and focus on getting comfortable.

Suddenly, the elderly volunteer from the desk reappeared and kindly offered, "Would you care for a blanket dear? I made these myself."

Amelia inspected the blankets; they were arguably the least appealing she'd ever seen.

"I don't think she wants one, Granny," the man muttered in his gruff English voice.

Amelia shot him an angry look and retorted, "No, that's not true. I would love one. Thank you. Can you just place it beside me, please?"

The volunteer set the blanket down next to her and then gazed sweetly into the man's face. "I understand you're going through a difficult time right now, but there is light at the end of all of this."

"Or dirt. Cold, dark, dirty dirt. But thank you for your kind words, Granny. I will treasure them always." He dramatically turned his head away from her and stared out the nearby window.

Amelia bit her lip hard as she watched the volunteer slowly walk back toward the lobby. It was challenging to resist casting another curious glance at the stranger. She began fidgeting with her book. The man let out a terrible cough. Immediately, she knew it was lung cancer.

He covered his mouth. "Bloody Hell, these masks. I can't breathe with them on. Enough of this."

He removed his mask and set it aside.

Amelia couldn't agree more. Though she wasn't about to say that. Her nurse approached her with the IV solution bags, and she felt queasy. She slowly began to reveal the port over her right chest, trembling as she fought back tears. In this moment, she felt more isolated than ever, wishing she could be anywhere else—maybe on a tranquil beach, somewhere in the Caribbean, sipping a watermelon daiquiri and reading the latest Sophie Kinsella novel. Yes, she'd think of the beach.

"So, what's your death sentence?" This man had certainly mastered the art of rudeness. Amelia stared into his blue eyes, forgetting about the sharp poke of the drip tube which had just pierced her skin.

"The hard part is over," the nurse reassured, returning her focus to the task of setting up Amelia's IV. Amelia was shocked by the nurse's response and glanced back at her in disbelief. When she looked back at the man he sat there, staring down at his hands, seemingly ashamed of what he had just asked, like a boy caught cheating on a test or something.

Amelia looked back to the nurse and asked, "It's over?"

"Your drip has started now. Just try to relax. Do you want the blanket on you?" the nurse asked, offering some solace.

"Yes, thank you." Amelia was grateful for the unsightly blanket at that moment. She arranged it around her shoulders and opened her book, trying to stave off the waves of loneliness which had started coursing through her.

"I'll be back to check on you in a second. And YOU..." the nurse pointed at the man.

"...behave yourself." He started coughing again, causing her to pause. "Do you mind putting your mask back on? I can get you some water as well," the nurse said firmly.

"It's lung cancer. No one's going to catch it," he snapped.

Amelia cut in. "I don't mind at all. He doesn't need to wear the mask. In fact, I'm taking mine off as well. I can't breathe with it on."

The English man seemed as surprised by her retaliation as Amelia was herself; the nurse, however, looked unimpressed. "I'm not going to argue with you both," she said, pursing her lips, then turned on her heel and left.

Amelia turned to the man and quickly introduced herself. "I'm Amelia."

He seemed taken aback by this gesture of friendliness. His face turned slightly red for a moment and he seemed to be searching for the right words.

"Why, I'm the Ghost of Christmas Present," he said eventually, raising his eyebrow then pointedly fidgeting with the brass Lion Head of his cane.

"And here I was thinking you were Ebenezer himself." Amelia replied, without hesitation.

"My name isn't Scrooge, it's Kinsey."

"I would say it's a pleasure, Kinsey, but we would both be lying to each other, wouldn't we?" She looked back down to her book to hide her smile.

He studied her face with what she perceived to be an impressed expression. "You are quite a young person to be fighting cancer. Let me guess, brain?" She frowned at him. "Because clearly you seemed to have damaged a part of it," he continued with a smirk.

"Not that it's any of your business..." she began to say.

"The business of dying," he finished for her. "That's all there is to talk about in here. Dying...death... the rainbow bridge... heaven's gates or hell, fire, and brimstone, depending on how naughty you've been." He raised that dark eyebrow again.

Frustrated, Amelia set her book down and looked deeply into the man's eyes. "If you're not scared of dying, why do you even bother with all of this torture?"

"Because I'm an optimist. Couldn't you tell? I'm a regular Fanny Price." He took his long cane and tapped her beloved book that rested on her lap.

"You're no Fanny Price. I can tell. You're more of a Mr. Rushworth."

Now *that* would irritate him to the core. Satisfied, she picked her book back up and tried to find the page she had left off.

"I am *no* Mr. Rushworth. Perhaps you need to read your book again."

She mimed a thoughtful expression. "Mm, you're right actually. I mean, your impeccably tailored suit suggests to me you have his money but you certainly aren't well-mannered." *You certainly aren't boring, either,* she thought privately.

The atmosphere in the clinic was quiet, almost haunted. It was no place to sit here making jokes like this. She wished that Kinsey would stop talking to her. She looked at his curious bowler hat on the chair next to him, imagining the initials he probably had stitched on the inside, and his polished leather shoes.

"I'm more of a Mary Crawford you see. Wanting what's best for everyone, no matter what the cost." His lip started to curl bitterly, but then it widened out into a grin and continued, "But one thing I know for certain is, you *are* Fanny Price."

He was also an asshole.

Elaine arrived with a piece of paper in her hand, looking slightly annoyed and handed it to Kinsey.

He read it to himself, his demeanor softening to a pitiful pout, looking a bit like a boy who has just found out Santa isn't real. Amelia felt a tug at her heart as she watched him fold the paper back up and place it in his jacket pocket but kept her eyes on her book.

After about ten minutes of random coughing bouts, Kinsey finally opened his mouth and said softly, "I see you are alone."

"How observant of you." Amelia continued reading her book.

"I don't see a ring on your finger."

She took a quick glance, returned to her book and replied, "I don't see one on yours."

"Where's your family?" he asked.

"Dead," Amelia closed her book for the *third* time during their conversation and gave him a hard stare, "and yours?"

Regret washed over his face and then he stared back out the window. "Far away."

She waited a moment then tested him. "Well?"

He snapped his head returning her questionable gaze. "Well, what?"

"Aren't you going ask *how* they died?"

"No. It's none of my business." They locked eyes at this. Amelia was beginning to feel like she was in a staring competition.

"No, it's not. However, because I'm a nicer person than you so I will let you know anyway."

"Fine."

"But you have to share first. Tell me, where does the Burton family hail from?" she teased.

"The Burton family? I'm not a Burton. Who are the Burtons?" he asked, confused.

She gestured with her hand toward his outfit and said, "Clearly you are a close relative of Tim Burton. What dark forest did you enter this world from?"

Kinsey laughed. It was a wonderful thing to witness. His whole body, every joint, seemed to erupt with movement. By now, the chemo lounge had started filling with other patients, and everyone was looking over at them. His laughing turned into coughing. After catching his breath and drinking some water, he looked at her, "I'm going keep you as my new favorite pet."

Amelia didn't know if she should be flattered or disgusted. The bleeping sound of the timer on his IV interrupted their conversation and the nurse reappeared, letting him know he was done for the day. Amelia averted her eyes as the nurse unhooked him from his port. He slowly stood up using his cane and bending over slightly to button his shirt.

"Until we meet again, Miss Amelia...?" He waited.

"Levingston. Amelia Levingston and for the sake of the human race, I hope we *don't* meet again, Kinsey."

He let out his gruff laugh, but it felt looser this time, almost boisterous. "Let's hope not. For the sake of the human race. Ha. Ha."

Watching him walk away, she felt relief, but then came the familiar return of sadness. With the departure of Kinsey, the room had fallen back into its haunted silence. Amelia looked around the circle of people. They all appeared dejected, but there was one crucial difference between her and them: she was alone. Kinsey and Amelia, perhaps, were more alike than she could ever have imagined. Yes, this strange creature from Dark Gables had something in common with her. She had no one, or at least that's how she felt. The truth is that she *did* have her awful Aunt Rita and her cousin Tessa as family. But she would be taking the bus home alone that day and every appointment after.

4

Two White Rabbits

HALLOWEEN LANDED ON a Monday that year. This was by far one of Amelia's favorite holidays. Most Hollywood celebrities would disguise themselves and enjoy the freedom from being chased down like animals by rabid fans. Others would embrace the season's spirit and dress in head-to-toe ghoulish couture for all the wild parties and charity events they had been invited to.

The salons of Beverly Hills would be fully booked from early morning and well past closing time. So of course, Dante was not pleased that Amelia's chemotherapy appointment was scheduled that afternoon. She arrived extra early that morning to make sure the salon was perfect for their busy day. When the glass entry door opened Amelia was greeted by what could only be described as an avant-garde runway show.

Every employee entering wore Oscar worthy costumes. Dante had gone as Marie Antoinette. His white wig stretched heavenward, and his dress was the most perfect bubblegum pink you could ever imagine. Paul and Roxanne, the salon's resident makeup artists, arrived in fantastic Sonny and Cher costumes and her personal favorite was a colorist named Lisa, who arrived dressed as Dolly Parton.

This year, Amelia had pushed herself to think out of the box. Flicking through her book collection, she had stumbled on her copy of *Alice in Wonderland* and the White Rabbit crossed her mind. Joshua loved the idea and decided to partner with her as the Mad Hatter. It was a success.

With her fragile budget, she thrifted and found pieces that worked perfectly. Black suiting pants, a white frilly top, and black vest. Bunny ears with a white curly wig. She even crafted a large clock, attaching a chain from one of her purses to it. The bunny tail took a while to come up with, and finally she stumbled on one of her old school pens that had a perfectly white fluffy ball attached. She pulled it off and hot glued it to her pants. When it was finished, she sat back on her aunt's living room carpet surrounded by glue sticks and breathed a satisfied sigh. It was the first time in weeks that she hadn't thought about the chemo.

When she showed up that day, everyone admired her perfect outfit. Some of them teased her by grabbing her bunny tail when she would pass by. Eventually it fell off when Dante took his turn a little too rowdily. The staff gasped collective "aw's" and "oh no's".

"I'm sorry about your bunny tail, *tesoro* Amelia, I will buy you cake. LET THEM EAT CAKE!" he proclaimed with a flourish of his pink silk glove, and everyone applauded him as he handed her bunny tail back.

Amelia didn't mind. Although it had crossed her mind that it was rather inappropriate for her coworkers to keep reaching for her backside, her attention today remained mostly on the clock on the wall. She was beginning to feel more and more like the white rabbit. *I'm late for a very important date... with chemo.*

When a lull in the salon finally arrived, thanks to the arrival of an elderly VIP customer, Oliver leaned towards Amelia and said in a hushed voice, "I have something exciting to share with you White Rabbit."

"What might that be, Mad Hatter?"

"I've received another job offer," he whispered.

Amelia's heart sank. "No, really? What for?"

"Believe it or not, I got an offer to be an assistant for Kelly Dublin's office."

Jealousy sunk into every cell in Amelia's body, poisoning her from the inside out. Could you get an IV drip to cure you of envy? Not only was Kelly one of Amelia's favorite interior designers, but she was also an absolute legend in the industry.

"Wow," she said, arranging her features into what she hoped was a genuine smile. She *was* happy for him, truly. The fact that he was completely underqualified, and she had studied for three painstaking years for a relevant masters' degree only niggled at her a tiny bit. Mostly, it was just difficult not to feel that a dream she held had been snagged by somebody else, that there was now a tiny bit less hope in the universe.

"That's incredible, Oliver," she said. "How did that happen?"

"Kelly showed up at a dinner party I attended the other night. We were sat across the table from each other, and we started chatting. She mentioned she was looking for a new assistant and I just took a chance and said I was available."

"Sounds like you were at the right place at the right time." Amelia forced a smile.

He lifted his top-hat in a triumphant and playful gesture. "I suppose I was."

Amelia's heart sank but took a deep breath and smiled, lying through her teeth, "I'm happy for you Oliver. That's great news."

He gave her a sidelong glance, his painted-red cheeks and whitened face making him look like a pensive clown. "Let's not pretend you're actually happy about it, Amelia."

"You're right. I'm really sad and jealous. I am extremely jealous." She felt relieved to tell him the truth.

"I'm sharing this with you because I promise that the next opportunity that becomes available, you are my person," Oliver whispered with sincerity.

"Seriously?"

"Of course. You deserve it. You are way more qualified than I will ever be. This is our foot in the door." Oliver grinned, "It's all about who you know, right?"

Right." Amelia smiled and hugged him. "Thank you for thinking of me."

"I'm always thinking of you." He looked at the clock and gasped. "It's nearly two, babe. You've got to go. Kick cancer's ass."

"Thanks Oliver." She was doubtful of her ability to kick any ass in this current state. But her friend's promise had opened up a small fissure of hope in her bitter heart. If by some miracle he could actually make a job at Kelly Dublin's office a possibility for Amelia, it would be life changing. What she had always worked for. The open door to the world she had imagined herself working in from the moment she picked up an interior design book at the library and knew: *Yes. That's what I want to do with my life.*

Every space she walked in from that day forward she imagined how she could transform it. Every bus ride she took to and from work she imagined the building's she passed at their full potential. She found the world to be a beautiful place. Even during this walk through the loneliest and hardest time of her adult life.

The clock struck two and the White Rabbit was off to her date. She walked down Rodeo Drive past witches, Jokers with lurid red-lipstick smiles and will'o'the'wisps, her costume choice attracting nods of approval—and the odd lecherous grin.

When she reached Wilshire Boulevard to turn right toward the medical offices, she looked across the street at the Beverly Wilshire Hotel. As usual, she was reminded of Julia Roberts in *Pretty Woman,* strutting into the hotel with her thigh high black boots and tiny skirt. But her imaginary vision was replaced by a real one as two beautifully dressed women exited the hotel entrance, giggling with each other. That was what life was like in Beverly Hills: life had a way of imitating the movies, rather than the other way around. For a moment, Amelia imagined herself walking out of the hotel dressed like them, in head-to-toe designer clothes and enjoying the afternoon without a care in the world. *In another life*, she thought.

After a short walk, she arrived at the dreaded chemo lounge. Today, Elaine the receptionist was wearing a Harry Potter costume, glasses and scar included. Amelia, remembering their awkward exchange last time, quickly placed her ID card on the counter.

Elaine looked at Amelia from under her glasses. "Great costume."

"Thank you," Amelia smiled brightly. "Big Harry Potter fan?"

The receptionist slid the card off the counter and replied: "Yes."

Not the friendliest woman, Amelia thought, as she made her way down the hallway.

As much as she was dreading chemo itself, her main focus of her attention was a certain gruff man dressed in odd clothes. Carefully, she listened down the hallway for a British accent, hoping against her better judgment that he would be there at the same time as her. Yes, he was terribly unpleasant. But he was interesting. As a sort of anthropological specimen.

Amelia always found people fascinating, and in her job she was privileged to meet many of them. She had met royalty, politicians, musicians, sports figures, yet this was the man she couldn't stop wondering about. He didn't seem entirely real to her; it was like he was a character from one of the thousands of books she'd read in her lifetime. *Who was he? Where was he from? What was his story?* She was so lost in her thoughts that she didn't even realized Elaine had been holding her cards out for her to take back for about a minute.

"Oh, sorry." She said as she took her cards back. Before she took a seat in the waiting room, the elevator opened, and she heard the familiar

CLACK of Kinsey's cane. There he was. This time fully dressed in a rich, plum-purple, double-breasted suit, bowler hat in a matching color, with two holes through which long white bunny ears protruded. Swinging in a circle from his hand was a long gold watch hanging from a chain. "I'm late for my important date with the devil," he deadpanned, making a show of taking his hat off and bowing to Elaine, who, as usual, was unimpressed.

Kinsey turned to see Amelia in her costume, erupted into a coughing fit, then proclaimed: "So Fanny Price has transformed herself into "The White Rabbit".

5

Tick Tock

AMELIA AND KINSEY studied each other's matching 'White Rabbit' costumes amused with themselves.

"Why, if it isn't *you*," Amelia said, then wished she had thought of something more original.

His face cracked open into that grinch-like grin. "Our stars must be crossed. Or is that ships? I can never remember how the saying goes."

The nurse arrived. "Amelia Levingston?"

Amelia stood up, holding her own watch. *It's time.* "Tick tock."

He grimaced holding his own watch in hand. "Tick tock indeed."

She felt Kinsey's eyes burning into her during the whole walk to the treatment room.

Later, after she had finished bloodwork and the nurse had connected her to her chemo drip, she attempted breathing exercises to calm her nerves. She felt a chill, most likely from the treatment. Or was it in fact that Kinsey was about to enter any moment? The circle of chairs, which were normally full of patients, was entirely empty except for Amelia.

I get it, she thought. *Everyone must be with their families for Halloween.*

There was a familiar clacking sound and soon Kinsey entered the room, the nurse gesturing for him to sit across from Amelia. He pointed in the opposite direction. "Oh no. Us rabbits must stick together."

The nurse looked at Amelia with an inscrutable expression. "Is this alright?"

Kinsey interjected: "Of course it's alright. Amelia insisted."

She opened her mouth to protest, but the nurse had already disappeared, and Kinsey was shaking out the creases in his plum trousers, readying himself to sit beside her. Amelia held her copy of Roald Dahl's *The Witches* tightly trying to read while the nurse hooked him into his therapy. It was awkward to say the least—until he interrupted the silence with that gravelling, low voice which—Amelia felt annoyed to realize this—sounded like honey, and the crunching of boots on dry pine.

"No Alice with you today?" he asked with a serious expression. She narrowed her eyes at him in confusion. "No Mad Hatter?" he continued in the same tone. "How about the Queen of Hearts? Where are all your visitors, my pet?"

Amelia indulged him and set her book down. "I'm not that interesting, I suppose."

He shook his head confidently, "Oh no, you are by far the most interesting person I've met in years and that says a lot." Here he raised his eyebrows and tried unsuccessfully to repress a cough. "That says quite a lot."

He removed his medical mask and Amelia did the same. "There's that beautiful face." He studied her for a moment. "Whoooo are youuuuu?" This Alice in Wonderland shtick was starting to spook her.

"I'm just Amelia," she said with a deliberate poker face. "Born and raised in Los Angeles. My story begins here and ends here."

This was a well-rehearsed answer for Amelia—one she regularly doled out when asked questions like 'What's your story?' or 'So who's the real

Amelia?' But today, for the first time ever, looking around the empty circle of chairs, she believed it. She had no story, no history. She was a page without writing on it. An image suddenly entered her mind of the frail woman who just one month before had been sleeping in her chair, trying to fend off the poisoned cells in her body.

"There is much more to you than that. I can tell." He stated without hesitation, with a cutthroat honesty that made her stomach flutter. He took his cane and used the brass end to point at her book, "And I see you are reading *The Witches*. Roald Dahl and his twisted imagination, how wonderful."

"I am."

"First *Mansfield Park*, now *The Witches*, I'm intrigued. Do you like to read or are you a Reader?"

"I'm a Reader," she answered, with total conviction in her words.

He smiled and his dark blue eyes seemed to brighten and glimmer with hope, "How many books would you say you read a week?"

She thought a moment and answered, "Maybe three. More when I'm not feeling like this." His eyebrows raised and he smiled, setting his hand on his chin and continuing to observe her like she was a rare oil painting or endangered flower. "You are a bit unnerving," she admitted.

"I get that all the time." He looked satisfied with himself. "Do tell me more. We have all the time. What makes you tick...tock?"

"I assume you are asking for my story?"

"Like you, I am a reader myself. I would love nothing more in this moment to read the autobiography of Amelia."

Amelia knew he wanted more and so she caved in and shared her sad story.

"My dad died when I was two. Cancer." She held her hands up to the room in mock surprise. "Shocker. Mom decided to become a nurse after that. She was on her way to her shift at the hospital and died in a car accident when I was ten." The humorous expression in his eyes dissolved a bit, and was replaced with something softer, something Amelia couldn't quite read. He rubbed his eyebrows. "I moved in with my Aunt Rita and my wicked cousin Tessa."

"Wicked you say? So not Fanny Price after all. More of a Cinderella story."

"No. I'm no princess."

"Yet. Your story hasn't finished yet, has it?" he asked. "You just haven't met your fairy godmother yet."

She was embarrassed to feel a warm buzz spark up in her chest and make its way to her cheeks. "I suppose not."

"No, your story is just beginning."

"I'm not so sure anymore." She sighed.

"So your parents have tragically died. You moved in with your aunt…"

"I live with my aunt. Presently." She corrected him.

Laughing, he replied, "No. How is that possible? You must be at least thirty."

"I'm twenty-seven."

"You still live with your aunt?" He laughed.

Slightly offended, she fought back, "Do you have any idea what it costs to live in Los Angeles?" She studied his outfit. He watched her look down to his shoes. "Oh, I see, I suppose money doesn't matter to you, does it? I can't even afford my treatments. I'm going to be paying off my medical bills for the rest of my life. However much longer that might be."

Kinsey corrected her, "It's never polite to discuss Money, Politics, or Religion with others."

The way he said it struck her heart. He was from a different time. An older world than hers, filled with confusing rules for how to behave, impeccable manners, stiff upper lips.

"Well, I'm Christian, between parties, and barely making ends meet. Thank you for *not* asking."

Her honesty must have hit a nerve. He avoided eye contact with her for a moment. His eyes closed and he coughed. "Do you hear that?"

"What?" she asked.

"That's Death calling my name. Not God."

He looked at her with his deep blue eyes. When she met them, she saw nothing but doubt. He looked like a lost boy. Not exactly sure what she should say, she was grateful when he changed the topic of conversation for them both. "Tell me, what do you do?"

"This isn't fair. I don't know anything about you," she protested.

"Answer my question and then I will grant you three questions. I warn you, don't waste them. Only three answers you will get." He grinned in delight at his own wit.

"Three questions?"

"Three." he repeated in delight while raising three long fingers in the air.

"Fine. I'll play your game. I work at a Salon in the Rodeo Collection as a receptionist."

"So that's your job. But that's not what you want to *do*. No one wants to be a receptionist. The woman at the front here wants to be a young wizard." he joked.

"I have a degree in interior design."

"Ah. So you have the rare gift of walking into a room and seeing it not as it is, but as it could be."

She couldn't help but smile at his comment. "It's my turn now to ask you a question."

Before she could finish he held up his long finger and warned, "Don't waste them, my pet."

He grinned again, waiting patiently for her question.

"Please don't call me your pet."

"Very well, we shall be friends." He declared.

She offered her hand and he grinned and took it shaking it. "Friends." she agreed. She smiled, leaned in and asked, "Now, friend, who is your family?"

Kinsey's face shifted and he suddenly looked though he was being tor-

tured from the inside. Amelia was filled with instant regret. Thankfully—
and she couldn't believe she was thankful for *this*—the nurse arrived at that
very moment. "How are you feeling Mr. Bonneville?"

Bonneville? Amelia thought.

"At this present moment, I'd love a stiff martini. One olive."

"Would you like some water?" the nurse asked evenly, her straight
face neither denying nor confirming that she got the joke.

"Fine," he doffed his bowler hat at her.

"And you, Miss Levingston?"

"I'm fine, thank you."

Once the nurse had left, Amelia turned to give Kinsey a hard stare.
He returned her stare and impatiently asked, "Well?"

"What?"

"Ask me a question?"

"I did!" she said, confused.

"Well then, you got your answer. Or were you not paying close attention? Don't waste your second question. Go ahead. I'll be waiting."

Amelia was finding it hard to focus on what he was saying because
ever since the nurse had spoken, she had been repeating the name *Bonneville* over and over in her head. She wasn't going to give him the satisfaction of knowing that, though. "Fine, what do you do for a living?"

He placed his hand lovingly on the brass lion head of his cane. "I like
to read," he gave her a meaningful sidelong glance at this, "To live. And
I love—well, *loved*, to laugh." He smirked again.

"That's not a job." Amelia jabbed, frustrated at his response. "And
are you aware you sound like a quote on a fridge magnet?"

"What's a fridge?" he said, then: "That's just what I do for a living,
Amelia darling. That's what I do." He closed his eyes. "No more questions today. I'm finished."

"Excuse me, I'm allowed two more questions, Mr. Bonneville."

His eyebrows raised but his eyes remained shut. Amelia felt tired as well. Her day had caught up with her and her eyes drooped shut. Before she knew it, she felt his hand on hers. Her eyes shot open, but his, she noticed, were firmly closed.

He looked exhausted. He looked like... he was dying.

What was it about him? An unfamiliar feeling stirred inside of her and suddenly she knew.

Trust. A word she hadn't felt since she was a twelve.

She held his hand and didn't let go. A perfect stranger, the strangest of strangers. But in that moment, that horrible moment, they were the same. Two white rabbits, watching time slowly ticking on their clocks, not knowing when their time would stop and Wonderland would call to them.

Amelia drifted asleep.

◈

IT WAS THE most terrible dream. She chased her Mother through the streets of Los Angeles and her mother wouldn't stop running from her. Her long brown hair blew behind her but Amelia couldn't see her face. She kept screaming for her to stop running but she wouldn't. When her mother finally stopped to turn around and face her, she held up a pocket watch for Amelia to see and pointed at it. Amelia awoke covered in sweat. Kinsey was gone.

As she reached for her water, something fell down the side of her leg onto the cold vinyl floor. She reached for it and picked it up. It was a business card. The card was black with an embossed gold lion head printed on its front. She turned the card over and printed on it was *Henry Bonneville XI, Marquess of Nottinghamshire* and a phone number.

The nurse approached and Amelia had to tear her eyes away from the card. "You are all finished. I was just letting you rest. Do you have a ride home today? Or do you need us to call someone for you?" the nurse asked.

Amelia's fibbed. "Of course. My aunt Rita is giving me a ride home. She's going to pick me up outside."

Amelia put her things together and stopped at the restroom. Her reflection was just as she imagined, a ghost of herself. Once she left the building, exhaustion started to set in. Trying her hardest, she pulled herself together and started walking toward Wilshire Boulevard to catch her first bus home.

6

The Marquess

IT WAS LATE morning, a beautiful November fall day, and Amelia was finally feeling better. Her previous chemotherapy session had taken a huge toll on her health and she missed several days of work. With Oliver's two-week notice, Dante scrambled to hold it together in her absence. He was so relieved to have her back. She gracefully directed their daily clientele, enjoying sipping on a green tea Dante had surprised her with earlier that morning. She was quite content to be at work and have her mind on something other than how sick she had been feeling.

Oliver was on the phone handling a very difficult client with the courage and poise of a kung fu master. She gave him a look of tacit encouragement, noticing that he was reaching his boiling point, "No, Mrs. Irving. She's not available today. I assure you that you are on the waitlist. Yes, I know it's your niece's wedding on Saturday. We are trying our best to get you in." He looked up for a second and exchanged a knowing look with Amelia. Given how exclusive Dante's salon was, part of their daily routine involved the constant ebb and flow of incoming requests for last-minute engagements followed by the commonly used excuse of, 'Don't you know who I am?' Like clockwork she heard Oliver reiterate, "Yes, I know who you are Mrs. Irving. Your family is very important to us and we will notify you as soon as we can get you in." Oliver hung up his phone and exhaled, "I'm getting an espresso."

"You are almost done! Just one more day." Amelia encouraged him.

"Yes, just one more day."

Oliver walked back to the break room for a moment to himself. The phones had quieted down some and Amelia glanced inside her purse that rested on the floor. She fished out the black card that had been haunting her thoughts. She still hadn't mustered the courage to phone Kinsey. Or should she be calling him Henry? Henry Bonneville the *Eleventh*. Her curious stranger must hail from a very old English family. Finally, she Googled him. She wanted to know what she was getting into with this new friendship. She typed in his name, and several photographs popped up on the screen of a much healthier and more handsome version of him.

She scrolled down and there was a photograph of Kinsey walking with a younger handsome man that had the same exact blue eyes. *Who is that?* After studying the photo for a minute, she moved on and noticed that the odd word which she had seen on the card cropped up multiple times on the screen of her computer. Marquess. Before she could do more research, she was interrupted.

"Who is this?" Dante asked, peering over her shoulder. Amelia tried to shrink down her screen, "No, no bring this up. I must see this man." Dante became the most Italian version of himself as he leaned in. "Henry Bonneville the Eleventh. He is handsome. How do we know this man."

"I don't especially know him *well*," Amelia replied, with deliberate nonchalance.

"Is he a new client? If he is, you must send him to me. Oh, he's a Marquess. How interesting." Dante said, just as an assistant who was struggling with a client's balayage called him over to the main salon. "I want to know more. We will talk," Dante said in a stage whisper, walking away.

Amelia continued to read about Kinsey. As speculated, he originated from an English family that had some social stature. The Bonneville's were a much more distinguished family than she could ever have imagined. Another photograph of Kinsey standing with his cane caught her attention, as he was holding the same Brass lion headed cane that she thought about during all hours of the day. *Click clack.* She could hear it as clearly as if he were in the room.

"My darling Amelia." She looked up in astonishment as Kinsey's voice suddenly sounded from the glass doorway. Dressed in a navy-blue double-breasted suit, a matching bowler hat, and matching dark blue leather shoes with his cane comfortably at his side, he stood with a warm smile staring at her. "You never called. So, I'm calling upon you."

Amelia's mouth dropped in surprise. Oliver returned to the desk studying Kinsey's dashing look. "Hello sir, how can we help you today?"

Before Amelia could speak up, Dante reappeared. "Oh, it's the man, The Marquess man."

Kinsey looked impressed and shocked, looking at Amelia's embarrassed face, "I see you've been talking about me."

Mortified, she explained: "No, I really haven't. I promise."

"Now now, don't lie, Amelia." Kinsey teased.

Before she could say another word, Dante took over their conversation in his confident circus-master way, hand out ready to greet them flirtatiously. "I'm Dante. This is my salon. You are most welcome. Would you care for an espresso? A haircut with me perhaps?" He waggled a suggestive eyebrow at the tall English man.

"I'm so flattered Dante, but alas," Kinsey removed his hat to reveal his bald head, "There is no hair to cut, darling."

Dante exchanged a knowing glance with Amelia and she shrugged her shoulders.

Breaking the growing silence, she said: "Kinsey, would you like to join me in the courtyard for a moment?"

"Dante darling," he returned with unusual charm, "may I borrow your Amelia for an hour or so? I would love to treat her to a cup of tea. I will make it worth your while." He winked at the smaller Italian man, who turned red and giggled nervously.

"Why of course, Amelia. Go, go and have your fun. Take as long as you need with your Marquess man." Dante waved them off.

"Marquess man!" Kinsey let out a guffaw.

Amelia kissed Dante's cheek and grabbed her purse.

Outside in the courtyard Kinsey offered his arm to Amelia and she took it, and together they strolled as if they had been friends for years. The clack of his cane echoed slightly on the tiles of the Rodeo Collection courtyard, at regular intervals, as if their walk together was choreographed. "Look at all these petals. Such a mess." He pointed with his cane at all the wilted Bouganvillea petals on the ground.

"I think they are perfectly lovely," Amelia said, petals floating around under her feet.

"Why didn't you call me?" he asked.

"I'm so sorry. I truly was going to," she replied, knowing she didn't quite mean it, because to call him would have been like admitting he was a real person and not a gothic concoction from the pages of one of her books.

He sighed, "I was hurt. Then I realized you must have had your head in a toilet like myself. Then I thought, why wait until we're dead. So here I am."

"How did you find me?" she asked.

"I have my ways."

He's enjoying this game, she thought. Being a bit mysterious was clearly his greatest pleasure, after laughing, living, and reading. They walked out to Rodeo Drive where an extremely handsome driver was waiting, standing proudly next to a silver Rolls- Royce Phantom parked on the curb. He opened the door for Amelia and Kinsey as they approached.

"After you, my pet," Kinsey smiled pointing his cane toward to the door.

"Please stop calling me that."

"My apologies. After you, Amelia darling."

Amelia squinted at him. "You have your own personal *driver*?" He shrugged as if to say, *no big deal.*

She looked over her shoulder, in the direction of the salon. "I really shouldn't be gone too long, Dante will start to worry..."

"I'll have you back in an hour." He took his cane and pointed inward to the car.

"Well, where are you taking me exactly?"

"We have a very important date and we shan't be long." She wasn't going to give him the satisfaction of jumping in the car with no questions asked, despite the fact that this seemed like an increasingly marvelous idea, so she waited a moment. "Well, what are you waiting for?" he asked.

"Well, are you sure this is *your* car? Shouldn't you be driving a hearse?" She smiled in anticipation of his reply while the driver snorted, seeming to fight back a laugh.

Kinsey, who looked like he was battling the grin which had just taken over his entire face, took his cane and pointed once more at the gleaming interior of his beautiful vehicle.

"Please get in, you clever girl."

Two finely dressed women walking past carrying Chanel shopping bags slowed to look at them and the car. More and more people were stopping to starting to stare. Amelia wasn't used to this kind of attention. She was beautiful, yes—but gorgeous women were common in Beverly Hills and she hardly drew glances except for when she was in the café. Amelia's curiosity and the pressure of the audience overwhelmed her. "Fine. But I must be back in one hour."

"I promise," he said with an unnerving ease.

She sat down on the luxurious leather seat. There was a lingering cigarette smell blended with a men's cologne that smelled like bergamot and mandarin orange. The interior of the car was like nothing she had ever experienced. Kinsey sat down next to her and slid his cane between them both. The brass lion head stared at her in an ominous way. She noticed how worn down the brass had become, almost a metallic color of gold. It seemed very old.

"That cane didn't originally belong to you, did it?" she asked him.

Kinsey's cleared his throat.

His driver sat down in his seat and closed his door. Without saying a word, he started their journey up Rodeo Drive. "You are very observant darling."

As they drove past the luxury brand stores she thought to herself, *so this is what this feels like, to arrive on Rodeo Drive.* Everyone they drove past tried to get a glimpse at who was inside this amazing ride. "So where are you really taking me, Henry Bonneville the Eleventh Marquess of Nottinghamshire?" she said scheming.

He cried out: "Oh, please don't call me Henry. Kinsey, always to you darling."

"Alright Kinsey where are we driving to?" she asked.

"We are off to meet our friend the Mad Hatter of course." He grinned in satisfaction.

"Isn't that supposed to be you?"

He touched his hat lovingly. "I do enjoy my hats, always have. But today we white rabbits are guests to a tea party."

"You weren't kidding? We truly are going to a tea party?"

"Yes, we truly are having afternoon tea."

"How very English of you."

7

The Antiquarian

IT WAS A short drive through Beverly Hills into a nearby neighborhood. After turning left onto Sunset Boulevard, the driver veered to the right, where a gate awaited them just off the road. He pulled up to a box near the car and spoke to it. "I have Lord Henry Bonneville and his guest Miss Amelia Levingston."

There was no reply, the gate simply opened, and they pulled up the road and into the private residence. It was a large, peaceful home. Nestled behind trees and large perfectly trimmed topiaries. This was an 'Old Hollywood' mansion standing timeless in its Tudor style, every inch of it surrounded by rose bushes of every color, just starting to fade with the arrival of fall. As their car slowly pulled up to the main entrance of the house and parked, Kinsey looked to Amelia in excitement, "We're here."

"Is this your home?" Amelia asked.

"I told you," he said, his gruff voice turning into a reassuring purr. "We are guests."

He had a difficult time getting out of the car and accepted his driver's arm willingly. Amelia waited until he was done, then slid out of the car discretely. Kinsey side-eyed her.

"Next time," he said quietly and quickly, "wait for your driver to open your own door and then step out."

"You British men and your etiquette," she teased.

A loud happy, "Hello my dears!" rang out as a jolly, robust man of about forty burst through his front doors. He man-waddled over to Kinsey, wearing long pink pants. His matching kimono floated gracefully behind him, giving the whole ensemble a look of effortless beauty. His arms were flung wide open, and he was giggling with infectious delight. When he reached Kinsey he raised his hands to his face and smiled, "My my, Henry Bonneville. What a delicious surprise."

The two men embraced each other and exchanged kisses on each cheek. Kinsey seemed overjoyed to see his friend. Amelia, unused to receiving such a warm welcome, felt strangely moved.

"Allow me to introduce you to my dear friend, Amelia Levingston." Kinsey held his hand out to Amelia.

"Hello sir." Amelia shyly greeted him.

He took her hand, kissed it violently, and smiled at her. "I'm Merry. You are very welcome here my dear."

"I've brought her for afternoon tea." Kinsey told him.

"And tea we shall have!" He clapped excitedly. "Ms Beaumont!"

A woman appeared outside his doorway. "Yes sir?"

"We shall be having tea at my round table please."

"Wonderful." Ms. Beaumont vanished back into the house as they walked toward it.

"Merry....?" Amelia asked.

"Just Merry, dear," he beamed. "And I am... the most *merry* to see you both. Kinsey, darling, it's been ages." He offered Kinsey the crook of his elbow in an adorable, old-school gentlemanly manner, and helped his friend walk slowly toward his house.

Looking back over her shoulder at the vaulting gates and the ornate garden fountains, Amelia thought of the VIP client at the salon who had refused to give a surname, and requested to be known as 'Jemima. Just Jemima.' She realized it was probably a similar deal with Merry, and that she would not be getting a surname out of him. Privacy was a luxury only money could buy, and she likely would be leaving the house today with more questions than answers.

"Merry my love," Kinsey crooned, "Amelia has a very busy schedule today but I promised her that you have the best tea in town, so I brought her straight here. Also..." Kinsey leaned in and whispered something into Merry's ear.

Merry's eyes got big as they lit up and he smiled. "Of course. Why, of course. How wonderful. Anything for you, my friend."

His home was a masterpiece, the perfect blend of Elizabethan and Californian—if there even is such a thing. Plants blending and weaving in and out of well-lit hallways, white oak with inspired royal blue walls and paintings that looked like they had been pulled straight from the Renaissance period—with an occasional modern splash of what she could only imagine was fresh out of Art Basel.

Two great Danes suddenly started galloping towards them, both wearing what looked like diamond-encrusted dog collars. Amelia leaned down to greet them. "And who are we?" she asked in delight.

Merry giggled happily, "These are my two children. May I introduce you to the *Great Dane* Judy Dench and the *Great Dane* Maggie Smith." He loved on Maggie, giggling at his wit.

Amelia petted Judy Dench. "Why, of course you are." She gestured at Kinsey to join in, but he was keeping his distance and looking rather sheepish.

"Kinsey isn't a fan of dogs," Merry explained teasingly.

"Oh come on," Amelia said. "You don't like dogs?"

"I like dogs, I just prefer a life without dogs in it. I do adore a good painting of a dog. Our late queen's Corgis were a wonder to behold." He looked over to Merry with concern. "I wonder what happened to them."

"I believe they are living with Fergie now."

Truly concerned, Kinsey replied, "No. Is that right?"

"Yes, I believe so."

Amelia squinted at the two men for signs of insincerity, but they were being serious, and both shook their head in sadness.

"Follow me everyone," Merry announced, appearing to shake off his grief at the prospect of Her Royal Highness's orphaned pooches. He led them through his house, gliding through the corridors dreamily, opening two glass doors which brought them out into a courtyard fit for the Queen herself. Roses of different colors bloomed in sumptuous garden beds, and a large round stone table awaited them with eight chairs.

There were various ornate stone sculptures dotted around the table, the most notable of which had a medieval-style sword growing from its center.

"Do have a seat you two," Merry said gleefully, watching her eyeing up the sword. "All seats are equal at *my* round table."

She sat across from Kinsey and Merry. The stone courtyard had an eerie stillness to it which reminded her of children's books by C S Lewis, and made her feel as if some ancient rite or sacrifice were about to take place. Floating in like a ghost right on cue, Ms. Beaumont reappeared pushing a cart carrying a large tea tray with a pot and three teacups, a sugar bowl, and milk as well as stacked plates that held sandwiches and little cakes, and then began to serve everyone in an exquisitely mannered way.

"Hello," Amelia greeted her.

She smiled back at her as both Kinsey and Merry whispered with one another. Ms. Beaumont poured her tea first. "Do you take milk or sugar, Miss?" she asked.

Thinking of the nutrition leaflet she'd received at the clinic, Amelia grimaced. "Neither," she sighed. "Thank you." As she began to serve Merry and Kinsey, Amelia turned to Merry. "Your home is wonderful," she said dreamily.

He smiled at her in genuine delight. "Thank you, Amelia, it's my refuge. An Englishman's house is his castle, after all. He smiled at Kinsey who nodded in agreement.

Ms. Beaumont left the courtyard in the same seamless way that she had entered.

"I'm so curious. How did you two meet?" Amelia asked.

"I met Ms Beaumont when I was holidaying in Cornwall. She was working for a friend of mine and I was in awe of her kind nature and wisdom. She changed my life. I couldn't bear to live another day without her helping me navigate my universe," Merry explained.

"I believe Amelia was enquiring about how *we* met, dear." Kinsey smiled over at his guests benignly.

"Oh, good heavens." Merry replied, giggling, "Kinsey and I met at an antique book auction about fifteen years ago back in London. Portobello Road, I think it was."

"Was it really that long ago?" Kinsey asked.

"Yes."

"Indeed. We were both after the same book, or books I should say," Kinsey scoffed.

Merry nodded and then threw his hands up in the air in victory, "I won."

Kinsey rolled his eyes in good humor at his friend, then sipped his tea. Amelia noticed this was the most relaxed she had ever seen him.

"Kinsey doesn't take loss well, so he tried to talk me out of it," Merry continued. "He couldn't, and so, we became dear friends."

"Did we?!" Kinsey said, raising his eyebrows in mock-surprised, but he looked fondly at his friend. It was obvious they were true friends and had been such for a long time.

Kinsey took out a cigarette and lit it. Merry quickly took it from him and threw it to the ground. "These will kill you, my friend."

"They already have." he muttered with a twinge of that gruffness

Amelia was surprised to find, she had started to miss. He took out another cigarette and lit it.

"It's never too late to make better choices." Merry crossed his arms and pouted in disapproval, looking like a wizened, orange child.

Kinsey looked over to Amelia, as if to get her consensus, and she nodded sadly in agreement. He rolled his eyes to the heavens, took one last inhale, and dropped the cigarette to the ground, squishing it out with the brass end of his cane.

Merry studied Kinsey's forlorn expression. "Perhaps we ought to see each other a bit more these days."

"Alas, Merry, this may be one of my last stops on the road to Mordor." Kinsey schemed.

Silence filled the courtyard. Feeling increasingly uncomfortable, Amelia asked in desperation, "What do you do for a living, Merry?"

"Amelia," Kinsey cut in, "it's never polite to discuss religion, politics, or *money*." He sat back in his chair with the look of an algebra teacher who has just delivered an important correction.

"Oh I'm sorry, Merry," she said, heat rushing to her face, "I didn't mean to pry."

"Tish tosh," the older English man said. "Don't pay any attention to *him* Amelia. First and foremost, I come from a very affluent family, much like Kinsey here." The man in question stared pointedly at the sword in the stone, perhaps wishing he could will it back into life. "But alas, our stories are so similar, we were not the children our families wished us to be. Two lost boys who much preferred Neverland to Parliament, if you know what I mean dear." He winked at her.

Amelia assumed that he meant they were both gay and nodded in agreement, with an expression she hoped seemed wise and knowing. "I understand."

"I fled my family to California to find some peace and sunshine," he continued in his pleasant, meandering way. "Now I mostly dabble in art dealing and antiquities, and perhaps I've also quietly produced an occasional film. The operative word being quiet."

Kinsey leaned in, almost seductively. "Now why don't you share with Amelia what your favorite hobby is?" he purred, and Amelia detected the glint of playfulness which had entered his eyes when he talked about living and laughing and the White Rabbit's lateness. "What you love more than anything in the world, Merry."

Merry leaned. in, staring deeply into Kinsey's eyes. "What's that Kinsey, my love?" he asked.

Kinsey smiled. "Why I've brought her *here* today."

Amelia leaned into their secret conversation, too intrigued by the outcome to feel left out as she normally would have. Merry smiled and wildly announced: "I'm a self-proclaimed Antiquarian."

8

Our Jane

ANTIQUARIAN. ONE OF Amelia's favorite words. A person who loves to deal with antiques, more specifically rare books. She had found herself sat at a stone table, with two people who loved and respected literature, just as she had all her life.

"Oh. Oh, how perfectly wonderful." Visions of her mottled editions of Austen, Carroll and du Maurier rose before her eyes. "Well, that makes sense as to how you both met."

"Amelia loves books, Merry. She's one of us. She's an *Inkling*." Kinsey smiled.

"I do," she said breathlessly, feeling at once like a child and also as if she had just been initiated into a secret club. I love to read. Books are the great love of my life."

"Wonderful, dear," said Merry.

"I also love architecture and design," she started saying, talking fast and excitedly. "I graduated with a Bachelors in Interior Design," Amelia proudly shared.

"Don't brag, Amelia," Kinsey teased.

"Tish tosh, Kinsey. You are horrid. My dear, that is wonderful for you," Merry told her. "I have *many* friends, with money, that are in desperate need of a house lift."

Kinsey finished his tea and struggled to stand up with his cane. "Shall we, Merry?" Kinsey said brightly to his friend, who had been watching his shaky ascent from the chair with concern. "I've promised to get Amelia back to her day job. I won't have her be in any trouble on my account."

Merry put a steadying hand on Kinsey's back and his friend mirrored the gesture.

Amelia's heart filled with tenderness. They walked slowly into Merry's home, the three of them, Kinsey relying more on his cane as they got to the stone steps leading down from the foyer.

When they arrived at a closed door, Merry stopped still in his tracks and shot Kinsey an interrogative glance. Kinsey made a harrumphing sound, but then shrugged his shoulders in acquiescence, and then both men turned to look at Amelia. She waited.

That beautiful, childlike smile broke out over Merry's plump, ruddy face and he gestured with a theatrical flourish towards the door. "Ladies first, darling."

Amelia obeyed and stepped into an enormous library. Books were stacked high to the ceiling on every wall, even inside the huge, unlit fireplace, no order to them at all, no rhyme, no reason. It was strange seeing such unashamed clutter in such a grand mansion which clearly wasn't lacking in space. Amelia felt like Belle when she walked into the Beast's library. She was at a loss for words, for they had all escaped into the pages of the bound marvels that bewitched her very eyes.

"Wonderland, Alice. Wonderland I dare say," Kinsey whispered in her ear as he walked past her.

"I have *never* seen so many books in one place." She quickly corrected herself, practical as usual. "Aside from the library or book store, of course." Her mouth hung agape in absolute wonder and delight as her eyes searched the room. She looked over at Kinsey who was watching her, an amused smile on his face. "This is a dream," she murmured.

"Just you wait."

Merry walked to the furthest, most cramped corner of the room—*ambitious*, Amelia thought, given the number of precariously piled tomes that threatened to give way at any second—and gently lifted up a stack of books, revealing a large wooden chest underneath. He opened the chest and pulled out a fireproof box. "Here they are."

He walked with the box to a nearby desk and turned on the reading light. Kinsey followed him and gestured for Amelia to do this same. "This is what you both came for," Merry said excitedly.

Amelia watched him open the box and looked inside to see some very old books. He then pulled a drawer open from his desk and brought out some white gloves, handed them to Amelia and pulled the chair out for her. "Sit down, Amelia, and put these on." She did as he said and looked at the old book, which stared back at her.

"What is this?"

"This is the first of three volumes I won at the auction that fateful day that ignited our friendship." He winked at Kinsey.

"And coincidentally Amelia," his friend continued for him, "it's how you and I first became friends."

Confused, Amelia studied the book in her hands. It had original brown boards with brown cloth spines. In handwritten words on the cover were faded words.

Mansfield Park

Jane Austen

She gasped as she realized she must be holding a first edition. "I can't believe this," and lovingly touched it.

"It is absolute perfection, is it not?"

Amelia nodded. "How old is it?"

"It's a first edition. Printed in 1814."

She had been right. She stared at the book in wonderment.

Merry offered some encouragement: "You may open it if you'd like."

"I can? My hand is almost shaking." Amelia could feel the goose-bumps up and down her arms as she contemplated that she was about to hold an extraordinary piece of literary history.

Merry exchanged knowing glances with Kinsey, "I understand you love Jane Austen." Merry smiled.

"Very much so," Amelia agreed. "I love her work, but I especially love *Mansfield Park*. It has a very special place in my heart as it was the last book my mother ever bought."

Kinsey and Merry both seemed moved by this information.

"*Every moment has its pleasures and its hope*," Kinsey quoted.

Merry, Amelia, and Kinsey shared a private moment of childlike fantasy as they leaned over their found treasure. "A young woman changing the literary world and she didn't even know it yet. Our Jane." Merry looked lovingly at his book.

"Our Jane." Amelia and Kinsey both repeated. Surprised, they met each other's eyes.

Amelia gently closed the book and handed it back to Merry. She didn't want to prolong the magic for too long in case it faded.

"Would you care to see the other volumes, Amelia?" Merry offered.

"Alas, we've run out of time Merry. I must return Amelia back to her world. Thank you, my dear friend, for sharing a mere glimmer of yours with us mortals."

"Very well then," he sighed, "I'll see you both out."

Merry's happy disposition quickly changed to sadness as reality began to sink in. Amelia took one last loving look at his library. She longed for his world, imagining how wonderful it must be to get lost in there for days searching for her next book. Every corner of the room was a wonderful mystery. Merry studied her expression on her face and they met each other's eyes.

"Merry, thank you so much," she said. "I will never forget this for as long as I live. This was my favorite day."

Her solemn words seemed to touch his heart and he took her hands in his, "I'm so very happy to meet another bibliophile. We are becoming rarer these days. Just like our books, you see. You are welcome to visit here any time my dear girl." He kissed her hands.

⁓ ✿ ⁓

AMELIA SAT WAITING in the car for Kinsey after her goodbye. She watched Kinsey and Merry speak at his front door together, their faces growing more serious and their bodies shifting protectively towards each other. Amelia could only assume it was to do with Kinsey's health.

Merry met her eyes through the car window and flung out a final wave goodbye which she returned. Kinsey stuck his hand out to shake Merry's, who stared at it a moment then reluctantly shook it with a huge smile. They embraced each other and Merry whispered something into his ear.

Kinsey broke their embrace first, walking back to his car where his driver was waiting to open the door.

Amelia took Kinsey's hand and said, "Thank you." She glanced back through the window at Merry, who seemed to be wiping away tears as their car pulled away.

Kinsey looked down at her hand and squeezed it. Then he removed his hand and put it on the lion of his cane.

"Off to Neverland we go, my dear Wendy," he said.

Grateful for an excuse to lighten the mood, Amelia followed suit. "Aye, Aye Captain Hook."

"Not Hook. Never have I been a Hook. I'm Pan. Peter. The boy who *never* grew up."

He looked out his window.

"I don't think that's true, Kinsey," Amelia replied.

Kinsey continued to stare out his window and, with a sigh, answered: "Nothing could be truer."

WHEN THEY ARRIVED back at Rodeo Drive, Amelia's hand instinctively fluttered towards the door handle, but she remembered Kinsey's instructions and waited for their driver to open it for her instead.

"Will I see you again?" she asked, casting a wistful look at Kinsey.

"Let's see, shall we?" he smirked.

She leaned to him and kissed his cheek. "Thank you, Kinsey. This was one of the best days of my life."

"You're welcome."

Amelia walked back to the salon, thinking about everything that had transpired that day. How had he known that she loved books so dearly? Her books were her private sanctuary. Her escape. Her refuge. *Mansfield Park* most of all. It was a book her mother had bought but never read—never had the *time* to read, because she was always working to support their life.

Now Amelia made time to read for herself and her mother. She did it to honor her mother and the time she had lost. Kinsey had seen this in her. He knew her in a way no one had ever known her. It was the material attachment that Amelia would miss the most if cancer won.

But cancer would not win. Something took hold of inside of her and as she walked through the door of her salon, she made an agreement with God. Amelia would not let cancer defeat her. She was going to do something important with her life. She just didn't know what that something was yet.

9

Thanksgiving

AUNT RITA WAS preparing Thanksgiving dinner with furious speed, clanking around in the kitchen like she was dismantling a tank, whilst Tessa had taken up permanent residence on the sofa and was scrolling through Tiktok, letting out the occasional giggle. However, for once, Amelia was too distracted to feel annoyed by either of them. The only thing occupying her thoughts was a single number, repeating over and over in her mind, like the chime of a clock.

Three.

Three.

Three.

Three more chemotherapy sessions remained until she was finished. Despite this, Amelia did not feel relief. She was incapable of feeling anything but exhaustion from the daily marathon she felt she was running. She could barely keep food down and everything irritated her. Despite her aunt, she couldn't be more thankful for Thanksgiving, as it gifted her an extra day off her job.

It was the salon's busiest season of the year, and Amelia was struggling.

Between the second week of November until the first of January, all bets were off. Clientele behavior was either at its worst or at its best—but mostly at its worst. The women of Beverly Hills didn't demand, they simply *expected* Amelia to work miracles with the salon's schedules, bending space and time to fit their will. She tried her best to accommodate the requests, but the hairdressing staff were being overbooked and overworked. It was uncertain if she was going to be able to push through, but she was giving everything she had, knowing Christmas was around the corner.

The silver lining about Christmas was that clients became considerably more generous with their gifts. Some even gave presents, but Amelia preferred cash, as she desperately needed it to pay off her growing debts.

Aunt Rita and Tessa's approach to Amelia's cancer was to pretend it wasn't happening, that it wasn't really a part of their lives, a minor inconvenience like an irritating background noise that could be drowned out with music. They had made no special allowances for her illness, and still expected her rent to be paid monthly as well as any medical debt her aunt was helping to cover.

Giving up were two words that did not exist in Amelia's vocabulary. Her Mother had raised her not to be a quitter. At the tender age of eight, Amelia had experienced a particularly rough day at school. Sitting together, Amelia tearfully confided about the art project she had poured her heart into, only to watch another student accidentally ruin it with a spill of paint.

Amelia's mother gently wiped away her tears, enveloping her in a comforting embrace. Even though Amelia was little, she could feel that the story her mother was sharing with her was deeply personal. "When your father passed away, I faced a crossroads, Amelia. I knew I had to provide for our future. So, I enrolled in nursing school, determined to forge ahead. I haven't looked back since. I'll continue to provide for us until you discover your dreams and can lead the life you've always envisioned. It's alright to feel sad, but we must discover our inner strength to persevere."

Amelia reabsorbed her mother's words as she sat on her bed, her gaze drifting toward the corner where a trash bin sat unceremoniously. She considered if she should throw up to feel better but decided against it. Her thoughts then turned to Kinsey, with whom she had spoken just a week prior. She had inquired about his plans for Thanksgiving, and he had revealed his fascination with the holiday. Taking a chance, she invited him, and to her immense delight, he accepted.

When she excitedly shared the news with her Aunt Rita, however, the response was less than enthusiastic. Rita questioned why she hadn't been consulted. Amelia assured her not to fret, explaining that neither of them had a hearty appetite. Rita seemed relieved, Amelia knowing it was largely due to the prospect of leftovers. Rita and her cousin Tessa cherished those post-holiday meals, stretching them as far as they could.

As the gentle drizzle began outside, its soft patter could be heard from her bedroom, where Amelia sought refuge from the rest of the apartment. Rain was a rare occurrence in Los Angeles, making it a welcome change of weather. It felt like the seasons were finally shifting, and something within her was changing too.

For the longest time, Amelia had felt as though she were trapped in a ceaseless cycle. However, chemotherapy held up a mirror to your life—a painful yet crystal-clear mirror—and she found herself unable to look away. The mirror, like Alice through the Looking Glass, beckoned her to step inside. Amelia was struggling to love herself and to see herself in any other way. The loss of her hair had been particularly devastating.

Back in August, it was Dante who had shaved her head for her. She couldn't bear to wait for her hair to fall out, so she'd asked him to help her take that step. On a busy day, he had escorted her to their private room, where two glasses of champagne were waiting for her. "Is this a celebration?" she had inquired.

Dante had smiled warmly and placed his hands on her shoulders. "No, *bellissima*, it's a toast. One for today and one for the days ahead. Now, let's raise our glasses." Amelia took the glass in her trembling hand, watching the bubbles rise for a moment before taking a sip. Dante draped a black cutting cape over her and asked, "Would you like to close your eyes?"

Amelia shook her head, a gesture of determination. Dante switched on the clippers and began to remove her long, luscious, brown locks. There was an odd beauty in the way they fell to the floor, piece by piece. She could hear her coworkers passing by and whispering, but she shed no tears. Devastation? Yes. It was painful to see her hair scattered on the floor around her chair, but something within her had ignited. She found the will to fight and survive this moment. It was an unexpectedly empowering experience. As Dante guided her to the shampoo bowl to cleanse her head, she couldn't help but wonder, 'Is there something different about me?'

Dante tenderly washed Amelia's head and gently dried it with a towel. He brought her back to her chair and removed the towel, as tears welled up in his eyes. He turned away, rubbing them. "I'm sorry. I must be allergic to the air today."

Amelia placed her hand on his reassuringly. "It's okay, Dante. I'll be okay."

He looked at the second glass of champagne and picked it up, saying, "I'm going to drink this for you," and quickly downed its contents. "You know what? I have a better idea. Let's just finish the whole bottle. What do you say?"

Amelia forced a grin, and agreed, "Sure."

With that, he darted behind a curtain into the break room. Amelia could hear the hushed whispers outside, gradually escalating into louder gossip. She closed her eyes, trying to block out the intrusive voices, and silently prayed, "God, if you are listening, I'll fight this battle. But I beg you, let it be worth it."

LOST IN THE memory, Amelia suddenly realized she had become so engrossed in it that she was losing track of time. In her small closet, she found the autumn-colored outfit she had planned to wear for dinner that evening. The sound of the front door opening startled her, and she felt a wave of anxiety. "Oh no? Could he already be here?" she fretted.

It was her cousin Tessa's voice in the living room on the other side of Amelia's door, which normally filled her with dread, this time brought a sigh of relief. Amelia continued to dress herself, but her confidence was at an all-time low. Lately, she had been feeling like she was losing herself more and more. It was a slow loss, like watching a beautiful golden ornament slowly lose its burnish and grow rusty.

She felt sad that Kinsey might look at her in her faded, post-chemo glory and be disappointed. But she also wondered if he might be the unlikely cure for her lack of confidence. She felt like there was something to live for in this new friendship. He saw her for her. No one else did. Despite the regret she felt when she inspected herself in the mirror, a feeling of anticipation at seeing her new friend accompanied it.

"Where is Amelia?" she heard Tessa call through to Rita in the kitchen. Her irritated tone was palpable. Spending the holiday with Amelia was just another annoyance for them.

"In her room. She's been in there all day," her Aunt replied, and Amelia could picture her eye roll perfectly, but she tried to ignore them both and focus on adjusting her wig. Then, she had an idea. She removed her beautiful wig and began to rifle through the closet, smiling to herself.

She could overhear her aunt and cousin. Tessa had clearly wandered into the kitchen—the sound of her nasal voice was a bit too audible for Amelia's liking.

"Everything smells so good, Mom."

"Thank you, precious. Where is your Thad?" Thad—which Amelia had always privately thought to be a ridiculous name– was Tessa's boy-friend.

"He couldn't join us. He is with his family tonight. Soon to be mine," Tessa said with typical unsubtlety.

Amelia could imagine Rita's surprise. Likely, she had nearly dropped the green beans she was carrying, whipped her head around and grabbed Tessa's left hand, searching for a ring.

"Are you engaged?" her mother screeched.

"Not yet," Amelia could hear Tessa sighing, "But any day now."

CLACK. CLACK. CLACK.

The sound of Kinsey's cane hitting the outside of the door announced his arrival.

10

Green Bean Casserole

CLACK.CLACK. CLACK.

"Are we expecting someone?" Tessa's voice, which was usually a drone, had gone shrill with confusion.

"Amelia's friend is coming. Go get the door. Amelia! Your friend is here," Rita called out.

Amelia ran out to greet him as Tessa opened the door, where—standing in a burnt orange suit, matching shoes, and bowler hat—was Kinsey. She opened the door wider and stumbled slightly as she stepped back and let him inside.

"Hello Kinsey," Amelia warmly greeted her friend.

Kinsey turned and a delighted smile slowly spread from his left cheek to his right.

Amelia had entered the living room wearing black pants, a orange tank top and a neon orange wig. She touched her wig, "What do we think?"

His smile grew even wider. "My oh my, aren't you a breath of fresh air."

"What in God's name are you wearing child?" Aunt Rita yelled.

"I suppose I felt like dressing up a bit. Orange is a fall color, after all. Isn't it?" she replied proudly. Kinsey and Amelia giggled together, and a warm feeling took over her insides, the feeling of having an ally against the world, a co-conspirator.

Kinsey removed his bowler hat, revealing his bald head, and doffed it like he was greeting a queen. "May I introduce myself? I'm Kinsey Bonneville."

"This is my cousin Tessa."

Tessa was at a loss for words.

"What a pleasure to meet you Tessa." He returned hat to head and walked, cane in hand, toward Aunt Rita, who was standing at the entrance to the kitchen. "You must be Amelia's dear Aunt Rita, what a pleasure it is to make your acquaintance." He took her hand and kissed it.

"Ew," Tessa said.

All Aunt Rita could manage was: "Hello."

Kinsey studied the small apartment. "What a lovely home you have. Quite cozy." He took his cane and casually strolled around, looking at all the obnoxious framed selfies of Tessa and Aunt Rita. "Where are the photographs of darling Amelia?" he asked, concern drawing a small line on his forehead.

Aunt Rita did not appear amused but wasn't about to cause a scene in front of this well- mannered Englishman. As well as being a toxic void of negativity, she was also a predatory social climber. "Well, everyone sit down," she said between clenched teeth. "Dinner is ready."

"Amelia," Kinsey beckoned, his voice carrying an air of effortless charisma. She obediently followed him to the table, where he gracefully gestured for her to occupy the head seat. Aunt Rita, bearing a platter of sliced turkey, cleared her throat just as Kinsey was about to sit down.

"No, that's my seat. You sit next to Amelia," Aunt Rita asserted.

Amelia quickly interjected, "Well, Aunt Rita, he is our esteemed guest. It's only fitting that he occupies the head of the table."

Kinsey rose to his feet with charm, saying, "Of course, Aunt Rita, your seat is secure. I want to express my gratitude for hosting such an exquisite event." He then seated himself beside Amelia, who whispered an apology.

He raised a hand gracefully. "No need to apologize."

Gazing at the vacant chair set next to Tessa, Kinsey inquired, "Are we expecting another guest?"

Tessa answered with a hint of regret, "Oh no, my boyfriend Thad couldn't make it; he's with his family tonight."

Aunt Rita momentarily observed the table before fixing an intense gaze on Kinsey. "Would you remove your hat for dinner?" she requested shrilly.

Kinsey, obliging, began to take off his hat, but Amelia intervened, "You really don't have to Kinsey."

"It's Auntie's house, Auntie's rules," he grinned at Aunt Rita.

He removed his hat revealing his bald head and Tessa and Rita exchanged uncomfortable looks with one another. Amelia took it and placed it on a small table nearby. She returned to her seat, saying, "Shall we?"

As Kinsey started to unfold his napkin, Aunt Rita declared, "In this house, we say grace before our meals."

"Please, feel free to invite Him to dine with us," Kinsey suggested with a wink, "The Lord is always welcome at the table."

"Are you mocking me?" Aunt Rita said.

"Of course not," he reassured her. "Would you like me, as your guest, to lead the Lord's prayer?"

Her lips had gone from tightly pursed to barely visible. "If you must."

He led without hesitation, "Our Father, who are in heaven, hallowed be thy name; thy kingdom come; thy will be done; on earth as it is in heaven. Give us this day our daily bread. And forgive us our trespasses, as we forgive those who trespass against us. And lead us not into temptation; but deliver us from evil. Amen."

After the prayer, Kinsey turned his attention to the delectable spread on the table: bread rolls, turkey, gravy, green bean casserole, mashed potatoes, and cranberry dressing. Tessa began passing the potatoes, expressing her gratitude to her mother for the meal. Kinsey and Amelia, however, took only meager portions, while Aunt Rita loaded her plate.

With each new dish's arrival, Kinsey and Amelia's portions remained consistent. When the green bean casserole reached him, Kinsey paused to appreciate its aroma. "What is this dish?" he inquired, intrigued.

Amelia smiled, "It's green bean casserole. Have you never tried it?"

"I haven't ever seen anything quite like it."

Amelia giggled, "You might be surprised. Looks can be deceiving."

Rita and Tessa observed him with great intrigue as Kinsey savored a bite, his curiosity piqued, "I can't quite describe it, but it's very satisfying." he remarked.

Tessa probed, "Where are you from?"

Teasingly, Kinsey responded, "I hail from a distant land known as England."

"Yeah, London, right?" Tessa guessed.

"Not London, actually. Although I've lived there," Kinsey clarified. "I'm from a place in England called Nottinghamshire."

Amelia chimed in, "Like Robin Hood?"

Kinsey grinned, "Exactly like that. I knew our resident bookworm would get it." He then turned his attention back to his plate, exploring the flavors. "This American Thanksgiving is absolutely fascinating."

Tessa, trying to engage him with her mouth filled with mashed potatoes asked, "How do you two know each other?"

Kinsey gently corrected her, "What did you ask?"

Amelia came to the rescue, saying, "She asked how we met."

"We met at a place called the chemo lounge," Kinsey explained. "It's quite an experience, really. You both should try to visit some time."

Tessa, undeterred, joked, "You're kind of a snob, aren't you?" Amelia gasped, but Tessa continued, "I mean, look at you. You give off major Willy Wonka vibes!"

Tessa and Aunt Rita burst into laughter, creating a light-hearted atmosphere. However, a sudden chill filled the room when Kinsey, with a slight grin, asked Aunt Rita, "And you? Aunt Rita? What have you been doing with your life?"

Taken aback, she retorted, "I beg your pardon?"

Kinsey persisted, "I'm just curious what you do with your time?"

Aunt Rita reluctantly replied, "I've been taking care of my daughter and my niece as a single parent."

Kinsey probed further, "you never pursued a career?"

Aunt Rita explained, "I had some savings from my late sister-in-law, and my divorce. It's been enough to get by."

"I see. You have mastered the art of existing."

"Are you married?" Tessa asked.

Kinsey became quiet, "I was engaged once."

"Didn't work out?"

"I'm afraid not."

"What happened?" Tessa probed.

Amelia interjected, "Tessa. It's none of our business."

Kinsey nodded. "It's not, but I'll entertain your question Tessa. I was given a certain set of rules and I broke them."

"Did you cheat?" Tessa asked.

"Tessa!" Amelia snapped.

Kinsey put his hand on Amelia's arm. "I was cheated. God had other plans I suppose."

"Let's leave religion off the table." Aunt Rita stated.

"I normally would agree with you however, we invited God to dine with us tonight, did we not?"

"Amelia, I think it's time for your guest to leave."

"What? Why?"

Kinsey brought out his very old pocket watch and looked down to it. "Ah, is that the time? I've overstayed my welcome. Amelia darling fetch me my hat." Kinsey used his cane to stand back up. Amelia handed him his bowler hat and he dashingly placed it on his head.

"You just got here, please don't go? I know they can be…"

Before she could finish, Kinsey stopped her putting his hand on her cheek, "Our families don't define us. Don't ever forget that." He took his hand off and looked back at the green bean casserole dish on the table. He then took his finger and raised his eyebrow toward Rita, "I really shouldn't but just I can't help myself."

Tessa and Rita watched in horror as he placed his finger directly in the middle of the casserole and brought it to his mouth in delight.

"I think you should leave!" Rita shouted.

"With pleasure, Madame." He tipped his hat to her and blew Amelia a kiss, "We will be in touch my darling girl." He walked toward the door and when he opened it, his driver waited on the other side.

"Who is that at the door?" Tessa asked.

"His driver," Amelia explained.

"He has a driver?"

"I'm going back to my room."

The familiar CLACK at the door stopped her. Amelia opened the door to see Kinsey standing behind with a smile. "I almost forgot something."

"What's that?"

"May I see your room?"

"No!" Rita yelled at him.

"I wasn't asking you."

Amelia smiled at his curious face and replied, "Of course. Follow me."

He followed her into the bedroom and she closed her door behind them. Amelia's room was more of a decorated library. Large hunter-green bookshelves lined the walls filled with books ranging from old to new. Even her gold-painted bedside table was stacked with books and a simple, elegant reading light. A small bible sat on her perfectly made bed. He walked over and touched it.

"That was my mother's," Amelia whispered.

"I see. Amelia, do you believe in God?"

"I thought we weren't supposed to discuss religion."

"Tonight, I broke all the rules. So let's skip to the end shall we? Do you?" His eyebrow raised and he looked deep into her eyes like a lost boy.

"Yes. There are countless things I'm uncertain of. But I know there is a God."

He turned away from her and continued searching her shelves and whispered back, "I do too." He stopped at a photograph of Amelia and her mother from her early childhood and picked it up. "Is this your Mum?"

"Yes."

"She was beautiful."

"She was." She took the photograph from him and put it just as it had been. It was an inspired space of her life collection... what she held dearest, the love of her mother and her love to read.

"You have a wonderful book collection."

"Thank you."

Aside from her aunt and cousin, she had never shown her room to anyone before this moment. This was her sanctuary and a rare invitation that so few had beheld. His smile warmed as he continued to admire her small room.

"I can very much tell you have a wonderful gift for design. You've done a marvelous job with this room. I can only dream of what you could do with an entire house."

"That would be the dream, perhaps someday. I've applied for several different design studios over the years, but it's so hard to find a job. Then I got cancer. I have a lot of medical bills so..."

He put his hand up. "Darling, no need to explain. I understand perfectly. One must do what's best for oneself." One smaller bookcase nearest to her bed caught his eye. Her small bookshelf was almost completely empty of books. Just a few lined its shelf. He used his long cane to point in its direction. "Why is *this* bookcase so empty?"

"Well, those are the books that belonged to my mother. They are *my* most prized possessions, and almost all I have left of her."

He took a step toward the shelf and read the familiar titles including the book she had brought to chemotherapy the first day that he had met, *Mansfield Park,* by Jane Austen. Along with it sat *Emma, Gulliver's Travels, David Copperfield, Jane Eyre, East of the Sun West of the Moon Old Tales From the North* as well as her mother's bible.

He looked deep in thought as Amelia continued, "My Aunt sold off everything. Aside from my clothes, I was only allowed one empty cardboard box to fill to bring back to live with her. So, I took her books and some photographs. That was all I could fit in my *one* box."

He coughed and seemed to be thinking deeply about something. He then took a final look around and said, "Thank you for sharing your world with me, Amelia. I will see myself out. Hide yourself away here, I'll close the door behind me. You don't need to face Tweedle Dee and Tweedle Dum again today."

With a final tip of his hat he vanished into the night. After the front door had shut behind him, Rita and Tessa's conversation erupted over their strange guest.

Mere moments later in the midst of Amelia's grief, her phone received a text message from Kinsey, *We two white rabbits are one and the same. No need to worry about anything. I've got it handled. XO- Kinsey*

11

Christmas Eve

SO, IT WAS Christmas Eve in sunny Los Angeles, an unexpected seventy-two degrees on the dial. Amelia was feeling strangely hopeful, a feeling that had eluded her for far too long. She had just one more brutal chemo session left, scheduled for January, and then she could bid adieu to this wretched cancer battle, hopefully forever.

She'd smartly scheduled her treatment a tad early this month, ensuring it wouldn't clash with the holiday festivities. With each passing day, she counted down to her sweet escape from that sterile hospital room, praying she'd never have to hear those chilling words, "You have cancer," ever again.

Life had taken on an entirely new hue. It's funny how a prognosis can shift your perspective. She realized that her days were numbered, shorter than she'd ever imagined. She'd existed, sure, but she hadn't truly lived.

Amelia hadn't crossed paths with Kinsey since Thanksgiving. They'd kept in touch, though. Post-dinner, he'd flown back to England for some mysterious family business, keeping tight-lipped about the details. Most of their conversations centered around books and their shared misery. Amelia had a sneaky feeling Kinsey's British jaunt had something to do with a secret rendezvous. She'd saved her last two questions for him but hadn't summoned the courage to ask. Kinsey had assured her he'd be back in Los Angeles by December, but as the month wound down, her anxiety cranked up, and he remained an enigma.

Tessa and her less-than-stimulating beau, Thad, had just made their grand entrance. Tessa had been ensnared in the throes of their relationship, seldom gracing their apartment, a mixed blessing that meant less Tessa and more Aunt Rita time. Tessa and Thad, they were a piece of work, the kind of couple you'd imagine sailing off into the sunset together, spawning a horde of rambunctious kids. Amelia stepped out of her room, where she'd buried herself in books all day, to greet them.

In the kitchen, Aunt Rita was working her culinary magic, the scent of roast beef and garlic wafted through the air. Now, that was a rarity, as Aunt Rita only whipped up culinary delights on three occasions: Easter, Thanksgiving, and Christmas Eve. For the rest of the year, it was all about quick- fix meals and fast-food deliveries. Amelia, juggling her job, relied heavily on store- bought soups and salads.

"Merry Christmas, Tessa and Thad."

Tessa paid Amelia no mind and threw herself at Thad. "We've got some big news! Thad popped the question during our lunch date today!" She gleefully flaunted her engagement ring.

"Oh, wow! Let me see!" Aunt Rita rushed over, inspected the ring with glee, and pulled them both into a hug. "I'm over the moon for you two! This is fantastic news. Let's crack open some wine and celebrate."

"Congrats, Tessa! That's amazing!" Amelia chimed in, giving the ring another once-over. "It's absolutely stunning!"

Tessa extended her heart- shaped diamond ring towards Amelia. "Yes, isn't it something?"

"It's beyond words," Amelia lied with grace masking any inkling of envy. Tessa, ever perceptive, called her out.

"You're totally jealous, aren't you, Amelia? It's written all over your face."

Caught red- handed, Amelia chuckled. "Guilty as charged, Tessa. I'll do my very best to hide my envy for your sake." Thad, lost in his phone since arrival, remained oblivious.

"Hey, babe, check out how many likes we've scored on Instagram!" Tessa dashed over to Thad, excitement in her voice "Over a hundred! Can you believe it, Amelia?"

"Hold on, you shared your engagement on your phone before telling your own mother?" Aunt Rita interjected, sparking a heated debate. Grateful for the diversion, Amelia felt her phone vibrate in her pocket. She raised it to signal her intention to take a call but thought better of it and answered, retreating to her room and closing the door behind her.

"Hello?" Amelia answered.

"Amelia, my dear," Kinsey's voice came through, softer and weaker than usual.

"Hi, Kinsey. It's so great to hear from you," Amelia said, her heart-warming at the sound of his voice. "Merry Christmas," she added.

"Merry Christmas, Amelia," Kinsey replied, his tone somber.

"I've got a little gift for you. Will I be seeing you soon?" Amelia sensed something amiss.

"I'm afraid not, darling. I've caught a bit of a cold," he coughed, confirming her suspicions.

"What's wrong, Kinsey?" Her heart raced, and a lump formed in her throat.

"Tell me all about your Christmas Eve plans. I want to hear every juicy detail," he deflected, clearly avoiding any serious discussion.

Amelia obliged, indulging his wish, but then paused. "You know, Kinsey, I still have two questions left for you."

"Ah, you do, indeed." He hesitated, "But first, spill the beans—what's your Christmas Eve plan with the 'charming' family of yours?"

Amelia leaned in, her voice hushed, "We're doing the classic dinner here, then off to mass." She confided, "Oh, and Tessa just strutted in with her beau, Thad. They got engaged today."

"Good Lord, how did he pop the question?"

Amelia chuckled softly, "Over lunch, of all things."

Kinsey couldn't help but laugh, "Lunch? Well, that's certainly unconventional."

"Right?" Amelia agreed with a grin.

Kinsey leaned in, curious, "So, what's this engagement ring like?"

Amelia sighed, "Okay, don't judge me for saying this, but it's a heart-shaped diamond."

"That's positively dreadful. Whatever happened to romantic proposals?"

Amelia quipped, "I'm probably the last person to have the answer to that question. Kinsey, can someone pick up your gift and bring it back to you tonight?"

Kinsey nodded, "Consider it done." After a pause, he coughed and changed the subject, "So, how have you been? How's your health?"

"I've got one more round of chemo in January, and then I'm finally free, except for those follow-ups and yearly scans," Amelia replied with a hint of relief.

"That's fantastic news, darling. Promise me..." Kinsey trailed off, unable to express what he really wanted to say.

"Promise you what, Kinsey?" Amelia prodded, urging him to continue.

Just as the conversation was getting deep, the door suddenly swung open, and Tessa appeared, clearly annoyed. "What are you doing in here?" she demanded, eyeing Amelia on the phone. "Who are you talking to?"

Amelia tried to maintain her composure. "Tessa, I'm on the phone. Give me a minute and close the door, please."

Tessa bargained, "It's my night, and I want you to join us for a glass of wine."

Amelia assured her, "I'll be there in a minute. Just close the door, please."

"Fine, one more minute, but that's it," Tessa agreed before closing the door.

Amelia quickly apologized to Kinsey, "I'm so sorry, Kinsey. Ignore what she just said. We can talk as long as we want."

Kinsey suggested, "I think it's time for you to have your own place."

Amelia sighed, "I wish, but maybe someday, when I can afford the rent. Anyway, what were you saying about proposals?"

Kinsey chuckled, "Darling, if a man ever proposes to you in a parking lot, a restaurant, or on a hike—God forbid—please make your excuses."

Amelia laughed, "Well, we don't have to worry about that, Kinsey. But I promise that if it ever happens, it must be Austen-worthy."

Kinsey's voice softened, "How about just worthy of you?"

Amelia agreed, "Okay, worthy of me."

Kinsey then reluctantly announced, "I must be going, I'm afraid."

Amelia halted him, "Kinsey, I have two questions left." She wanted to prolong their conversation, sensing it might be their last.

"Don't waste your tears on me, my love. Put them back in your pocket," he comforted her as he overheard her emotions.

"What is the Lion?" she finally asked.

Kinsey responded, deeply moved, "What a marvel you are, Amelia Levingston. You've asked perhaps the most significant question of all. The Lion holds great importance to me, you see. But the gates have been closed for far too long, until you entered my life. I believe it may be time to open them once more."

Amelia was baffled, "I don't understand, Kinsey. You're speaking in riddles."

Kinsey inquired, "Do you trust me?"

Amelia pondered for a moment and then replied, "Yes, I do."

"Good. Now, run off and pretend to enjoy dinner with your family."

Amelia felt a sudden rush of guilt. "They're not that terrible, Kinsey."

He responded with a truth that stung, "Any family member who leaves you alone at chemotherapy, by definition, is terrible."

The weight of his words sank in, and Amelia realized the painful truth about her family. "I don't want to say goodbye yet, Kinsey."

Kinsey coughed, masking his emotions. "And for your last question?"

Amelia's face reddened as tears welled up. She cleared her throat, "Who do you trust in your life?"

He paused. "For me, the one person I can trust whose heart seems to always be in the right place is my brother Arthur."

"Arthur." Amelia repeated.

"Our time together is up my friend." He softly spoke.

"Goodbye, White Rabbit," she choked out.

"Tick tock," Kinsey whispered before hanging up.

Amelia dropped her phone to the floor. Tessa entered her room with two glasses of wine and saw Amelia in tears. "Honestly, Amelia, I know you're jealous, but I didn't think you'd cry about it. Don't be so pathetic." Tessa handed her a glass of wine and returned to the living room. Amelia stared at her drink, feeling sick to her stomach. She walked to her bathroom sink and poured the wine down the drain.

12

Happy Christmas

LATER THAT NIGHT, as they were still savoring their Christmas Eve dinner, the doorbell chimed. Tessa sprang from her chair with gleeful anticipation, exclaiming, "I've got it! Probably some congratulatory flowers or something." She swung open the door, only to find Kinsey's driver standing there.

"Hello there, is Amelia Levingston available?"

"Amelia? You have a friend here."

Tessa opened the door allowing him to enter.

"Miss Levingston? Mr. Bonneville sent me," he stated. "I believe you have something for him."

Amelia stood up from the table, her curiosity piqued. "Yes, I do. Thank you for coming. I'll be right back."

She retrieved a wrapped canvas from her room and handed it to the driver. "Thank you for taking this to him. How is he doing?" Amelia inquired.

The driver hesitated, a hint of sadness in his eyes. "There have been better days." He remained composed, tipping his hat slightly as he said, "Have a Happy Christmas, Miss Levingston."

Amelia watched him as he walked away with Kinsey's gift, whispering, "Happy Christmas."

Returning to the dining room, Aunt Rita couldn't contain her curiosity. "What was that all about?"

Amelia brushed off the question, saying firmly, "It's none of anyone's business."

⁂

THE CHRISTMAS EVE church service had concluded, a beautiful and solemn affair. Before leaving, Amelia went to light a prayer candle. Her family was already heading out, but she needed this private moment. She held a small white candle in her hand, pausing to reflect.

Originally, she had intended to light the candle for Kinsey, but then she thought, "Why not for me too?" She placed another offering and took a second candle. One was for Kinsey, and one was for herself.

Closing her eyes, she prayed for peace to find Kinsey and for peace of her own. After lighting both candles, she placed them apart from the others, side by side. She watched them flicker for a moment. Glancing at the multitude of lit candles, she wondered about the prayers and the people who had lit them. A wave of peace washed over her, and she felt grateful for being alive. Yet, the thought of Kinsey's impending fate loomed in her mind, bringing tears to her eyes.

Suddenly, she sensed someone standing beside her—it was the priest.

"Why do you cry, child?" he asked.

Amelia confessed, "My friend is about to die."

"I'm sorry to hear that," the priest said kindly. "We shall pray for this soul, and you will need to live on for them."

Amelia contemplated his words as she left the church. "Live on for them." Not just for Kinsey, but for all those souls whose candles had flickered that night in the church.

Walking towards Thad's car, where Aunt Rita and Tessa impatiently waited, she felt her phone buzz in her pocket. Stopping in her tracks, she pulled it out and saw a text message from Kinsey. It read, "It's perfect. I know just where it will hang. Happy Christmas. XO- Kinsey."

Amelia texted back, "Happy Christmas."

Another text followed, "Happy Christmas, eh? I'll make a Brit out of you yet."

Little did she know, this would be the last text message she would ever receive from

Kinsey.

13

A New Year

ON NEW YEAR'S Eve, the salon was in complete chaos. Everyone was getting ready for the night's festivities, and Amelia had been running around without a moment's rest. When her new coworker, Stephan, handed her the phone and announced it was for her, she didn't expect the voice on the other end.

"Amelia Levingston?" a man with a distinguished English accent inquired.

"This is she. How may I help you?" Amelia replied.

The caller introduced himself as Mr Field, the solicitor for The Marquess Henry Bonneville the Eleventh. The name sent shivers down Amelia's spine. Her coworker Steven looked irritated as their phones kept ringing off the hook, but she couldn't tear her attention away.

Mr Field continued, "I'll be flying into Los Angeles on January second and would like to schedule a meeting with you. Can that be arranged?"

Stephan gestured urgently at the ringing phones, but Dante approached, concerned. "Why aren't you answering the phones?"

Amelia covered the phone and told Dante, "One second."

Mr Field prompted, "Can that be arranged, Miss Levingston?"

Amelia, overwhelmed, finally agreed, "Yes."

Mr Field provided further instructions, "Let's meet at the Peninsula Hotel restaurant at three o'clock on January second."

Amelia quickly realized she had a conflicting work shift and blurted out, "I work that day until six."

Mr Field adjusted, "Let's meet at six thirty, then. Will that work for you?"

Amelia, feeling the pressure, agreed hastily, "Yes."

After hanging up the phone, she rushed to manage the phones while smoothly checking clients in and out. It was a mad dash, and she was relieved when the workday ended.

As the last one out, she walked through the deserted salon, switching off the lights. In the quiet, her thoughts turned back to Kinsey. His absence felt heavier than ever, and she couldn't shake the feeling that he was gone. She locked the salon's front door and noticed the dried-up Bougainvillea petals, which once floated gracefully, now scattered on the floor. It filled her with a sense of melancholy and loss.

Alongside the sadness, curiosity began to bubble within her. She couldn't help but wonder who Mr Field was and what he might want with her.

WHEN JANUARY SECOND finally arrived, Amelia's nerves were in overdrive. The day dragged on, and work felt interminable. Everyone was still recovering from the holiday season, and her coworkers moved sluggishly through their near-empty schedules. When it was time to lock up, her stomach churned with anticipation.

When she had dressed that morning, she had thought that the green two-piece would give her an air of sophistication. Now, she worried it made her look a bit *lady of the night,* especially in context of her mysterious hotel focused on relaxing. This was made difficult by the fact that her anxiety was, at present, out of control; nonetheless, she gave deep yogic breathing her best shot on the short Uber ride to the Peninsula hotel.

The hotel was every bit as luxurious as she had imagined and confirmed her worst fears about the outfit: as she entered the grand doors, she immediately felt underdressed. She walked in, self-consciously trying to pull down the back hem of her skirt and asked a Bellman for directions to the Belvedere restaurant. He guided her effortlessly to the entrance. A stunning hostess greeted her with a smile. Amelia adjusted her skirt for the last time. "My name is Amelia Levingston and I'm meeting Mr Field?"

"Yes, welcome. Right this way."

Amelia followed the hostess to a quiet corner table, where a large man with salt and pepper hair was sitting, seemingly waiting for her. As the two women approached, he stood up to greet Amelia, holding out his hand to shake hers.

"Miss Levingston, it's a pleasure to meet you."

Amelia took his hand willingly; it swallowed hers in a firm grip. She noticed his large briefcase sitting beside him as his grip released and sat down at the table. The breadbasket was empty. He must have arrived early, she thought to herself.

"It's a pleasure to meet you as well Mr Field."

He put his hand to his briefcase and then seemed to have a change of mind, just as the waiter arrived. "Good evening, my name is Tony and I will be your server this evening. May I start you both out with something to drink?" he asked.

"Ladies first," Mr Field offered.

"I'll have a mineral water, please," said Amelia.

"And for you, sir?" he asked Mr Field.

"I'll have flat water. Thank you, and will you please bring us some more bread."

"Of course, sir."

Amelia looked around the room as Tony walked away. The tables were mostly filled with men who looked as though they were plotting their next Hollywood deals. Mr Field's demeanor turned professional very suddenly. "Miss Levingston..."

"Amelia," she said, taken aback by his formality. "You can call me Amelia."

"Amelia, he sighed heavily, "I understand you were a close acquaintance of the late Marquess."

She paused, took a breath and then mustered up the courage to ask the question which had been brewing in her head and heart all morning, the question she couldn't bear to ask, the question she *had* to ask.

"When did he die?" she asked finally.

"He died on December twenty fifth."

Amelia's heart sank and she bit her lip so that she wouldn't cry. She held it in. She held it in just like she had held in all her feelings most of her life.

"Christmas Day." She shook her head in disbelief. "I knew it."

"Were you quite close?" he asked.

She thought for a moment, "He meant something to me." She met Mr Field's eyes; they had become a bit softer.

"I'm the late Marquess' solicitor," he explained. "In November he came to meet with me at my office in London. At that time he amended his will. He appointed me to be his executor for his estate, and I am pleased to tell you the late Marquess has left you a great deal."

14

Keys

AMELIA WAS TRYING to swallow the words she had just heard arrive from Mr Field. She felt as if she might have heard him wrong. Then he stated them again, clearly.

"The late Marquess has left you a great deal indeed."

He studied her reaction as she nervously nodded along.

Tony returned to their table carrying their drink order. "Here we are. Now may I offer some appetizers?"

"Ummmm..." Amelia was choked up.

"I think she may need a moment," Mr Field answered. "Will you please bring us your favorite three appetizers. Thank you."

Tony nodded and walked away. Amelia was still at a loss for words. "Are you alright, Amelia?"

"I don't know why he would leave *me* anything."

Mr Field pulled a large thick packet from his briefcase with Amelia's name printed on the outside.

"He did. The late Marquess has left very specific instructions for you to follow with me. His first request from you is to return his ashes to his family."

Her stomach dropped, "I don't know anyone from his family. He would barely share anything with me about them."

"I will provide you with his mother. The Marchioness, Lady Edith Bonneville's current address. You will need to address her as your Lady-ship. But we will go over those formalities in due course."

Amelia's face was ghost white. "Okay," was all she managed.

"Shall I continue, or do you want to eat a piece of bread?" he asked, looking embarrassed. "You seem a bit pale."

"I'm fine," she said, collecting herself. "Please continue."

"He has also left you a few personal items that he would like you to keep—but with special instruction that you bring them to the Park House."

"The Park House?" These words meant nothing to Amelia.

He opened the mysterious envelope and removed a large brass set of skeleton keys, setting them on the table with a loud *Clank!* She stared at them. "What are those?"

"These now belong to you. You are the rightful owner of The Park House in Nottinghamshire, England. This was *his* gift to you." He smiled at her.

"Kinsey left me a house?" Amelia, still utterly baffled, picked up the heavy keys. "These look like they fit into Hogwarts."

"It's a very... very old home," he replied and rubbed his eyebrows. "It needs *work*, so prepare yourself."

Tony returned as requested with three appetizers. A plate of fresh oysters on ice, a beef tartar, and a charcuterie board. Both Mr Field and Amelia stared at the food in front of them. "These are my favorite appe-tizers. Have you both had a chance to look over the menu? I'm happy to take your entrée order." He smiled.

Amelia felt nauseated looking at the oysters, "I think this is plenty for now."

"Nonsense." Mr Field smiled. "I would love the duck."

Tony was impressed, "And you Miss?"

"I think I will just work on this cheese board."

"Excellent." Tony returned back to work.

"Do we need a break? These oysters look fantastic, I can't help my-self."

Amelia wasn't sure it was watching Mr Field eat the oyster or the incredible news that was making her nauseous. She looked away and decided to take his advice and eat some bread. It started to settle her stomach.

Exhaling a satisfied, "Mmmmm" after eating his oyster, Mr Field wiped his hands on his napkin and returned to his work, "Alright, where was I?"

"The Park House."

"Ah yes, The Park House. The Park House and the four hundred and ninety- two acres of land that it sits on now belongs to you. This gift comes with some stipulations. First, as I mentioned it is a very old home and requires a lot of work. His instructions to you are to move into The Park House and bring the home back to life. He told me you were an incredible interior designer and that you would bring love into this es-tate which it so desperately needs."

"He said that?" she asked.

"Yes, and he also told me that you must quit your job at Salon Roma..."

"Wait no. I can't quit my job."

He stopped her by putting his finger up. "Let me finish. He told me that you must quit your job. You don't need to worry about a thing. Flower arrangements have been ordered for every employee at your workplace and shall be arriving tomorrow. He also arranged for the owner Mr Dante and a guest to stay at an inclusive resort of his choice. All expenses paid to ease the blow of the loss of his favorite employee, you."

"This is crazy." She shook her head in disbelief. "This is just crazy. This doesn't happen in real life."

"Well, Kinsey as you know was always a bit, what's the word I'm searching for. eccentric."

"Very." Amelia agreed.

Reading from his notes he looked up at her, concerned, "I just want to apologize to you before I read this next part. These are his words."

She braced herself, "Alright."

He read from the document, "You will tell your horrible Aunt Rita and Cousin Tessa that their past behavior has been despicable and that they will enjoy the rest of their miserable existence without the gift of your presence. As of today, you are an independently wealthy woman and are moving to England where you will live your happily ever after."

He looked up from the paper. She nodded along. "That sounds exactly like what Kinsey would say."

Mr Field continued. "Now I understand that you have one last round of treatment this month. I'm aware you might not feel well enough to travel yet. But when you feel ready, all travel expenses will be provided for your journey to England. My assistant will be in charge of helping make those arrangements for you."

"Wow this is actually happening." Amelia let out a deep breath.

"Yes. Now listen carefully. This is very important. The Park House and its land can't be sold. If, for some reason Amelia, you are to refuse the Park House, it will then be returned to the present Marquess Arthur Bonneville, and so on in the lineage that has been provided for me."

"Arthur?"

"Yes, *Arthur Bonneville.*"

"Okay. "She smiled and nodded toward the keys. "The thing is, Mr. Field. I don't have any money. I can't just pick up my life and move to England."

"Oh no, the late Marquess took care of all of that for you. I just haven't gotten to that part yet." He ate a piece of cheese and started flipping through his paperwork. "Ah yes, here we are. The late Marquess left you a total of four million pounds to restore The Park House. In addition, he has left you two million pounds of personal allowance. Once the Park House has been completed, an additional one million pounds will be wired to your account. I will visit the house myself when you are ready and then I will have that paperwork signed."

The room was spinning.

"Eat more bread Amelia, you look like you are going to faint."

"I think I need a glass of wine," she said helplessly.

He took another oyster, placing some horseradish and Tabasco on it while he continued speaking. "I understand that this is a lot of information and it's going to take a while to process."

"So, is that everything?" Amelia said weakly. "Or did he leave me Atlantis as well?"

He laughed. "Well. You will need to provide me with your banking information so I can have those funds transferred to your account tomorrow. We will continue to work together in the foreseeable future as we finalize the estate, and I will provide you further details about your travel plans. But yes, that is all for today."

Tony arrived with Mr Field's duck. "I see you are still working on those appetizers."

"Yes. You can just leave everything, but Amelia would like to order some wine."

"The house Chardonnay is fine." Amelia nodded.

"Bring the bottle," Mr Field told Tony.

Tony walked away happily and Mr Field smiled back at Amelia, probably relieved that he didn't have a fainting woman on his hands.

"Thank you," she said.

"Before that arrives, I need you to sign this paperwork. This just stipulates that I've provided everything to you. After signing, I will then hand over the keys and the plans to the estate. In my room I have the late Marquis' personal items he left you. I will retrieve them for you to begin his specific instructions. He didn't want you to start crying in front of everyone and cause a scene."

"Well, he's not wrong."

As she signed the documents Tony arrived with the bottle and poured her a small amount into her wine glass. Amelia shook her head no. "Just go ahead and pour the whole glass."

Tony smiled and poured the glass and she took it and slammed it back. Mr Field's and Tony's eyebrows both raised and Amelia handed the glass back. "Go ahead." Tony refilled it and left the table.

Mr Field started eating his duck, noticeably content. He looked relieved to have his paperwork signed off and Amelia then shared with him, "I've been so unlucky my whole life."

"It seems that your luck has turned for the better." He smiled.

⁂

THE REST OF the dinner was a complete blur. When they finally finished, he handed her the envelope and keys and instructed her to wait in the lobby while fetched Kinsey's belongings. While waiting she ordered her Uber and nervously fidgeted with the large set of keys. Mr Field returned shortly, clutching Kinsey's lion cane and bowler hat. As soon as Amelia saw these familiar items, she started to choke back tears.

He handed her the cane, the hat and a bag. "Inside the bag are his..." he looked over to the valet that were listening and changed his voice to a whisper, "his ashes."

Tears rolled down her face. He took a handkerchief from his pocket and handed it to her. It's... it's alright to cry Amelia," he said awkwardly. He retrieved a letter out of his inner jacket pocket and handed it to her. "This is the last piece I leave with you. The instruction is that you are not allowed to read this letter until you are on the plane for England."

Amelia's Uber drive pulled up and the Valet asked for Amelia, "Miss?"

"I'll be right there," Amelia called over to him in tears. Turning back to Mr Field she wiped her tears away and offered his handkerchief back. "Thank you Mr Field."

"Oh no please, keep it. You have all my information, and we will be in touch."

"Goodbye." Amelia said, hands full of Kinsey's strange, beautiful possessions.

"I will see you in England, Miss Levingston."

As Amelia drove away from the Peninsula hotel there was much she was uncertain of, but the one thing she did know was that her world was about to change. In that envelope were the keys, the keys to the chapter of an entirely new life.

15

Survivor

AMELIA KICKED THE door open to her apartment and was immediately assaulted by the unmistakable fragrance of greasy fast food. There sat Aunt Rita, performing her three favorite activities: drinking red wine, watching a travel show, and shooting daggers with her eyes.

Rita's icy greeting cut the air, "Where were you all day?"

Balancing her armful of stuff, Amelia figured her best bet was to go incognito with Kinsey's bowler hat. But Rita, like a hawk spotting a field mouse, pounced on that hat.

"I was at a meeting." Amelia explained, her voice oozing with as much enthusiasm as a soggy sandwich.

"What's with all that stuff? And why the heck do you have that man's cane and hat?" Rita demanded, leaning in for the inquisition.

Amelia staggered to her room, dumping everything on her bed. But Aunt Rita, impatiently waiting for answers, wasn't about to let her off easy. "Well, explain?"

Amelia sighed, dreaming of nothing more than collapsing onto her bed for a well-deserved escape. Rita however, kept up her relentless questioning. "Hello? Did you go brain dead or something?"

Then, something peculiar happened. Amelia felt a surge of empowerment that she hadn't experienced in eons. She caught a glimpse of herself in the mirror and decided it was time to face her aunt head-on. "Aunt Rita, I've got something big to drop on you."

Rita, not one to beat around the bush, shot back, "Well, don't keep me in suspense. What is it?"

"I'm going to be moving out," Amelia announced, her voice a mix conviction and disbelief.

"What in the world?" Rita exclaimed wine glass abandoned on the table. "You can't just up and leave. You've got no place to go!"

"I didn't before, but now I do."

"Oh yeah? And where's that supposed to be?" Rita prodded.

"England," Amelia replied with a grin, relishing the word and watching as Rita's face contorted in confusion.

"I hate to break it to you, but you're a tad short on cash," Rita remarked.

"Once true, but not anymore, Aunt Rita. I'll even pay you back every last dime I owe you by the end of this week."

The look of shock on Rita's face was priceless. "Have you lost your marbles?

Did the cancer finally make a detour to your brain?"

In that moment, something clicked for Amelia. She'd always given her aunt credit for providing a roof over her head, but she'd never really felt any love from her. Even when she was at her lowest, battling cancer, Aunt Rita had been AWOL, blaming her aversion to doctors and hospitals.

"It's been a long day, Aunt Rita. I need some sleep."

"But why England?" her Aunt pressed on.

"Why England you ask?" Amelia knew it was best not to share about the Park House to her aunt, so she took a moment and then replied,

"Because, it's time for me to start a new chapter of my life. One that doesn't include you or Tessa."

Rita's jaw practically hit the floor. "What on earth does that mean?"

"I think you know what I mean. Now, I'm beat, and I've got an early shift tomorrow."

"What's that supposed to mean?" Rita continued to press.

"Exactly what it sounds like. Goodnight, Aunt Rita." Amelia strolled into her bedroom and shut the door. Leaning against it, she couldn't help but overhear Aunt Rita on the phone with Tessa, gossiping about their little showdown.

Amelia picked up the paperwork from her bed and placed it on her bedside table.

Grabbing Kinsey's cane, she looked at the lion head with affection and then held it up in front of her bedroom mirror. Finally, she snatched Kinsey's hat and plunked it on her head, feeling an adrenaline rush of adventure.

Aunt Rita burst in with the phone and stopped when she saw the expression on Amelia's face—and the cane in her hand.

"Get out of my room!" Amelia told her, brandishing Kinsey's cane at the door like a pirate's cutlass.

In the hyper-careful, steady way that you approach a lunatic or dangerous animal,

Aunt Rita came closer to Amelia, holding the phone in her hand. "You can't just leave, girl. You don't have any money. You also have the chemo and the doctors appointments. You are fantasizing and Tessa agrees."

"My last treatment is coming up. You'd be aware of that if you ever paid attention to anything I told you." Amelia shared with aunt, her voice tinged with frustration.

"I'll fill you in on my plans in the coming days."

Aunt Rita remained frozen, phone pressed to her ear, and repeated Tessa's words, "What about Tessa's wedding?"

Amelia's response was swift, with a hint of indifference. "What about it?"

Rita couldn't contain her exasperation. "What do you mean, 'what about it'? You're going to be in it! You need to help her with all the planning."

Amelia couldn't help but chuckle. "I have a feeling you two are going to have a blast on this wedding journey together. Every moment will be a memory. But for now, I really need to get some sleep. Goodnight." She gestured toward her bedroom door, signaling for her aunt to leave.

Rita, in utter disbelief, protested, "You don't turn your back on your family. I've given you everything!"

Amelia met her aunt's gaze, a sense of determination in her eyes. "I'm going to. respectfully disagree with you and take that chance. Goodnight."

Aunt Rita stood there, shocked and speechless, before finally exiting the room.

Amelia locked the door behind her and felt an overwhelming sense of relief wash over her. Mixed with that relief was a touch of excitement at the prospect of choosing her own family.

Kinsey had chosen her and granted her this precious gift—a chance to start a new life, a future she had never dared to imagine until that very night.

"Thank you, Kinsey." Tears welled up in her eyes, "Thank you, Kinsey." She said again and again. She removed her wig and walked into her bathroom for a much-needed shower, and a retreat to solitude from what might be the craziest day of her entire existence.

OVER THE FOLLOWING days, Amelia's life underwent a whirlwind of change. The news of her inheritance and Kinsey's unexpected passing sent shockwaves through her family and friends. Aunt Rita and Tessa were less than pleased, but Amelia stood her ground, ready to embark on this new chapter.

The arrangements for her departure were made swiftly, and she focused on preparing for her last round of treatment. She decided to fly to England the first week of June. That would give her plenty of time to recover and make final decisions with her belongings. The thought of leaving her job at Salon Roma, a place where she had spent so much of her life, was bittersweet. The flower arrangements and the trip for Mr. Dante were a thoughtful gesture from Kinsey, one that showed his caring nature even in his absence.

The day she rang the last chemo "bell" the sound of freedom announced her new life. Nurses cheered and tears ran down her face as she left the medical offices for the last time. Her recovery was not without challenges, but the freedom of not having her work schedule gave her the rest she needed to fully grasp what she had been through. She had walked through hell and back and had stayed so busy that she had never had the time to process what she had survived.

For Amelia Levingston was a SURVIVOR.

As the day of her departure to England approached, Amelia's emotions were a mix of excitement, anxiety, and sadness. She knew she had a challenging journey ahead, both in terms of restoring The Park House and coming to terms with Kinsey's passing. She had a letter waiting for her, one that held the promise of answers to her third question.

Amelia Levingston was about to step into a new life, one filled with unexpected opportunities and challenges. She couldn't help but wonder what adventures and mysteries awaited her in the grand estate of The Park House and in the letter that Kinsey had left for her.

16

First Class

AS THE BRITISH Airways employee announced the first-class boarding, Amelia confidently handed over her boarding pass at the gate. After a quick scan, she joined the line of pre-board passengers making their way down the ramp. The roar of the airplane engines were somewhat disconcerting, but she concealed her unease, determined to appear composed among seasoned travelers. There was a momentary pause as passengers began to board the aircraft, and Amelia cautiously stepped across the gap between the plane and the covered ramp, adjusting Kinsey's bowler hat, which had slipped slightly forward on her head.

With a sense of pride, she presented her boarding pass to the flight attendant at the entrance to the first-class section. A quick glance at Kinsey's cane, which she carried, and the attendant directed her further inside while helping the other passengers to their seats.

Amelia had never been on an airplane before. Mr. Field's guidance had been invaluable, but firsthand experience was an entirely different matter. She noticed the spacious enclosed pods lining the aisle, each equipped with plush pillows and neatly rolled blankets. Spotting her window seat, a wave of relief washed over her.

With a contented smile, she placed her bag, along with Kinsey's cane, next to her pillow and blanket. The other first-class passengers moved with practiced ease. She observed as they stored their belongings in the overhead compartments and decided to follow suit, placing her backpack among the others. She retained her purse, wanting to keep it close.

Unzipping her backpack, she glanced at Kinsey's urn nestled among her important documents, her fingers brushing it gently as she whispered, "Almost home, Kinsey." Retrieving her headphones and an *Architectural Digest* magazine she had picked up at LAX, she also noticed the one thing that had haunted her since the initial meeting with Mr. Field: the letter Kinsey had entrusted to him. It was intended for Amelia to open once her journey to England officially began.

Her thoughts then turned to Kinsey's hat. She decided against wearing it during the flight and removed it, contemplating where to place it. Just then, a cheerful English accent sounded behind her.

"May I offer to take your hat, Miss?"

Amelia turned to find a friendly flight attendant standing beside her. "Oh, um, is it safe?"

The attendant laughed warmly. "Yes, of course. I'll place it in the smaller overhead compartment near the front of the aircraft. That way, it won't get crushed if luggage shifts."

"Okay, then. Yes, please. Thank you," Amelia agreed, handing over the hat. She watched as the flight attendant carefully stowed it near the front of the first-class cabin. Finally, she settled contentedly into her seat, moving her pillow and blanket to the floor by her feet. There was a TV screen and a small amenity bag waiting for her on the seat next to hers.

Curious, she opened the bag and found toiletries and a sleep mask. "Wow," Amelia said aloud.

Across the aisle from her, a cute honeymooning couple sat down in the center of two pods. She listened to them joking with each other about raising the partition between them. The attendant joined Amelia again with a tray of champagne. "Champagne?"

"Why, yes. Thank you," Amelia replied, biting her lip as she accepted the glass. She was pinching herself. This was a dream come true. She looked around, watching the other passengers settle in, and began to enjoy her champagne. Finally, she could wait no longer and opened the mysterious envelope, reading the letter to herself.

Dearest Amelia,

I'm writing to you from the dead. I've fallen down the rabbit hole, and you see, I can't get out. Wonderland is a magnificent place. You must come to visit. But not too soon, you've been granted the greatest gift, a second chance at life. When I met you, I saw a beautiful girl with a glimmer of hope in her eyes, even in the darkest of places. You have a keen sense of humor, a strong wit, and a heart that beats a little bit faster than everyone else's. But what stood out the most to me was that you noticed things others didn't. You stop and appreciate things. I had forgotten to do that until I met you. In these last days, I started to appreciate things a bit more. You made an impression on me, and I decided to be a little bit kinder with what time I had left. Alas, I'm afraid I did have to die, as many stories go. But this isn't the end of your story, my darling; it is just the beginning for you. You see, you've been given my greatest gift I could leave you. My home. But like me, my home has rotted from the inside out from a place of abandonment and fear. Our time was much too short. Thank you for your Christmas gift. I did manage to have it mounted. I hope you like the placement.

Until we meet again... in Wonderland,
Kinsey
Your White Rabbit

P.S. Please forgive my family. They will behave terribly. Worse than myself, if you can imagine. Give them time... now that you have it. Don't waste it.

The flight attendant came by to collect Amelia's glass. "Are you finished, Miss?" Amelia handed her the empty glass.

"Thank you. May I have another?"

"Nervous flyer?"

"First time flyer," Amelia shyly admitted.

"Oh, how wonderful. Everything will be just lovely. I'll be right back with another glass for you."

Amelia stared back down at the letter. Her brain was on fire, and her heart was pounding in her chest. Taking a deep breath, she decided that no matter what happened, she could not fail him.

The flight attendant returned quickly and said, "Here is your champagne. Make sure you drink quickly because I'm going to have to take that before our departure."

A flight attendant's voice began to speak on the intercom, drawing Amelia's attention upward. "On behalf of British Airways, it is my pleasure to welcome you aboard flight twenty-two with service to London. Federal regulations require that carry-on items are stowed prior to closing the aircraft door. We will be arriving in London at approximately twelve fifteen tomorrow. I hope you all brought umbrellas, as it's going to be a very rainy welcome."

"Well, shit," Amelia muttered to herself.

17

London

IT WAS INDEED a foggy and rainy day in London, just as one would expect in June. But Amelia wasn't going to let the weather dampen her spirits. In fact, she welcomed the rain. Los Angeles needed more of it, or any of it, for that matter. She had a long travel day ahead of her and was worried about the wig she was wearing. It was one of her most expensive, and she was afraid to damage it. After disembarking the aircraft, she quickly located a travel shop and wisely purchased an umbrella.

After successfully clearing customs, she was overcome with relief. Mr. Field had provided all the information she could possibly need, and she faced far fewer questions than she had anticipated. Her very first passport stamp, and just like that, she had entered Great Britain. An elderly, burly man stood patiently holding a sign with "Miss Levingston" written across it. He had a hearty gray beard and was dressed in a houndstooth suit and tweed flat cap. A luggage cart stood by his side. Her excitement overcame the exhaustion she was battling, and when she saw her name, she was absolutely thrilled. She approached him with a smile and introduced herself, "Hello, I'm Miss Levingston."

He greeted her warmly, "Ah, Miss Levingston. Welcome to London. How were your travels?"

"Wonderful. This was my first experience flying," she told him.

He burst into a laugh like Santa Claus. "Ho. Ha. Ha! You don't say? Can I take that pack from ya?" he asked, pointing to her backpack.

"Yes, but please be careful," she warned. "There are some delicate items packed inside."

"Always 'em. Always 'em. Follow me so we can collect yer baggage."

"Wonderful," Amelia replied, grateful for the company and not having to carry the weight. She felt tired but grateful to have someone help navigate her out of the busy airport. "What is your name?" she asked.

"Did I not say? Sorry 'bout that. Me name is Mr Grover. I work for Mr Field."

"It's a pleasure to meet you, Mr. Grover."

"I must say, that is quite the bowler hat which you are sporting." He smiled at her hat and gave a big laugh, "Ho. Ha. Ha. Me Dad wore something a bit like that."

Amelia smiled, "It belonged to my dear friend. I didn't want to smash it in my luggage, so I thought I would just wear it to get it here safely."

"Very smart of yeh." He stopped at the baggage claim. "Alright. Here we are." Mr Grover collected her first large rollaway and nearly dropped it. "My goodness. What's in here? Ho. Ha. Ha."

"Books," Amelia giggled.

"Ah, I see," he grunted.

After collecting her bags, she followed him to his town car, and they were off. Amelia stared out the window with delight. Her body was feeling the jet lag, and her last session of chemo had taken a lot out of her. She felt her eyes closing as she leaned her head against the cold window, listening to the rain. "Miss Levingston? Miss?"

Amelia opened her eyes and realized the car had parked, and they were at their next stop on her journey.

"I'm sorry to wake ya, Miss. We've arrived at your hotel."

The car had parked at the entrance of The Four Seasons Hotel in London. There was a valet holding an umbrella, patiently waiting to open her car door. She quickly wiped the slight drool from her mouth, adjusted herself, and nodded, allowing the young man to open her door. She took Kinsey's cane and her purse and stepped out onto the red carpet that led to a black-framed door.

"Sorry about that," she said stepping out, "I'm a bit tired from traveling." She told him.

He smiled and said, "Welcome to The Four Seasons. May I please have the name for your reservation?"

Mr Grover presented paperwork to the valet, and he took it from him. Amelia looked up at her hotel in dreamy excitement. She felt like she was right back in Beverly Hills again. But now it was her turn to be the guest.

"Excellent, Miss Levingston. Enter the lobby through those doors, and you will be welcomed straight away. We will handle all of your luggage."

Amelia approached Mr Grover and began to open her purse, but he stopped her, putting his hand up.

"Oh no, Miss Levingston, everyone has been taken care of on your behalf. Please go inside and enjoy yourself. I'll be out front here tomorrow morning at nine to give you a ride to the train station."

"Oh, okay, great," Amelia replied, relieved. "I'll be outside at nine then. Thank you, Mr. Grover."

"It's been a pleasure. Get some rest. You look like you need it. Ho ha ha." He laughed to himself with his hand on his stomach. She nodded and held out her hand to shake his hand.

Surprised, he looked at it and took it warmly with a firm shake.

Amelia entered the beautiful lobby. She immediately smelled the fresh flowers that filled a large vase at the entry. A dashing gentleman approached her, wearing a gold name badge. "Miss Levingston, I'm William Murray, the manager of this hotel." He handed her his card.

"Oh. How nice to meet you," Amelia replied, a little stunned.

"I'll be showing you to your suite," he stated.

"Oh, don't I need to leave my credit card to check in?" she asked.

"No, Miss Levingston. It's all been handled. It's a pleasure to welcome you to our hotel. Please follow me to the lift right this way." He politely escorted her toward the elevators and used his master key card to select Hotel Suites.

Amelia's mouth nearly dropped. She tried to hide the thrill of her excitement.

"You will find that this is a beautiful suite. If there is anything you may need, feel free to reach me directly on the number I've provided for you." The elevator door opened, and he stepped out, holding it open. "After you, please."

Amelia followed him down the hallway. "This is like a dream," she said with a smile, "Your hotel is so beautiful."

"You haven't stayed at a Four Seasons before, Mum?" He inquired.

"No, I haven't." She looked around wide-eyed and said, "It's truly incredible." He led her to her room and opened the door for her.

"After you, Miss. Levingston."

Upon entering the suite, she was stunned to see that her luggage had already been delivered. She whispered, "Wow."

"This is our grand one-bedroom suite," the manager welcomed her as she stepped inside and placed a door stopper to leave the door open behind them. There was a sitting room with a small library and a television in front of her. She wandered over to look at the books.

"This is perfect. I wish I could stay longer than one night," she said.

"If you would care to follow me."

"Of course." She followed him into another room and saw a lovely sitting room area with gold and ivory furniture adorned with floral arrangements. Toward the back of the suite, she saw the bedroom area. There was a dining area with a glass table and four chairs, and she could see a beautiful terrace just outside. He began his tour, "This suite has separate areas, including the library, the bedroom in the back, adjoined to the ensuite." He led her to the terrace doors and opened them. "As well as a private terrace." He pointed out a complimentary bottle of champagne and two glasses on a table nearby. "Compliments of the Four Seasons."

She stepped out to the terrace to look at the view of the park. The rain had finally stopped. Everything was so green and fresh. She didn't miss Los Angeles for even a moment. The smell from the mossy air was intoxicating.

"If there is anything else you may need, please feel free to call the number on the card I gave you. That is my direct line. Do you have any further questions for me, Miss. Levingston?"

"Actually, I do have a question."

"How may I be of service?" he asked.

"I need a fashionable raincoat."

"I would suggest Burberry. I can arrange a car, compliments of the hotel," he told her.

"That would be wonderful. I just need an hour to freshen up a bit."

"Very well, Miss Levingston. I will take my leave. Your room keys are on the entry table. Enjoy everything the Four Seasons has to offer you, Miss. Levingston."

"Thank you, Mr. Murray." She watched him leave. When the door closed, she squealed with excitement. She practically skipped into her bedroom and into her bathroom, where she saw an enormous bathtub, separate from the shower. She took her wig off and immediately began to undress herself. "Hello, Heaven."

18

Raincoat

AFTER A LUXURIOUS bath, Amelia elegantly dressed herself, her excitement palpable. Today was a day she had long awaited, a day that held the promise of transformation. When Mr. Field's assistant had booked her flight to London, one of her first thoughts had been, "I need new clothes." Years of working on Rodeo Drive, observing the jubilant shoppers with their designer bags, had fueled her daydream of one day becoming one of them.

Today, that dream was becoming a reality as she made her way to Burberry with a heart full of anticipation.

Upon entering the hotel lobby, Amelia quickly located Mr Murray engaged in a conversation with a staff member. As their eyes met, he extended a welcoming hand, "Miss Levingston, right this way."

"Hello again, Mr Murray," she greeted him.

"We have a car waiting to take you directly to Burberry," he informed her. "If you wish to continue shopping afterward, the driver will be at your disposal, ready to take you wherever you desire, and return you to the hotel when you're ready."

A few curious guests checking in nearby cast a glance in her direction. Amelia had never experienced such attention before. "You're making me feel like royalty," she remarked.

"We strive to treat all our guests as such," he replied warmly.

Pretty Woman, eat your heart out.

A lady emerged from the driver's seat of a luxurious town car, opening the door for Amelia. Mr Murray introduced her, "This is Ms. Hood, your driver for the afternoon."

"Miss Levingston, I understand our first stop is Burberry today?" Ms Hood greeted her with a friendly smile.

"Yes, indeed. Thank you," Amelia responded, taking her seat in the opulent town car.

"Enjoy your time," Mr Murray bid her farewell.

Moments later, as the vibrant streets of London unfolded before her, Ms Hood inquired, "Is there any other shopping you'd like to do later?"

Amelia considered, "You know, I'm quite tired from my journey, so I think Burberry will be my sole destination for today. I'm from Los Angeles, so I don't have a proper raincoat. I had to buy an umbrella at the airport."

Ms Hood chuckled, "Well, you'll find an excellent raincoat at Burberry."

"And do they sell rain boots?" Amelia inquired.

"Certainly! You'll love it. I'm taking you to the flagship store; it's extraordinary."

"I'm so excited. I worked on Rodeo Drive for years, but I never once walked into any of those stores. Can you believe it?" Amelia confessed, warm delight spreading from her heart to the tips of her limbs. It was fantastic what a bit of retail therapy could do for a girl.

"You're kidding?" Ms Hood's eyes widened in surprise.

"I never had the means, so I always thought, what's the point? Years of staring in those gorgeous windows. But not today," Amelia said jubilantly.

"Not today, Miss!" Ms Hood joined in her excitement.

"Today I'm going shopping."

"Yes you are."

Arriving at 121 Regent Street, Ms. Hood handed Amelia her card. "My number is on there. Just text or call me when you're finished, and I'll be waiting outside for you."

Amelia stepped out, grateful for the respite from the rain. With eagerness, she made her way to the entrance, where a security guard opened one of the grand doors for her. As she stepped inside, she was greeted by the enchanting fragrance of perfumes. A saleswoman approached her, asking, "How may I assist you today?"

"I'm here to buy a raincoat and some rain boots, please," Amelia replied.

"Wonderful," the saleswoman led her further into the store. "Do you have a particular coat in mind?"

"Honestly, I just want to look like a local," Amelia chuckled, though the saleswoman remained composed.

"Are you visiting London?"

"I'm here for the night, but I'm moving to Nottingham tomorrow," Amelia said, her nerves inexplicably flaring up.

"Ah, I see," the saleswoman led her to a magnificent display of Burberry trench coats. "This is what you're looking for."

Amelia spotted it—an embodiment of her desires. She pointed at it with certainty. "That one."

"Excellent choice. This is the Long Waterloo Heritage Trench Coat," the saleswoman explained.

"That's the one. It's perfect," Amelia affirmed, feeling a profound connection with the coat.

"There are three colors available: Honey, Black, or Coal Blue," the saleswoman noted.

"Oh, honey, it's honey, without a doubt," Amelia declared. "In a size six, if available."

The saleswoman signaled to a colleague to join them. "May I have your name, please?" she asked.

With newfound confidence, Amelia replied, "Amelia Levingston."

Suddenly, her colleague's demeanor shifted. "Miss Levingston, of course. We were expecting you today." She turned to her colleague and said, "Miss Levingston requires the Long Waterloo Trench Coat in Honey, size six." Her colleague hurried off.

"Forgive me, Miss Levingston, would you like a coffee, a glass of wine, or champagne?" the saleswoman asked, now taking Amelia seriously.

Amelia smiled, feeling empowered by the attention and opportunity before her. She had never been so self-assured. It was a novel and exhilarating experience to shop without scrutinizing price tags.

Amelia grinned, thinking, *so this is how Vivian Ward felt.* "How about pizza?" she quipped.

Without hesitation, the saleswoman replied, "I suppose I can arrange that if you wish."

Amelia laughed, "Oh no, I wasn't being serious."

Slightly bemused, the saleswoman said, "Well, if you'd like something, I'm happy to arrange it for you. Now, if you'd care to follow me, I'll take you to our shoe section, where we have some wonderful boots for you to choose from."

The shoe selection exceeded Amelia's expectations. She pointed to the Vintage Check Detail Leather Chelsea Boots—black with the Burberry print running down the ankle. Amelia knew she had to have them.

"Those. Can I try a size thirty-eight? I think that's right. Sorry, I'm still figuring out the sizing here," Amelia said.

"What size are you currently wearing?" the saleswoman inquired, eyeing Amelia's faux leather boots.

"These are eights," Amelia replied.

"Very well, let's try a thirty-nine. We'll also bring you a size forty, just in case you want to wear thicker socks during winter," the saleswoman advised.

Amelia waited while the boots were retrieved. Slipping her feet into the larger pair, she realized the saleswoman's suggestion was spot-on. She happily settled on the size forty.

About two hours later, after a quick text to her driver explaining her extended shopping excursion, Amelia found herself comfortably seated on a sofa. The saleswoman swiped her new card, and Amelia enjoyed a cup of tea provided by the store. She was unburdened by any concerns as she spent more money than she had ever imagined.

The saleswoman returned, and even the store manager joined them to express gratitude for Amelia's patronage. Amelia responded with grace and thankfulness as she made her way back to the store's entrance. Her hands held four large Burberry bags, and her smile was as wide as can be.

Stepping outside, she immediately spotted her waiting driver. As she glanced around, she noticed curious onlookers eyeing her shopping bags. She felt like somebody because she was somebody—Amelia Levingston. This was her new life, and she couldn't be more thrilled.

"How was it?" Ms Hood asked as she opened the car's trunk and began placing Amelia's bags inside.

Amelia couldn't contain her excitement, "That was so much fun."

"Well, if you loved shopping at Burberry, wait until you experience Harrods."

"Do they have food?" Amelia inquired eagerly.

"Oh, yes," Ms Hood affirmed.

"Then let's go."

LATER THAT NIGHT, as she snuggled into those warm, buttery sheets, Amelia let her imagination run wild. She dreamed about the adventures life had in store for her, ones where she'd truly live life to the fullest. For dinner, she treated herself to some room service, and then had the entire hotel room all to herself. She'd never really had that kind of space before. Sure, she'd shared it with her mother, which was a treasured part of her past, but the rest of her life had been spent with her dreadful aunt and cousin. But now, she felt like she was finally shedding that heavy weight she'd carried for as long as she could remember. She could almost see her mother up in heaven, giving her a standing ovation as she went on her Burberry and Harrods shopping spree, reveling in the joy of swiping her card and knowing there was no debt to follow. She was free to make her own choices, and she intended to do just that.

Amelia adjusted her head on the pillow, staring up at the ceiling as her eyelids grew heavy. She closed them, knowing that come morning, she'd be off to The Park House—her new home.

<h1 style="text-align:center">19</h1>

<h1 style="text-align:center">Drifting</h1>

THE NEXT MORNING, Amelia woke up to the gentle sound of rain pattering on her terrace. She stretched in bed, feeling like she'd had the best night's sleep ever. It was a new day, and her excitement for what lay ahead was infectious. She checked her phone—it was only six-thirty. She could've snuggled back under those cozy sheets, but her excitement for the day was just too much.

She threw on some jeans and a brand-new shirt, then headed down to the hotel's restaurant for breakfast. Sipping on her warm tea and gazing out the window at the never-ending rain, she felt a sense of tranquility. Her own little table, the peaceful atmosphere, and some fantastic people-watching—it was the perfect start to her day. The diversity of people around her was like something out of a storybook. It was as if all those novels she'd read had come to life, and she was now a part of the narrative. It was a dream; a wonderful one she had no intention of waking up from.

Amelia went all out with breakfast, ordering a full English breakfast with black bacon, eggs, British sausage, bubble and squeak, fried tomato, fried mushrooms, black pudding, and toasted bread. She savored each bite, trying a little bit of everything. It was a culinary experience to remember, leaving her feeling full and ready for the day ahead.

Despite the relentless rain outside, Amelia refused to let it dampen her spirits. Today, she'd finally lay eyes on her new home. She'd packed everything the night before in anticipation of this grand adventure. Her heart was brimming with excitement.

The day would be long, but it marked the final leg of her incredible journey. She couldn't resist adding a touch of lipstick as she looked at herself in the mirror. She reached into her purse and pulled out the special shade she'd picked up at Harrods. Today, she felt beautiful.

With her new raincoat on and her new rain boots giving her a playful bounce, she felt like a kid ready to jump in the biggest puddle. A knock at the door signaled the start of her day.

Amelia greeted the young porter named Peter with a warm smile, thanking him as he led her to her luggage. He made a move to grab the bag with Kinsey's hat, but she stopped him, saying, "Oh, don't worry about that one; I'll carry it."

She picked up Kinsey's cane and her purse, handing the porter her backpack. As the hotel door shut behind her, she couldn't help but feel a bit sentimental about saying goodbye to the comfiest bed she'd ever slept in.

Peter inquired, "How was your stay with us, Miss Levingston?"

She beamed at him, genuinely grateful, "It was a dream. That was the most comfortable bed I've ever slept in."

"Delighted to hear that, Miss. Headed home today?" he asked.

Amelia took a moment to think as they approached the elevator, and he pressed the button. She finally replied with enthusiasm, "Yes, that's the plan. Going home." Those words felt strange in her mouth. It had been so long since going home meant anything other than stony silences and emotional neglect.

The elevator doors slid open, and they stepped inside together. Amelia suggested, "Peter, this one's all yours; there's plenty of room."

Peter shook his head, insisting, "Nonsense, hop on in; there's space for both of us. Where's home Miss?"

"Nottinghamshire." She answered.

"That's where my whole family is from."

Surprised, Amelia asked, "Does your family perhaps know the name Bonneville."

"Of course. Everyone knows the Bonneville family. My family has worked for them for many years. In fact, my brother Charlie works for Lady Edith herself at Oak Hall."

Amelia nearly fell over as they ascended in the elevator. She couldn't believe her luck. How could this even be possible. Amelia felt an immense feeling of gratitude, accompanied by the feeling that a new chapter of her life was beginning.

When they reached the lobby, Peter led the way with her luggage. As they made their way through the hotel, they encountered Mr Murray, the hotel manager.

"Thank you, Peter. If you could take that to the front," he said in a low tone.

Amelia sensed the situation's gravity. Having worked in a first-class environment for years, she knew the importance of maintaining impeccable behavior when the boss was around. She didn't want Peter to get into any trouble. She called out to him, "Peter, could you wait by the car for a moment? I'd like to chat with you."

Peter blushed but nodded, saying, "Yes, Miss."

As she continued walking, Amelia picked up Kinsey's cane and her purse, handing the porter her backpack. Mr Murray, seemed genuinely surprised by her hug. He looked at the other hotel staff to see if anyone had noticed, then gave her a pat on the back.

Amelia playfully teased, "I'm sure I'm not supposed to hug you, but I just don't care."

"It's perfectly fine," he assured her. "Allow me to walk you to your car."

Outside, the temperature had noticeably dropped since the previous day, and Amelia was thankful for her new coat as she watched the rain pouring down. Mr Murray wished her a safe and pleasant journey.

Peter had started loading the luggage into the car, and the rain had intensified. Amelia, holding an umbrella, offered it to him, showing unexpected kindness. Peter was taken aback but gratefully accepted. "Thank you, Miss."

"I'm actually on my way to visit Lady Edith at Oak Hall." Amelia admitted.

"You're kidding." His whole body shifted.

Peter's reaction made her nervous. Mr Grover opened the car door for Amelia, and she stepped inside. She noticed the growing traffic and the impatient glares of other drivers.

"Is she expecting you Miss?" Peter called out to her.

"No, it's a surprise sort of." She sheepishly admitted.

Mr Grover closed her door and Peter knocked at her window. Don't just show up unannounced." He pled. Mr Grover started to drive away from the busy hotel.

"Did he say, 'Don't show up'?"

Mr Grover, growing impatient himself, clarified, "He said, 'Don't just show up.'"

Amelia took a deep breath and felt her nerves creeping in. "Great."

"Next stop... Waterloo Station."

"Here we go," she replied, her gaze fixed outside. She sensed the shift in energy, her excitement tinged with apprehension.

"So how are you this morning?"

She contemplated his question very seriously. In chemo, people had asked her this question all the time. *How are you? On a level of one to ten, how much pain are you feeling?* Being asked it genuinely, as a friendly off-hand comment, felt like a luxury Amelia was unused to.

"Good. Well, I think. I suppose I'll find out soon enough," she murmured, glancing at the bustling streets.

⁓⁂⁓

WATERLOO STATION WAS like a madhouse with all sorts of folks hustling around. Amelia, armed with her ticket details, weaved through the chaos, and a friendly cop gave her a hand by pointing her in the right direction at the security post. Juggling her bags, she knew this was the final stretch of her journey, the last leg. She was almost there, and excitement surged through her as she dropped off her stuff and hopped on the train for a two-hour ride.

She kicked back, loving the view passing by her window. The rain added a touch of drama to everything. Amelia ordered a glass of wine and a cheese plate to keep her nerves in check. Every now and then, anxiety would sneak in, but she pushed it out the door.

Kinsey's bowler hat and cane sat beside her, almost like her travel buddies. She'd glance over at them from time to time, thinking of her dear friend and his grand plans for her. The thought put a big, happy grin on her face.

This whole journey had been a massive leap of faith, and Amelia couldn't help but mull it over. While she checked her phone, she couldn't ignore the fact that most of her former coworkers hadn't dropped her a line. Eight years at the salon and it seemed like the job meant nothing to them. Aside from Dante, only Oliver had stayed connected with her since his departure. They had their differences, but she always rooted for him. She'd peek at his Instagram stories, getting a glimpse of the design-filled life she'd always dreamt of.

Her thoughts circled back to The Park House. She dug out the blueprints from her bag. The house was an absolute stunner, not just in size but in layout too. Excitement and her imagination ran wild as she thought about what it would look like in real life. Maybe it just needed a modern touch—some electrical and plumbing upgrades. She hadn't felt overwhelmed about bringing the house back to life until now, but she couldn't let Kinsey down. His faith in her meant the world.

As she finished off her glass of wine and stared at the blueprints, a text message popped up on her phone. It was Mr Field, checking in to make sure she'd caught the train. She fired back a message, letting him know she was on track. Having him as her lifeline in England gave her a sense of security. Funny how she didn't miss her aunt or cousin one bit, even though they were her only family. Her escape from their toxic clutches was a breath of fresh air.

About ten minutes from her destination, she began rounding up her gear, and trying not to panic. Nottingham, England—her new stomping grounds—was just around the bend. The name alone stirred up thoughts of legends, from Robin Hood and Maid Marion to the infamous Sheriff of Nottingham. This was where her new life would unfold. She eyed the bag holding Kinsey's urn and whispered, "Almost there, my friend." The weight of returning his ashes to his family hung over her, a mix of fear and determination.

As the train chugged to a halt, darker thoughts crept in. What if this whole thing was a colossal mistake, not hers, but Kinsey's? Had he picked the wrong person for this job? Why hadn't he entrusted his family with it? What was their story? Kinsey's father was an enigma, and she barely knew a thing about his other relatives. Doubt gave way to sadness. Mysteries and uncertainties aside, Kinsey had been her friend. She gazed out the window as sunlight pierced through the clouds.

She pulled out and glanced at her phone checking the time as Peter's words before she left the hotel echoed in her mind. The train had pulled into the station, and it was time to face her new destination head-on.

20

Nottingham

NOTTINGHAM RAILWAY STATION greeted Amelia with a lungful of fresh air as she stepped outside, luggage cart in tow. Fortunately, that endless English rain had let up, and she felt elated to be in her new city. She took her coat off and enjoyed the sun that was starting to peek through the clouds. Navigating through the station was a breeze, and she swiftly found her way to the taxi line. While waiting, she pulled out her phone and located the address Mr. Field had provided as Lady Edith Bonneville's current residence. She squinted at her surroundings— nothing but green, leafy trees and tiny shops with thatch roofs. Not a salon or plastic surgeon's office in sight. *We're not in Beverly Hills anymore, Toto,* she thought to herself.

Her plan was straightforward: go directly to Lady Edith before checking out The Park House, carting along everything she owned. Amelia didn't want to postpone delivering Kinsey's ashes any longer. She felt a mix of anticipation and anxiety about finally meeting Kinsey's family, something she had wondered and worried about for many months. It was time to bring Kinsey home.

The cab driver pulled up, and he hopped out to assist Amelia with her luggage. "Looks like you're moving here. Are you a student at the university?" he inquired.

"I am moving here, but I'm not a student," she replied with a smile.

The cab driver continued to load her luggage and then asked, "Where to then, Miss?"

Amelia replied, "Can you please take me to Oak Hall? The address is…"

But the cab driver interrupted her, saying, "That's not a hotel. That's a private residence."

He closed the trunk of his car and glanced at the address on her phone.

Amelia nodded, "Oh, you know it. Yes, I'm visiting the Bonneville family."

The driver gave her a sidelong look. He seemed surprised. "Are you expected Miss?"

"No, but that's where I would like you to take me, please," she told him firmly.

"Very well, Miss." He opened her door, and she stepped inside, putting her phone away.

As they left the city behind and entered the countryside, Amelia noticed the sky opening up and marveled at the various types of trees. Coming from Los Angeles, where the urban environment dominated, the lush green surroundings felt like a different world. The air was damp and sweet, and Amelia could feel a weight she didn't know she had been carrying slowly lifting.

"Are you a friend of the family, Miss?" The cab driver's curious eyes were visible in the rearview mirror. Amelia hesitated, unsure of how much information to reveal. Sensing her discomfort, the driver quickly picked up on the cue and said, "Sorry, Miss. It's not my business."

Amelia felt bad, she didn't want to come across rude—this was a nation of politeness after all, Kinsey had taught her that—so she indulged him. "Yes, I guess I am. In a way."

"No, Miss. I just read it in the paper that he had died. He wasn't living here. He was in America. Is that where you're from?" the cab driver replied.

Amelia nodded, "Yes, that's right. I'm curious, what else did the paper say?"

The driver thought for a moment, then said, "Let me think. It's been a while. It said he had died, young he was. Just thirty-six. Wasn't married, so his brother Arthur will get the title and everything else, I suppose."

"He was only thirty-six? I always thought he was older. Did it say how he died?"

"No, Miss. I felt bad for her ladyship. First her husband and now her eldest, and both died on Christmas Day, no less."

"Christmas Day?"

"Yes, both of them. That's what the paper read, they both died on Christmas Day exactly ten years apart from each other. Poor Lady Edith, I have three sons myself. I couldn't imagine that kind of heartbreak," the cab driver said.

Amelia bit her lip. "You said 'her ladyship.' How do you address her exactly? Like, say, if you are meeting them for the first time?"

"Um, I would address her as 'your ladyship.'"

"'Ladyship,'" Amelia repeated. She was uncomfortable with such formalities. "Lady? Like 'your ladyship' or 'Lady Edith'? What's best?"

"Um, I suppose you would say, 'your ladyship, I'm so and so,' or 'Lady Edith, I'm such and such.' However, I wouldn't just speak to her without being spoken to first."

"Do I have to curtsey?" It hadn't occurred to Amelia until this moment, just as he turned off the main road onto a private one lined with huge oak trees.

Her nerves started to tighten up.

"No, don't curtsy. But be on your best behavior. You didn't hear this from me, but I've heard she isn't the nicest of people."

"Oh... great," Amelia muttered, and then she saw it as they approached the enormous driveway. Her face became as white as a ghost. She felt as if she could faint.

21

Oak Hall

IT WAS A seventeenth-century marvel. A feast for the eyes. Her imagination ran wild as they approached the historic home, and she felt the presence of old-world beauty that was a wonder to behold. To the right, there was a large horse stable, and she imagined this must have been a royal family's hunting escape.

The garden was alive and Amelia could see rows of finely pruned rose bushes lining the exterior of the home in perfect harmony.

"This is Oak Hall, miss," the driver murmured as he slowly approached the home.

"Wow. That is quite a home," she said.

"I'm a bit nervous for you, miss. If Lady Edith isn't expecting a guest, she might..."

"Shoot me?!" Amelia yelped.

"No, of course not. This is England. We don't shoot people here. She will ask you to leave her property, and you won't have a ride. That's why I think I should wait for you."

"No, no. I have to be here. I have to see her."

A handsome man in outdoor work clothing exited the nearby stable, curious at the unexpected visit. She watched him grab a nearby towel and wipe his hands as they drove up the pebbled driveway toward the main entrance. When she stepped out of the cab, he slowly started to approach them.

The driver stepped out and started collecting her things, placing them outside. "Okay, thank you," Amelia quickly paid him.

"Are you sure you don't want me to stay?"

"Yes, just go. Thank you again." The driver got into his cab and drove away just as the man from the stable approached her.

"Hello, Miss," he said with a warm smile. "I think you may be lost."

He was tall and had a kind face, reminding her of a schoolteacher she had when she was younger. His voice was just as warm.

"I'm not lost. No, I'm Amelia, sorry, my name is Amelia. I came here to speak with the Bonneville family."

"Are they expecting you?" he asked, throwing his towel over his shoulder.

"No, but..." she picked up Kinsey's cane, "...I..."

He took one look at the cane and took a step back, startled. "Where did you get that?"

"I'm so sorry, who are you? Are you Kinsey's family?" Amelia felt like she was a fumbling idiot. This was not going very smoothly. She accidentally let go of Kinsey's cane. "Oh no." He caught it and looked at it. The door opened, and there at the top of the stairs stood an elegant woman with a tightly pulled-back bun and a white suit which seemed to reflect the glare of the weak winter sun.

"Who is it, Charlie?" she said in an unnervingly soft tone.

"Hi!" Amelia took Kinsey's cane back, leaving her pile of luggage in the driveway, and approached her.

The woman saw the cane and stepped back, her elegant features tightening. "Oh."

Amelia stopped dead in her tracks. "I'm Amelia Levingston." She quivered, "Are you Lady Edith?"

"Yes."

"Um..." Amelia gave a terrible curtsy with Kinsey's cane and looked at her. "I'm so sorry. I forgot I wasn't supposed to curtsy. Unless I'm supposed to."

Amelia sensed she should just stop talking. Lady Edith studied her in a way that made Amelia feel cold to the core. It felt like minutes until she spoke. "How very American you are."

"I'm so sorry for not writing to you first, but I thought it would be best to just show up."

"Again, how incredibly American of you," Lady Edith quietly muttered. She turned to Charlie and said, "Charlie, can you please collect her things so they aren't just sitting in the drive. You can put them inside by the door."

Charlie nodded and started to collect everything.

"Oh, he doesn't have to do that," Amelia told him, walking over. Charlie was already taking her things inside.

Lady Edith gestured with her finger for Amelia to follow her, "Come with me, child." Amelia nervously took the bag that held Kinsey's ashes, his bowler hat, and the cane. Charlie offered to help, saying, "I can take all of that for yeh."

"Oh no, I'll handle it," she replied.

She followed Lady Edith into the ground floor of the baroque-styled interior hallway. A large round table with fresh roses filled the entry with the sweetest floral scent.

"Follow me," Lady Edith coldly welcomed her into a formal sitting room off the hallway. Large velvet chairs awaited them. Amelia's mouth was wide open as she stared up at the high ceiling and the ornate crystal chandelier that hung above her.

Lady Edith sat down and pointed to a chair for Amelia. She obeyed like a scared animal, her eyes darting around the surrounding walls that held family painted portraits. There was no sign of Kinsey in any of them.

Suddenly, a woman who had the vibrance of a young Gwyneth Paltrow entered the room. Her long blonde ponytail swung side to side, and her piercing blue eyes met Amelia's in curiosity as she asked with a snobbish tone, "Who is this?"

"Hello," Amelia interrupted Lady Edith from answering. She realized this was a mistake as Edith stared back at Amelia with the same piercing blue eyes.

With an equally snobbish look in her eyes, Lady Edith icily announced, "Why, this is Amelia Levingston."

The young woman leaned into the arm of the chair Lady Edith was sitting on. She studied Amelia up and down and said, "So *this* is the American girl."

Aware that she was not welcome, Amelia lowered her voice to a soft and caring tone. She spoke from her heart, "I'm very sorry to just show up here. But I thought it would be best just to meet with you so you knew..."

"That you stole our families' inheritance from us and apparently spent it all at Burberry?" the girl asked in a harsh tone.

"Rosie, be civilized," Edith hissed.

Rosie's phone buzzed and she looked down at it. "I've got to take this."

"Go tell Henrietta to fetch Miss Levingston and myself some tea, please."

"You must be joking," Rosie looked at her mother, but Lady Edith raised one finger at her, and Rosie submitted without argument. "Yes, Mum."

Rosie sulked off, leaving as quickly as she had entered, and Lady Edith watched her with those same blue eyes. Between Kinsey and Rosie, Amelia knew that this was a dominant family trait. Lady Edith returned her gaze to Amelia, saying, "As you were saying?" She motioned her hand once again for Amelia to continue.

Her palms were becoming sweaty, and she wiped them on her pants. "I was friends with Kinsey," she began.

"The Marquess or his late Lordship?" Lady Edith corrected her.

"That's right, the... Marquess," Amelia continued. "I'm assuming now, you've read his will?"

"Of course." Lady Edith pursed her lips together and crossed her legs, leaning slightly.

Amelia was certainly not the only person uncomfortable with this conversation. Rosie reentered and sat down, crossing her legs and arms, staring at Amelia with a cold gaze.

"Well?" Lady Edith asked Rosie.

"She's bringing it," Rosie told her mother.

Amelia continued, "I just wanted to meet with you and tell you I didn't expect any of this."

Rosie coughed, and Lady Edith put one finger in the air. Amelia wasn't sure if she wanted to continue. "I... I... wanted to bring Kins... The late Marquess' remains home to you." Amelia reached for her backpack and hastily brought out his urn. Her hands were shaking. A well-dressed woman, whom Amelia assumed was Henrietta, entered with a tea tray.

Henrietta glanced at the urn Amelia was holding in her hands and nervously poured the tea. "Do you take milk or sugar miss?"

"No thank you."

"Thank you, Henrietta," Lady Edith told her without breaking her gaze with Amelia. Amelia gulped, not knowing where to place the urn, and decided to set it on the tea tray.

Rosie gasped and started to laugh. Lady Edith raised her finger up to Rosie, and she covered her mouth to keep from laughing. Amelia quickly picked the urn back up. "I don't know where to put him, it, ... him."

Lady Edith took a slow turn of her head and gave Rosie a long look as Rosie fought back her laughter. Knowing full well she would just get in trouble, she stood up and left the room, grabbing her cell phone out of her pocket as if to call someone.

"I brought you his hat and cane, as well, you see." Amelia started to hug the urn. She hugged it like it was the only hug she would ever receive in the world again. This all felt like a mistake she couldn't correct.

"Perhaps you should set the urn somewhere away from our tea," Lady Edith suggested coldly.

Amelia looked around the vast room and spotted a nearby table. She stood up and placed it there after moving a very antique and expensive-looking lamp an inch to set it down. As she moved it, she could feel Lady Edith's eyes staring at her with total disgust. Amelia felt like she might throw up.

In total defeat, she sat back down, staring at the tea.

"How did you know my son?" Lady Edith asked as she reached for her cup of tea. She gestured for Amelia to take her cup. Amelia, with shaking hands, took it and tried her hardest not to spill. It felt warm in her hand, and she took a sip of it. Her throat had become quite dry, and she welcomed the tea. She drank it quickly and set it back down.

"Sorry, I was quite thirsty," Amelia told her.

"Shall I have Henrietta pour you some more?" Lady Edith offered.

"Oh no, thank you. I... met your son in chemotherapy."

Lady Edith's body language changed. There was a shift in the already cold energy of the room. She seemed startled. She took a long sip of her tea and thought for a moment and then asked, "You were his nurse?"

"Oh no. I was a patient as well," Amelia told her.

"Are you dying?" Lady Edith asked coldly.

"We all are, I guess," Amelia joked. Lady Edith didn't laugh. Amelia continued, "No, I'm in remission."

"So, may I assume my son gave you his inheritance out of pity?" she claimed.

"No. Well, I don't think so. I don't know, really."

Lady Edith abruptly stood up and walked to a nearby window and stared out of it. She crossed her arms and muttered, "Kinsey."

"I was very surprised when his attorney told me what Kinsey had left me."

"The Marquess," Lady Edith corrected her.

"Yes, but to me, he was Kinsey."

"No." She turned coldly to her.

Amelia sighed deeply, her nerves still on edge from the awkward encounter. "Okay. Well, I'm returning his ashes to you by his request. I also brought his cane and hat. He left them to me, but I thought you might want them."

Lady Edith's response was cold and unwavering. "He left them to you, not to me. I have no desire for those belongings."

With determination, Amelia insisted, "Well, I've brought him back home to you."

Lady Edith's stern demeanor remained unshaken as she delivered a history lesson that left Amelia stunned. "This was never his home, Amelia. This home, Oak Hall, belongs to my family, and it has for over three hundred years. He left you the Park House, which belonged to my late husband and his family. What the late Marquess did was another blasphemous stain on his already trail of mistakes that have haunted our family these last ten years."

Suddenly, a new voice broke the tension from behind Amelia. "Mother." She turned to find a tall, handsome man dressed in a crisp white shirt and dark jeans. He had light brown hair, a groomed beard, and the same remarkable blue eyes as his mother. It could only be Arthur.

With a warm and welcoming smile, Arthur extended his hand towards Amelia. "Hello," he greeted her.

Lady Edith acknowledged Amelia, "Arthur, this is Miss Levingston. She was a friend of your brothers."

"I'm very pleased to meet you. I'm Arthur Bonneville."

Amelia felt some of the tension dissipate as she shook Arthur's hand. "Lord Bonneville to you, Amelia," Lady Edith corrected him with a cold tone.

Arthur, unfazed by his mother's correction, kept his friendly demeanor. "Please call me Arthur. I insist."

With a shy smile, Amelia agreed, "Arthur."

Arthur then turned his attention to Amelia. "Mother, she's had quite a journey here today. May we offer you something to eat? Do you know where you are staying?"

Lady Edith remained adamant. "She isn't staying here."

Amelia could feel the tension thick in the air as the Bonneville family's dynamics played out before her. Amelia walked over to the urn, picked it up, and showed it to Arthur, her voice quivering with emotion. "I'm not staying. I just wanted to bring you your brother's ashes and offer my sincere sympathy." Tears welled up in her eyes, but she fought them back. "And... apologize if I've caused any sort of trouble." She carefully placed the urn back on the table.

In a gentle and comforting gesture, Arthur pulled a handkerchief from his pocket and handed it to Amelia. "Please. Allow me," he said.

Amelia wiped her tears with the handkerchief and managed a grateful, "Thank you."

Arthur persisted in his concern for her plans. "Where will you be staying Miss Levingston?"

Amelia didn't waver. "I'm going straight to The Park House," she told him.

Lady Edith's frustration reached its peak as she threw her hands up in exasperation. "It's time for you to leave, Miss Levingston. Take your things and go."

Arthur intervened, trying to mediate the situation. "Mother, honestly."

Lady Edith's anger was palpable as she continued, "And take his things with you."

Arthur addressed Amelia again. "You can't stay there," he told her with genuine worry in his voice.

Amelia, however, remained determined. "Well, that's where I'll be living," she informed him.

Lady Edith's anger flared once more as she scolded Amelia. "Take his ashes with you. They don't belong here. They belong there, with the rest of the ashes." Her tone dripped with anger and disdain. "You've outstayed your welcome. Now take them and go."

Amelia glanced at Lady Edith, who was pacing nervously, and whispered to Arthur, "Kinsey left the house to me."

Arthur remained concerned for Amelia's safety. "I'm perfectly aware of that, but you can't possibly stay there in the condition it's in," he cautioned.

Amelia responded to Arthur with determination, "Well, I know it requires some renovation."

Arthur exchanged an incredulous glance with his mother and then turned back to Amelia, concerned. "Do you not know?" He looked at Lady Edith. "Does she not know?"

Amelia was taken aback by their reactions. "Know what?" she asked, her voice trembling.

Arthur delivered the shocking news with a heavy heart. "The house is in ruin from fire damage. There's nothing left. There is no place to live."

Lady Edith's patience wore thin as she shouted at Amelia, "Please leave. Now!"

Amelia's stomach churned with a sinking feeling. She hurriedly gathered Kinsey's cane and hat, then picked up the urn. Tears welled up in her eyes as she took one last, apologetic look at Lady Edith. "I really am so very sorry for your loss. Kinsey was my friend, and for some reason, he left all of this to me, and... not to you. I know that doesn't seem fair to you. But I wanted to pay my respects... and—"

Lady Edith's tone turned bitter, and her words were laced with disdain. "What did you think? You would come here, and we would welcome you with open arms and accept you as our equal? My son died ten years ago. I buried him then. Please take those remains and go."

Amelia was at a loss, but a familiar voice broke through the tension. Charlie offered his assistance, "I'll drive her." He stood nearby, ready to support Amelia.

With her icy glare fixed on Amelia, Lady Edith reiterated her unwelcome status. "You are not welcome here, Amelia Levingston. Do not ever visit us ever again." She stormed out of the room, disappearing into the depths of her home.

Amelia knew she needed to leave immediately.

22

Retreat

AMELIA FOLLOWED CHARLIE out the door, her heart heavy with disappointment and embarrassment. Arthur pursued her, desperately calling out, "Please stop. You really don't understand."

Tears blurred Amelia's vision as she attempted to flee, but the gravel beneath her feet proved treacherous. She lost her grip on her belongings while trying to break her fall, and the urn shattered upon impact, releasing Kinsey's ashes into the air like a thick cloud of smoke. With ashes in her hair, on her shirt, and covering her, Amelia cried out in horror, "OH MY GOD."

Arthur swiftly caught up to her and knelt beside her, while Charlie rushed over to help. Amelia's hands were scraped and bleeding, with one hand sporting a deep cut. The ashes had settled all over her, creating a disheveled and distressing sight. Amelia wept uncontrollably and looked at Arthur with deep regret, saying, "I'm so sorry." Tears mixed with ashes streaked her cheeks.

"Oh no, your hands are bleeding," Arthur observed, gently taking her injured hand. "I'll run and get the first aid kit." Charlie hurried away to retrieve it.

Amelia, in her panic, tried to collect some of the ashes back into a remaining section of the broken urn. However, Arthur stopped her, advising, "Oh no, stop. Don't do that."

As Amelia looked back toward the house, she noticed Lady Edith staring out of a window with a pulled-back curtain, her expression one of disgust and contempt. Disheartened, Amelia shook her head in response before turning her attention back to Arthur and Charlie, who were there to help her through this difficult moment. Rosie, observing the chaos from a nearby second floor window, had her hand covering her face. Amelia continued to cry, her emotions a tumultuous mix of embarrassment and sorrow. She turned back to Arthur, tearful and apologetic. "I'm so... so sorry."

Arthur offered comfort, reassuring her, "It was just an accident. Here, please, let me help you stand up." He gently assisted her to her feet and guided her to sit on the front marble steps leading up to the house. Charlie reappeared, rushing over with bottles of water and a first aid kit in hand. Arthur, in his attempt to clean her shirt, accidentally touched her chest. Flustered, he muttered, "What am I doing? I'm so sorry."

Amelia bit her lip between tears, suppressing a laugh. "It's okay. I mean, it's not okay."

Charlie knelt beside her, and all three of them looked at the urn and the pile of ashes that had spilled out. The wind picked up and scattered the ashes everywhere. Panic set in as Amelia exclaimed, "Oh no! I have a bag in the car." Charlie hurried to the vehicle and retrieved a paper shopping bag from the back seat, using it to gather the remaining ashes.

Amelia winced as Arthur poured water over her bleeding hands, causing a stinging sensation. "Ouch," she cried.

Arthur examined her hand with the deeper cut, his concern evident. "This one is pretty bad."

Amelia sighed, feeling overwhelmed by the situation. She gazed into

Arthur's beautiful blue eyes, appreciating his kindness. "Why don't we take you back inside and get you cleaned up?" Arthur suggested, trying to lift her spirits.

Amelia refused; her embarrassment still too fresh. "I would rather die. I can't go back in there. I'm mortified."

Charlie, meanwhile, had returned with the bag containing the ashes and the broken urn. He gently placed them beside Amelia. He looked at her hands and proposed, "Maybe we should take you to the clinic. You might need a stitch or two." Charlie then opened a bottle of water and used it to rinse away the ashes and dried blood.

Amelia winced again at the sting of alcohol, but she appreciated Charlie's care. "Ouch," she repeated.

As Charlie finished bandaging her hands, Arthur turned to Amelia with a concerned expression. "Blood doesn't seem to bother you much."

Amelia smiled weakly through her tears. "Oh, I'm so used to medical stuff. I've had about a million blood tests in the last year." She explained, surprising both Arthur and Charlie.

Arthur was taken aback. "Really, why?" he asked, his curiosity piqued. Charlie, equally surprised, turned to Amelia.

Charlie looked up at the sky which had started to fill with angry clouds. "It's starting to get late and it looks like rain. We really should be off."

"Charlie, take her to The Lace Factory." Amelia looked at him confused "It's a hotel in town that has a pub next door. You can have a nice dinner and a good place to sleep. At least for tonight."

Charlie nodded in agreement whilst Amelia was simply too tired to argue.

"Fine. But tomorrow I will start living at the Park House," she said firmly. "Or at least, assess what I need to do next."

"I'll call ahead for you and make arrangements, Amelia," Arthur said sternly.

Charlie helped Amelia stand up. "Are you alright?" He asked.

"No." Amelia forced a smile. "But I'm tough."

Charlie walked her over to his car door and opened it for her. Amelia turned back to Arthur, "Don't worry about making arrangements. I can take care of myself."

"I insist." Arthur told her.

Charlie closed her door and ran to the other side and got in. Arthur waved goodbye to Amelia through her window and she nodded at him with a forced grin.

As they drove away, she watched Arthur go back to where the ashes had been and kneel down near them. He put his hand to his face. Amelia wasn't sure how anything was going to play out, but she felt like this experience was most likely as bad as it was going to get.

Charlie turned and said to her, "I got a text message from my brother as I was running to the barn, He said he met you at the hotel in London."

"Yes Peter. We met very quickly, and he was right to warn me."

"Are you going to be alright?" Charlie asked.

Amelia looked over to him, "I hope so." As they drove from Oak Hall Amelia's phone started to ring. She took it out of her purse and read the caller display. Mr Field.

"I'm sorry, I have to take this." She answered the phone. "Hi, Mr. Field."

"Hello Miss Levingston. I just wanted to check in and see how the meeting with the family went?"

"Not well."

There was a pause.

"Oh?"

Amelia looked at her hand and her shirt that was still covered in ashes. "Um, I did bring his ashes to them as you requested."

"Excellent."

"But..."

"Yes?"

Charlie gave her an encouraging glance as she mustered the courage to tell him.

"Well, she didn't want to keep them. So, I took the urn with me and I, um... fell."

"Okay?"

"So now, some... of the ashes are in the driveway, some are in a paper bag, and most... are covering me right now."

A long pause followed.

"Hmmmm. I'm not usually at a loss for words. So, I'll notate that you did... return the ashes to their family... and... we will just leave it at that."

"Okay."

"Call me if you need anything. I'll check in with you next week after you've gotten settled."

"Alright. Thank you, Mr. Field."

"You're welcome, Miss Levingston." He hung up and Amelia buried her injured hands into her dirty face in total defeat.

"Things will turn around for you." Charlie said optimistically, one of those men who couldn't stand to see a hopeless woman.

Amelia gazed at Charlie with a faint glimmer of hope in her eyes. Blood from her hands had smudged onto her face, but her focus was on Charlie's reassuring words.

He bit his lip, clearly concerned for her, and replied, "It... will. I'm certain of it. Because this was... pretty terrible."

Amelia managed a small, grateful smile. "From your lips to God's ears, Charlie." She turned her attention back to the passing scenery outside the car window, her primary goal now to reach the hotel as quickly as possible so she could wash away the day's traumatic events.

23

Safe Haven

THE LOOK ON the receptionist's face said it all. Amelia was covered in ashes with bloodied bandages on her hands and was, frankly, a disheveled, hopeless mess. But her arrival at the boutique hotel was expected. Arthur had kept his word and called to make the arrangements for her stay. She was handed her room key the moment she arrived and that was that.

Charlie insisted on helping her up to her room which Amelia was very thankful for and after a quick goodbye, the sound of her hotel room door closing behind her was one of the best sounds she had ever known. It brought her back to living with Aunt Rita and Cousin Tessa, that sweet sound of solitude when the door was shut and the lock was turned.

She ran into the hotel bathroom. Her right hand had been throbbing in pain and she had hid it all the way to the hotel. She knew it was a deep cut and could feel the warmth of the blood that was still slowly seeping through her bandage.

Instead of going to urgent care which she knew she should, she called downstairs and asked for a first aid kit to be brought up. A member of the staff swiftly did as requested and she stoically assured him she was fine and just needed a Band-Aid. She let her hand run with cold water over it for a while and the pain began to lessen. Her other hand was scraped up, but not like this one. Her hand needed a stitch or two, but the butterfly bandages she located would have to do that evening. After doing her best to cover it with a large bandage, she began to undress.

Her wig was a disaster. She tried her best to get the remainder of the ashes into the sink and hung it gently behind on the bathroom door hook. She stepped into the shower and undressed the rest of herself, shook off her clothing, and watched the remainder of the ashes fall to the floor.

When she finally was able to turn the shower on the water felt so amazing on her tired and aching body. She bent over and leaned with her left hand on the tile and looked down watching Kinsey's ashes floats down the drain. Then the tears started and didn't stop. It had been a very long day, turning into an even longer night.

⁂

THE NEXT DAY Amelia awoke to the sound of someone knocking at her door. She had slept so deeply she could barely open her eyes. She looked over at her clock. Ten a.m.

"Who is it?" She called out.

"Amelia, it's Arthur Bonneville." His voice said through the other side of her door.

Amelia sat up, feeling a sense of surprise. Her fingers grazed her short hair on her head, and it struck her that she wasn't wearing a wig. She quickly got out of bed, retrieved a robe from the nearby closet, and then opened her suitcase to search for a wig. After locating a bag containing a long blonde wig, she put it on, adjusting it carefully in front of the mirror. Taking a deep breath, she composed herself and opened the door, ready to face whoever was on the other side.

"Yes?" Amelia answered, finding Arthur standing there. He looked handsome in a white collared shirt and a sport coat. She met his piercing blue eyes, which left her feeling somewhat unnerved. He held two white paper cups and had a bag sitting on the floor beside him. "What are you doing here?"

The man's cheeks reddened slightly as he responded, "I don't want to disturb you, but I thought we all got off on the wrong foot yesterday."

Amelia glanced at the cups he was holding. "Is that coffee?"

"Well, I wasn't sure what you drank, so I brought a coffee and a tea," he explained, offering them to her.

A warm smile crossed her face. "That's very sweet of you." As he continued to study her, Amelia sensed he might be looking at her hair. "What?" She reached up to touch her wig to ensure it was in place. It felt secure.

"Is your hair a bit longer than yesterday?" he inquired.

Amelia nodded. "Oh, um, yes. I wear a wig."

His face reddened further as he stammered, "Oh. I'm terribly sorry for asking."

She immediately tried to put him at ease. "Please, don't be embarrassed." Amelia reached out and lightly touched his arm, hoping to convey her understanding.

He observed her hand as she removed it from his arm. "I'm going to get dressed now," she informed him.

"Of course. Here, I'll just leave these with you," he replied, handing her the drinks.

"Thank you," Amelia said gratefully. The door closed, and she stood there holding the tea and coffee, somewhat bewildered by the interaction. As she moved to set the cups on the table, there was another knock on the door. Opening it again, she found Arthur still standing there, looking somewhat like a schoolboy, holding a bag.

"I brought you breakfast as well," he announced.

"That is very kind of you. But you really didn't need to do this, what with arranging the hotel and everything," Amelia responded, beginning to explain her situation.

"Oh, yes I did. I'm very embarrassed by the way my family treated you yesterday," Arthur admitted.

Amelia nodded in agreement. "Yes, that was pretty awful."

He inquired about her hands. "How are your hands, by the way?"

She offered a reassuring lie. "Fine. I'll be fine. I'm tougher than I look."

"I'm sure you are," he replied, his light eyes shining with an inscrutable expression. "Well, I wanted to offer to drive you to The Park House this morning."

Amelia was taken aback. "Really? You would take me there? I was just going to grab a taxi."

"Oh no, I insist, really," Arthur persisted.

Amelia sensed there was more to his offer, perhaps something he needed to hear from her. She was becoming enchanted by his presence with a swiftness that felt fated, as if she had always known him in some way, in a past life. Maybe it was the similarities she was starting to notice between Kinsey and his brother, particularly their smile.

"I would appreciate that very much," she agreed, hoping he hadn't noticed her gazing dreamily into the middle distance. "Let me just get dressed and pack everything up."

Arthur seemed to have different plans. "Oh, there is no need to pack up," he informed her. "Well, I'm sure I need to check out this morning," Amelia protested.

"No, I've made arrangements with the hotel. You can stay as long as you like," he assured her with ease.

Amelia started to feel a bit perturbed by his insistence. "Um, well, we will discuss that later, but for now, I'm going to get dressed. I'll meet you downstairs shortly," she said firmly, quickly closing the door. Leaning her body against it, she rested her head and heard him walking away, muttering something like, "you idiot." Groggy from the previous night's events, she welcomed the coffee with enthusiasm, feeling the effects of the time change weighing on her today more than ever.

24

It's Been A Long Road

SHE KNEW ARTHUR was waiting but took her time getting dressed anyway. Once she had decided she was ready, she looked back at Kinsey's cane and hat, deciding she would bring them with her, along with the remainder of his ashes.

When she arrived downstairs in the hotel lobby, Arthur wasn't anywhere to be found. She approached a woman working at the desk, hoping to ask if she had any visitors, but then saw Arthur standing outside on the street, smoking by the window. Amelia walked straight up to him, pulled the cigarette out of his mouth and threw it on the curb, crushing it with her boot heel.

Arthur looked both shocked and impressed.

"Don't smoke," Amelia said quietly.

The same mixed expression on his face, Arthur looked at the cane and hat in her hand.

"Why do you have those with you?" The subject was being negated.

"I'm bringing them to The Park House. Where they belong."

"Very well. Follow me," he said, and turned away before she had a chance to reply. She followed him to his dark green land rover and stepped in when he opened her door for her.

"It is so strange to get in on the left side," she remarked.

He rolled his eyes, but in a good-natured way, then closed her door and went to the driver side, stepping in to start the engine.

"Thank you for driving me today."

"Well, the only way to get there would be a taxi and I'm not sure you want to drive with a total stranger into a private estate, alone, with no one for miles."

"Well, I'm not overly concerned," she said, sitting upright.

"Didn't your mother ever warn you about strangers?" he jested.

"Well, yes. But after seeing the size of your house—and the…determination of your mother—I don't think I have anything to worry about. It would be all over the news before you were halfway to the kidnapping spot."

He nodded, grinning, and then started to drive. She looked to the backseat of his car, which contained a stack of teaching books and his satchel.

"I'm curious, it's a Monday," she said. "Shouldn't you be at work or something?"

"A colleague is filling in for me today."

"Oh? And what do you do exactly?" she asked.

Caught off guard, he replied in a mumble. "I am a professor at Nottingham University."

"You're a teacher?" she asked, surprised.

"Yes. A professor of English Literature," he said, seeming to look shy.

Her heart started pounding in her chest. That was not what she expected. It was in fact, the perfect answer. "Wow."

"Wow, what?" he asked.

"I think that's wonderful."

He laughed to himself. "Not the usual response people give when you tell them you're an English teacher. Normally they're all, *Oh, so a failed novelist then?*"

"It's June though. Shouldn't you be on summer break?"

"Normally yes, but I offered to help with their summer semester. I needed to stay busy. It's been a healthy distraction from... everything."

She glanced over at him playing with his beard as he drove. Until now, she had never really thought anyone with a beard was attractive, but there was something about him that was so confident it was making her a bit nervous. He met her eyes and she quickly turned her head back to her window. Everything was wet from the rain—the buildings, the people—but it didn't look overcast or dreary. It seemed just right.

"It really is a beautiful city."

"It is," he said with a smile. "May I ask you a question, Amelia?"

Amelia could feel that he wanted more from her. She nodded, then realized he couldn't see her properly because his eyes were on the road, so added "Yes."

"Were you with Kinsey when he died?" he asked.

"You call him Kinsey too?" Amelia was surprised. "You don't call him Henry? Or... "The Marquess." She mocked Lady Edith.

Arthur laughed. "No, I always called him Kinsey. Since we were very young. We all had such English names we joked around about what we would rather be called, and Kinsey stuck for some sort of reason. He's always been Kinsey. Except for formal events, and such."

"You mean royal events?" Amelia joked.

"And such." Arthur agreed.

Amelia studied his face. He had such a good-looking short beard. She noticed he had very clearly trimmed it today. He looked very clean and dapper. She wondered if he had tried to look this good for her. She then thought about his previous question and before Arthur could ask her again, she told him, "To answer your question. No, I wasn't with him"

"I don't want to be impertinent but how close were you?" he asked.

"Well, he wasn't my boyfriend if that's what you mean." She laughed.

"Well, of course not," he replied.

"Did you know your brother was gay?" she softly asked him.

The energy shifted dramatically in the car. "Yes, of course." He replied. "He kept a lot of secrets from our family, but that wasn't one of them. Keeping cancer a secret must have been very hard for him. I really don't understand why he would never tell me. He was always good at hiding things."

"I would agree with that." Amelia said as she reached into her bag and pulled out the keys.

Arthur looked over at them and shook his head, "I haven't seen those keys in years."

"They look like keys to a castle."

"It's a very old house."

"And who did it belong to?"

"My Father's side of the family. For centuries. It was built as a country house for hunting and that sort of thing. When my father married my mother, she fell madly in love with it, mostly because of the land and her love for gardening. He sold off some other properties he owned and together they brought it into this century. That's where Kinsey, Rosie and myself grew up."

"Your mother must hate me."

"She doesn't hate you Amelia. How could she? She doesn't even know you."

"Neither do you."

"Let's change that, shall we?" His eyes found hers and she smiled. "So tell me, Amelia Levingston. How old are you?"

"How old am I? Now you're being impertinent! How old are you?"

"Perhaps, but I asked first." He grinned.

"Fine. I just turned twenty-eight in February."

"I'm thirty-one." He told her.

"Really?"

"What's that supposed to mean?" He asked.

"I thought you were a bit older. Perhaps it's the facial hair."

He scoffed, "Well, I like this look." She bit her lip to keep herself from giggling and looked back out her window. He started to slow down, and she looked around as he turned off the main road.

His voice changed to a more serious tone, "We're here."

As they drove down the graveled pathway, Amelia turned to look behind her at the main road. "Isn't this near where your house is" she asked.

"Oak Hall?"

"Yes."

"That's my mother's home. Technically speaking, it's her family's house. Her mother, my Gran, lives in London now with her second husband Barnaby. When we lost the Park House, my Gran offered for us to live there with her, so we did. Now it's just Rosie and Mum."

"So it doesn't belong to her?"

"No and it never will. That house will pass onto my uncle when Gran dies." He sighed.

"Hmmm."

"But yes, to answer your question we are very near to Oak Hall." He answered as he focused driving slowly up the road which was unkept, and littered with branches that must have been falling over many years. They were pushed to the side as though recently someone had moved them out of the way.

"Where do you live, Arthur?"

"I have a place near the University where I work."

They approached a large wrought iron gate between two rocked pillars He parked the car in front of the gate and stepped out.

Amelia stepped out of the car as well and they walked toward a large lion head padlock that was keeping the gate secure. The lion reminded her of Kinsey's cane. In the center of the lion face was the keyhole to a lock. Arthur looked at her. Amelia gazed back. She felt chills.

"Well?" he asked.

"Well what?" she said.

"May I have the keys?" he asked.

"Oh. Oh yes." She went back to the car and pulled the large set of keys out of her bag and ran back to hand them to him. He picked a brass key and unlocked the lion and removed the chain attached. The gate began to creak loudly as he pulled each side open and wedged it into the nearby bushes. Amelia followed him back to his car and joked, "I feel like we're in an Agatha Christy novel."

He didn't laugh, instead he nodded in agreement and continued to drive up the oak tree lined road. As they began to approach the Park House, Amelia saw some white deer in a clearing to their left. "Oh my goodness look Arthur!"

He slowed the car to a stop on the gravel and they watched as a small herd of deer lifted their heads to them. Quickly, they started to scatter off into the forest that surrounded them.

"Those are Fallow deer. They live here on the grounds. There are hundreds of them."

"They are so enchanting." She watched in awe as they scurried off.

"Enchanting, eh?"

"Yes. I've never seen a deer before in real life."

"You're joking." He said surprised.

"I wish I was." She looked eagerly out the car windows trying to see more.

He continued to follow the long road. "There is some amazing wildlife here. It was once a truly a special place."

"This is a long driveway." She commented.

"It's a mile all together between The Park House and the main road." He told her.

Then they turned a corner and the house that had been completely hidden, suddenly stood before them.

"Wow." Amelia gasped.

Arthur seemed just as surprised, "Good Lord."

25

The Park House

THE PARK HOUSE stood in its former glory. It was dark and over-grown, slowly being taken over by vines, however, there was a magnifi-cence that still remained. The two-story Tudor home stood timeless. The right side had clearly been burned with cracked walls and a crumbling roof but otherwise the integrity of the home stood. Not only was there damage to the house from a fire but distress from the elements as well. A large window that might have once been stained glass had been broken.

As Arthur parked the car at the entry way, she studied his face which was in absolute awe. "Are you alright?" she asked.

"I... I just, I thought it was all gone." He told her.

"What do you mean?"

He opened his car door and stepped onto the gravel. His eyes were fixated on the house that stood before him as he grasped the magnitude of what remained. "I had no idea so much was still here." He said.

"I don't understand. When was the last time you were here?" She asked confused.

"It's been ten years or so."

"Ten years?"

"Yes, ten years this past Christmas." he remembered.

"Oh. So, I don't understand, why haven't you been back here?"

"It didn't belong to us anymore. It belonged to Kinsey. Mother told us it had burnt to the ground. I always thought there was just nothing here."

"You thought the house was gone?" she asked.

"Yes. I thought it was all gone. But clearly, I mean, look at it. Did you know?"

"I was given the plans of the house by Mr. Field. I was told that it was in need of repair, nothing more." She replied honestly.

She looked at the gravity of the home and the project that stood before her. It was huge. A sight to behold. She had seen the layout of what had been provided to her by Mr Field and was aware that it was a large estate. But she had no idea of the weight of the home or the magnitude of its presence. It was daunting. She wouldn't allow Arthur to see how terrified she was feeling, so instead she put on a brave face and with confidence said, "Let's go take a look around."

Arthur quietly followed her as they walked around the exterior of the home, taking pictures along the way. It was going to be a huge project. At every corner of the exterior, she imagined what she could do and envisioned how it once was. He patiently waited for her to finish and then asked, "What are you going to do?"

Amelia turned to face him, "What do you mean what am I going to do?"

"With the house? Do you plan on selling it?" he asked.

"Why of course not Arthur."

He took a step back. "You're not?"

She looked back to the incredible home that stood before her and collected her thoughts. "Just because it's a mess, doesn't mean it not worth fighting for." She turned around to face him and continued, "I'm going to restore it to its former glory."

Her soul cried out with those words. This was *her* purpose. It was *her* chance at something great.

"This is a lot to take on." Arthur muttered.

Amelia was surprised by him. Arthur seemed to care so little about this house. "You grew up here. Don't you want to see your home restored?"

"Yes, but this house..." She could tell he was searching for the right words, "It has so much tragedy attached to it." There was a lot of weight to what he had just shared with her.

Amelia held her hand out to one of the stone walls and touched the house with care, "Well, the Park House and I have that in common. Doesn't mean you should give up on it."

After assessing the outside of the house, it was obvious that the East wing carried the majority of the damage. Aside from an infestation of ivy, the Park House looked surprisingly well off.

"How old is the house?" Amelia asked as they walked toward the main door.

"Old. It was built sometime during the seventeenth century."

They climbed the two wide stone steps toward the door squeezing the keys in her hand in disbelief that Kinsey had left all of this to her. It didn't feel right. It didn't feel like it belonged to her or should belong to her.

The door was huge with a large brass lion head door knocker. "Aslan." She muttered to herself as she knocked twice.

"What's that?" Arthur asked.

"Aslan." she pointed to the face.

"Ah yes. It is quite the Narnian door. The lions were my father's personal contribution to the estate. You will find them everywhere." He pointed out the head key she held in her hand and she took it to unlock the large bolt. The door opened with a loud creak. The fresh air poured into the space. Dust began to blow all around them. The floors were covered in heavy soot from the fire, however, the entry hall otherwise remained in near perfect condition. Amelia took her foot and swiped the soot to the right revealing the unique tile below. It was exquisite.

He pointed to the smoke damage that was evident throughout the surfaces of the ceilings and throughout the home and said, "You won't be able to live here in this condition."

"No, I'll have to figure that out." She agreed.

She took out her phone and turned the flashlight on so she could see better. Amelia couldn't stop smiling, "It clearly has a lot of smoke damage but otherwise it's magnificent."

She could see the beauty. She imagined how it once stood. Such a proud home. She envisioned it at its finest. "I'm going to walk around."

But before she took another step forward her smile washed from her face when she saw a long marble table to her left. Her stomach twisted. The immense marble table had recently been wiped down and mounted above it on the wall, was the painting that Amelia had given Kinsey for Christmas.

It was a replica canvas of "The Son of Man" by Belgian artist Rene Magritte. Below sat a large metal box with an envelope that read *'For Amelia'* Arthur and Amelia exchanged glances and Amelia slowly walked over and picked up the envelope. Arthur recognized his brother's handwriting and angrily grabbed it from her wounded hand, "He was here?"

"Ow." she pulled her hand back and accidentally dropped her phone. She could feel her hand start to bleed again and she held it tightly.

In shameful regret he gently reached for her hand. "Oh, I'm so sorry." He pleaded, as she took a step back looking at it. "No really, I'm so sorry, let me look at it." He reached down and picked up her phone and wiped it on his shirt. Then shined the phone light towards the wound.

The band-aid was starting to turn red.

"It's fine." She said.

"It's not fine. I can see you're bleeding." He pulled out a handkerchief out of his pocket and held it out as a peace offering. "Please allow me."

She looked at her hand and could see blood was starting to seep out. "Fine." She held out her hand and he gently wrapped his handkerchief and tied it. It hurt, however his quick action made her heart skip a beat.

He met her gaze and said, "That's a bit better. You know we might want to take you to have that looked at. If it's still bleeding perhaps you really do need a stitch."

"Oh no, really it's fine. I'm fine. Plus, I think it's too late for stitches." She told him.

"I truly am sorry."

"I know." They both looked down at the envelope that sat on the soot covered floor and he leaned down to pick it up and after looking at it handed it to her.

"Do you see that painting? That was my Christmas present to him. That was the last day we ever spoke."

"Why *that* painting?" He asked staring at it.

"Because, it's *him*."

They both stared at the painting for a minute then she looked down to the envelope in her hand and stored at it.

"Are you going to read it now?" He asked.

"No, I will later." she replied, looking back up to the painting, "I'm not sure if he came here." She told him.

"But how is all of this here?" he asked.

"Maybe Mr Field? I really don't know," Amelia told him honestly.

"What's that metal box then?" he asked desperate to change the subject.

"I have no idea," she opened the mysterious metal box and looked inside. When she recognized what it was, she let out a gasp, "Oh. Wow. Okay."

"What is it?" Arthur looked inside.

Inside sat the three volumes of Mansfield Park, that Amelia had encountered several months ago at Merry's home.

"These are very old. What are they?" Arthur asked.

"You won't believe me when I tell you." She put the lid back onto the metal box. "Let's just say, they belong in a museum."

Amelia looked down the hallway and slowly walked through. A great arch opened to her right, revealing a very similar large sitting room Lady Edith had in her current home. Inside the room was a haunted reminder filled with old Christmas decor. Stockings still hung lifeless on the mantle, and the remains of a Christmas tree stood in the corner. It was a tragic scene.

Amelia looked to the paintings on the wall that were covered in soot and could see a family portrait. "All these paintings. I'm fairly confident that I can send them off to be professionally cleaned and touched up." By the hopeless look on his face, it offered little to no comfort to him. He stood staring into his past at the remains of the Christmas tree. He felt trapped in time until Amelia put her hand on his shoulder, "Let's move forward."

He followed solemnly. Just down the large hallway and to the left stood two large, armored guard suits standing at attention outside a large wooden door.

"My goodness. Look at these." She smiled looking at them.

"That's Harry and Hank." He told her.

"Harry and Hank?" she laughed.

"That's what Kinsey and I called them." He smirked.

"What can Harry and Hank possibly be guarding?" She asked Arthur. Looking down there was a lion head brass handle and another keyhole.

"My late father's study." He grew weary as he held his hand out to hers. She gave him the keys and he found the one that fit the lock and handed it back to her.

"Oh." She spoke carefully. "Well, do you want to wait here?"

He looked like a frightened child. "No. Let's go in." He said in a bitter voice.

She unlocked the large wood door with its ornate brass lion head handle pushing it open with a loud *CREAK*. They both were taken aback by the study and library space they stood in. The floors were coated in a layer of dust but they were still in amazing condition. As Amelia entered, she wasn't looking at the dust she was looking at the books. Thousands of them. "Oh, my goodness." She said putting her hand to her mouth.

"I can't believe it." he said.

"This is wonderful. Look at all these beautiful books." She pulled one off the shelf blowing away the dust and read the title out loud. "*The Hound of the Baskervilles.* This is a first edition Arthur, look!" As she held it out in excitement his dark stare stopped her. "What are you looking at?" She followed his gaze and saw a broken bottle that sat on the floor in front of a large wooden desk.

He couldn't stop staring at it. Then he looked at her. "I have to get some air."

Gently she put the book back in its place and closed the office door behind her. Amelia decided to not follow him out. She instead took a few more minutes to look around. The right wing would be in dire need of repair, however, the rest of the home stood in worthy condition.

Worried a bit for Arthur, she decided to cut things short. She stopped to pick up the metal box and walked outside to look for him. She started to set the box back down and yelped, "Ouch." To her hand.

"I'll help you lock it in a minute!" Arthur called over to her with a cigarette in his mouth as he inhaled and exhaled his stress away. Worried for him she left the box on the doorsteps and went to comfort him. He was standing near a large elm tree far across the lawn. She was nervous to approach him but felt like she had no other option and walked slowly toward him.

"Is everything alright?" Amelia asked.

He finished his cigarette and took a pack out to light a second. Amelia took it straight from him mouth and threw it on the ground. Stunned and angry he accused her, "Stop doing that!"

In a worried voice she pled, "I'm sorry. I just don't want you to smoke."

He didn't fight her. She turned away from him and crossed her arms. She felt him looking at her as she stared out into the vast fields in awe and wonderment. She worried about what he must be thinking about her and everything that had transpired.

Her worries faded a bit from the view before her. The fields met a long line of mature trees in the distance. The land the Park House stood on was aristocratic legacy. She was standing on the land of a long line of English nobility and felt its presence. The garden was extensive, complete with a fountain behind the house which was overgrown and dry. Amelia imagined the simple bliss from the sound of water. "It really is beautiful here." She sighed.

He looked out to the land and memories flooded him. "Yes, it is." He agreed.

"It's a big job and it's not going to be easy. But I am going to bring the Park House back to life.

"You're very ambitious." Arthur said with a bitterness that Amelia couldn't understand.

"It could be a home again. It could have a whole new life. That's what *Kinsey* wanted."

He growled and angrily walked back toward the front door of the house, fetching a cigarette from his pack and lighting it on his way. This time Amelia didn't scold him but she did chase after him.

"Am I missing something here?" Amelia asked. "What are you not telling me?"

"Can you hand me the keys?" He asked impatiently.

"If you stop smoking." She muttered.

He took his cigarette and tossed it angerly. "Keys... please."

She pulled them out and handed them back to him. After locking the door he picked up the metal box and brought it back to his car opening the back to place it in. Quietly she followed and remembered Kinsey's ashes she had brought. Arthur opened the door for her to get in.

"I have to do one more thing." She took the bag of what remained of his ashes and walked away from the car and toward the house. Arthur watched her from a distance and she looked around. To the right of the house she saw a tree and she walked to it. She put her hand on the tree and looked over to the house. Opening the bag and looking at the ashes she whispered,

"I'm sorry this wasn't perfect my friend. But you are home now." She opened the bag and poured what remained of his ashes out. A gust of wind picked them up and they flew toward the house and Amelia watched.

After a moment she walked back to Arthur's car where he was waiting for her, holding the door open and she sat back inside. He sat down next to her and started the car.

"What is it that you aren't sharing with me?"

He thought a moment and said, "Did Kinsey tell you what started the fire?" Amelia shook her head no. He looked into her eyes and said, "*He did.*"

26

Brothers

THE SILENCE WAS deafening as Arthur drove Amelia back to her hotel. Amelia sat impatiently fidgeting with Kinsey's letter in her hands. Amelia couldn't take the silence anymore, "Do you want to tell me why Kinsey started the fire?"

"Not today."

She stared back down to the letter and her hands began to tremble.

"Well, when you're ready, I would like to know what happened."

He nodded. As they continued their journey into Nottingham Amelia admired the many homes they passed. There were so many unique buildings, especially as they began to get closer into town. Los Angeles was so bland and dirty, she thought. Yes there were many beautiful buildings but all tucked away by large hedges. Here it felt like everything was exposed... besides the largest of estates that were down private roads such as the Park House.

The Park House plagued her imagination. She was still shaking her head in disbelief of the gift Kinsey had left her. Her thoughts returned to the letter, curious about its contents, but astutely aware this was not the appropriate time to read it.

"Aren't you going to open that?" he demanded.

"Don't raise your voice at me. You sound like your mother," she spat.

His mouth hung open. Arthur couldn't believe she said that, and neither could Amelia. She had never spoken like that before to anyone. Though she had wanted to several times.

"I don't sound like my mother." He said starkly.

"You sounded *exactly* like your mother." She said scowling.

"Well, when do you plan on reading it?" He sounded like a petulant child excluded from a game by the other children. He started fidgeting with his beard. She looked at him for a moment and then back down at her envelope.

She whispered, "I am going to read it, but I'll wait until I'm alone."

He huffed and continued fidgeting with his beard.

"Okay fine, I'll read it now."

He sighed. "You don't have to. I'm sorry. It was meant for you."

"No, I'll read it. If I were you, I would want to know what's inside too."

"Thank you." he said with a sincere relief to his voice. He glanced over as she carefully opened the envelope and began to read it out loud.

'My Dearest Amelia, there will not be any more surprises I'm afraid. My time has run short. The book was a gift from our dearest friend. He insisted. He told me he had his turn and now it was yours. You can decide what's best for its future. I know you will.

I'm sure by now you have met my family. They aren't all bad. Give them time. My mother may carry many thorns, but she is the most beautiful rose. Lean on Arthur. I trust him to help you make the right decisions in the days ahead.

Take as much creative liberty as possible. I loved the Park House until I didn't. It's time for it to have a second life. It deserves that at the very least. Just like you.

- Your's truly-
The White Rabbit'

"White rabbit?" Arthur asked. They were approaching Amelia's hotel.

"It's a sort of, personal joke. He told me to lean on you. But I've just met you."

"You can trust me." He assured her. After parking his car they sat for a moment. Amelia searched his face, and he assured her again, "You *can* trust me."

Amelia didn't trust anyone. That was the truth of it. How could she trust a man she had just met. However, he *was* Kinsey's favorite after all.

She collected all of her things and closed the door and he continued to follow her. Amelia turned surprised. "What are you doing?"

"How can I help you with The Park House?" he pleaded.

"Are you serious?" she asked.

"Yes. I'm very serious. I would very much like to help you."

She could tell he was being earnest. She felt his nervousness, like he was worried she might turn him away.

"I need to think about that." She told him.

"Why?" he asked.

"Well, I'm just a bit hesitant to..." she looked at his kind face. Something inside her shifted and she couldn't refuse him. She considered his offer and then told him, "Well first, I need to hire a general contractor."

He smiled and returned to his car. "Wonderful, I will be in touch with you first thing tomorrow." He left quickly. Almost like he was worried if he stayed any longer, she would change her mind.

As she entered her hotel, she felt nervous. She was greeted by the receptionist and Amelia was thankful to not be alone. Once she entered her hotel room and shut the door behind her, she felt a sense of relief and thought, 'Maybe I'm better off being alone.'

After setting her things down, she retreated to her bed and pulled the covers on. Her wig was hot and itchy and she took it off and laid it down next to her, running her fingers through her very short and sweaty hair. A warm bubble bath might be the best thing to calm her nerves.

⁂

THE BATH MADE her hands sting. It took a moment for it to stop and once they did, she sunk down into the tub and leaned her body back submerging past her ears. Silence. It had been quite a journey to get to here, and now that she had finally arrived, the stress consumed her. She touched her port. Feeling the scars with the tips of her fingers, she thought of the first time she met Kinsey.

When she heard him scream at the nurse for being clumsy with his IV down the hallway. His grinch-like smile which was hiding who he truly was, a scared man.

She was scared too. Why did he entrust this to her? Her mind drifted to Arthur. Could she truly trust him? Perhaps he was Lady Edith's spy, and they were all set out against her.

She closed her eyes and cleared her mind of negative thoughts. Focusing on the good, two words entered her mind. *Thank you.*

Her body relaxed. She stretched out her back and then slowly sat up resting her head against the porcelain tub. "Thank you, God." She whispered. "Thank you for this second chance." It was wonderfully quiet. A quiet that until this point in her lifetime, she had never experienced. It was perfect.

27

The Bonnevilles

"HAVE YOU LOST your mind completely?" Lady Edith snapped.

Arthur and Lady Edith were in her stately home's study. She had just been enjoying a quiet moment to herself putting a flower arrangement together in a vase when her son had revealed his determined decision.

Arthur casually sat in a large leather sofa chair drinking a glass of scotch and smoking his cigarette. "I'm going to help her." He said decidedly.

"That is out of the question" she demanded. She felt betrayed as she set the flowers she was holding down on the table in outrage. She started to pace, trying to decide if she should just leave the room. She didn't want to run away from this. After the fire something had shifted inside of her and she knew she needed to face any problem straight on. So instead, she went over to some books on a nearby shelf and started reorganizing them with her nervous energy.

"I understand you might be upset mother. But you do understand we have no power over the decision that Kinsey made."

She turned to face him. Her eyes changed as she shared, "I've hired someone to investigate all of this. We might not have to live with Kinsey's wasteful and absurd decisions for the rest of our lives."

Irritated, Arthur put out his cigarette and stood up, following her across the room, "I think you are wasting your time and money if that's true. His will was iron clad other, and he was of sound mind. If you need to ask any more questions you need to contact Mr. Field, but there's nothing more to be done."

"Sound mind?" she sputtered, "Sound mind? He was at death's doorstep. He wasn't thinking clearly. How could he have been? No, no, Kinsey was just trying to send off one more middle finger in my direction." She walked away from him toward a nearby window and stared out.

He followed her, "Did you know he was here?"

She turned confused to face Arthur, "Who was?"

His voice softened, "He was."

"What do you mean he was here?" she couldn't believe what he just told her. Her face shifted into a fearful and uneasy manner as her throat tightened from grief.

"I mean Kinsey came home to England before he died. Sometime in the fall," he said, gently, "most likely to make his final arrangements."

"How do you know that?" she was becoming more and more flush as her blood rushed to her head.

"Amelia told me that he had returned."

"Why are you even speaking with that girl?" she demanded.

"I drove her to the Park House yesterday."

The room went ice cold. Lady Edith could barely turn to face her son.

"You did what?" she asked.

"Why didn't you tell us the truth about the Park House?" he asked.

She tried to change the subject and shrugged her shoulders defensively ignoring his question completely, "So, you mean to tell me, for the first time in ten years Kinsey came back to England, knowing he's dying, and doesn't even have the courage to face us."

"Yes."

Lady Edith retreated to a nearby chair staring at the floor. Arthur stood up and walked to a decanter sitting on a table. Instead of refilling his glass he picked up another and filled it for her. She sat quietly with her hand on her face and eyes closed. Arthur handed her the glass. She shook her head no to him. He gently took her hand and opened it and placed the glass in-between her fingers. She took a much-needed drink from it and sighed in admission, "I will never forgive him for any of it."

Arthur kneeled next to her, and she looked into his eyes. Quietly he spoke with deep consideration, "I'm struggling with forgiving you for lying to all of us as well."

"I didn't lie to you?" she replied slamming her glass down on the table.

"Did you hear what I said? I went with Amelia to the Park House. I walked inside and saw it all with my own eyes." He took a step back distancing himself from her and waited for her reply.

Lady Edith stood to face him. Fear grew in her eyes as she cried out to him, "Saw what?"

"You told us the house was burnt to the ground. Not a single book was left, you said. It was *all ashes* you said. Mum, over half the house is still standing. It's been repairable all this time. Dad's belongings are still there! His study is just as it was, slowly being swallowed by dust."

Bitterly, her voice shook in fear and anger, "That place is a tomb. It should have been bulldozed with what remained and sold off."

"But why? I don't understand. That was *our* home and you lied to us when you said we could never go back. That there was nothing to go back to? Why? Why lie?" he asked.

She walked back to her roses that lay on the counter and looked at them. She stood in silence.

"Why Mum? Why did you lie to us all these years?" he said.

She faced her son who stood looking at her with the same blue eyes that always melted her heart, just like Kinsey's had, and Rosie's still.

Anything they could possibly ask of her it was impossible to say no. She knew it was time.

"Because I had no control over any of those decisions." she answered.

"What are you saying?" Arthur asked.

"You honestly never knew? Kinsey never told you the truth?"

"I don't know what you mean."

Until this point she had never been certain, but in that moment, she felt a sense of relief that Arthur had always been honest with her. Reluctantly, she continued to share the dreaded truth, "I have been shocked and frankly hurt that you've continued to speak with your brother these last ten years."

"We spoke because we are brothers. It had nothing to do with you." Arthur told her.

"It has *everything* to do with me, Arthur. It has absolutely *everything* to do with us. You, me, and your sister." Arthur sat down in the sofa chair in defeat as he listened carefully to his mother. "You see. Your father left everything to Kinsey. *Everything,* every brick, every stone, every tree, and every rose. His will was ironclad."

She crossed her arms standing above him as she looked down to her son who suddenly looked like her little boy again.

"What do you mean *everything*? Father wouldn't have left you with nothing." He solemnly stated.

"Not a single book." she looked around the room.

"How are you able to afford...?"

"Because Kinsey refused to accept it all. He gave a mere quarter of it back to me."

She picked up the glass of scotch that Arthur had previously poured for her and finished drinking it. Gently, she set her glass down. She wondered if she needed to continue onward.

"But why wouldn't we go back to the house? After all, Kinsey ran off to America, I'm sure he wouldn't have minded us living there after it was repaired."

With bitterness in every word she continued, "In writing, delivered by his barrister, I learned I should never be allowed to step foot at The Park House again. The grounds, the house, any of it, and so I have never been allowed to return there."

"Truly?" Arthur asked.

"Truly." She muttered, "According to Mr Field, if I step even, just one foot on that property, all of my assets would be seized."

Silence filled the room. Lady Edith went to refill her glass with scotch. Arthur shook his head, "I had no idea."

Lady Edith took another sip and reluctantly shared, "Anything that remained of your fathers, of ours, it *all* belonged to Kinsey. Even though all of it was *Kinsey's fault.*" She fought back the tears that were forming in her eyes. Quickly wiping them away, she proclaimed shaking her left finger at Arthur, "I will never forgive him. Never." She drank the rest of her second glass. Wiping away another tear and refusing to let Arthur watch her cry, then angrily fled the room taking the glass with her.

Arthur felt as if the wind had been knocked out of him. What little of a relationship he had shared with his brother over the last ten years had been not entirely truthful. Kinsey had failed to tell him about everything. He felt betrayed but then he thought to himself, *perhaps it wasn't Kinsey's truth to tell after all.*

Lady Edith entered back into the study almost as quickly as she had fled, pleading, "Arthur darling, you mustn't speak to Amelia about any of this. She has no right to know."

"She should know the truth." he pled.

"She can *never* know. You must promise me." Her disposition had changed from a pleading mother to her 'Ladyship.' "Promise me," she demanded.

He couldn't believe the two words he was about to say but they escaped his lips before he could even think upon it, "I promise." He said in a defeated whisper.

"Good. Oh, and you mustn't tell Rosie either." She commanded.

"No. You *have* to tell her."

"Tell me what?" Rosie walked into the study with her phone in hand. Lady Edith and Arthur exchanged nervous glances. "Well, tell me what?"

Lady Edith gave Arthur a hard stare. He went and poured himself another glass of scotch and lit cigarette retreating to his chair.

"It's nothing darling," Lady Edith replied, and left the study.

"What was all that about?" Rosie enquired as she approached her brother. "You were both so serious with one another."

"It's nothing." He said as he inhaled.

"You should really quit smoking." Rosie scolded him while taking away his cigarette.

"Why does everyone keep doing that?" Arthur said as he took another drink.

Rosie sat down in the adjacent chair with his cigarette and put it out on a nearby ash tray.

"Because I don't want you to die like Kinsey did," she replied.

He wasn't sure why, but it had never occurred to him. He realized in that moment why Amelia had been so upset each time he had started to smoke in front of her. They didn't want him to have lung cancer and end up like Kinsey. He took his pack and threw it in a nearby trash bin.

"Fine. I quit."

"Good for you." Rosie slowly applauded him. "I hope you quit for good. You are after all, my favorite brother. My only brother."

Her phone buzzed in her lap and she looked down to check it. Arthur took his glass and began to swirl his scotch thinking about all that had occurred between himself and his mother.

"What are we going to do about this girl. Mother is obviously quite upset by her presence. I think perhaps we need to scare her off or something." Rosie plotted.

"Leave her alone." Arthur scolded her. "This isn't her fault. Any of it."

"You're no fun."

"I mean it Rosie, leave her alone." He told her sternly.

Rosie threw her hands up in defeat and stood up, "Fine. I don't have time for this drama anyway."

"You and mother both, need to stay far away from her. Just let her be. Her intentions are good."

Rosie's manner changed and she fought back, "You can't possibly believe that it's alright for some American nobody to live in our family's estate. It belongs to us and what's next? A title of some sort?"

"The Park House doesn't belong to us anymore. You both need to accept this and move forward. It all belonged to Kinsey, and he chose to leave it to her. I don't know why yet, but there must be a very good reason for choosing Amelia Levingston" He finished his glass and set it down as he left the room, "I'll be damned if I don't find out."

Rosie was left all alone. She threw her hands up in the air in utter frustration. "This is too much for my life. I've got to get out of here." Rosie walked into the grand entryway and yelled, "I'm going to go to London, Mummy."

Her mother appeared at the top of the staircase, "You're what?"

"This has all been such a drag. I need to get out of this house." Rosie begged.

"Out of the question." Lady Edith said.

"I just need a long weekend, or a week, or like a month." Rosie begged "I need some time to myself. I feel trapped with you two fighting all the time."

"We were not fighting." Lady Edith walked down the staircase to face her. "Let me make that clear, we are not fighting."

"Yes, you are." Rosie said. "You sound like Kinsey and Daddy all over again."

Lady Edith taken aback asked. "How would... how could you possibly remember that?"

"Mum. Give me a bit more credit. I was nine years old. I was old enough to remember *the* fight," she said. "I really do want to get away though. Just give me the weekend at the very least."

Lady Edith considered. "Well, I can't argue that things haven't been hard for all of us."

"They've been terrible." Rosie took her mother's hands. "It's been especially difficult to be around you lately. I'm just being honest with you. Let me take a few days. You can wallow some more, and when I get back, I hope you will be your chipper self once again."

Lady Edith realized she might have been a little hard on Rosie lately. She gave in and politely disagreed, "I'm never chipper."

"Oh Mummy, of course you are," she joked. Lady Edith gave into her request, "The weekend."

"The week," she begged.

"The *weekend*."

Rosie kissed her mother's cheek. "Thanks Mum." She ran back upstairs to her room to start packing.

"Where will you be staying."

"The Four Seasons of course."

"Of course." Lady Edith whispered rolling her eyes at her daughter.

Rosie happily ran to her room as Lady Edith stood quietly in the foyer listening to her daughter on her phone sharing her good fortune with a friend, "Yes I'm coming to London!" The squeals of excitement that followed. She fought back a smile knowing her daughters joy and then felt someone staring down at her. She looked above to a large portrait of her late husband hanging on the wall. She pointed her finger at him and said, "This is all your fault." Then sulked away shaking her head buried in grief once again as memories of her husband and late son crept back into her spirit. Her grief quickly turned to anger, and her anger to a brewing revenge.

28

A New Life

THE NEXT DAY Amelia was in brighter spirits and decided to take a short walk to a nearby coffee shop for a light breakfast. She sat near the window enjoying a scone with a warm cup of tea and a little people watching. Lots of locals were out walking and on their bicycles as they made their way to work and school. It was a nice morning for a stroll so after she finished eating she continued wondering around the neighborhood.

The walk felt wonderful and soon she made her way to Nottingham Castle. Amelia had to pinch herself staring at the castle before her. A lifetime of reading and using her imagination to transport herself to places like this. She carried a permanent smile as she walked around the castle grounds, reading every sign and soaking up the information attached. She felt the cold stone walls and closed her eyes imagining what events must have transpired on these grounds over the past thousand years.

When she felt like she had experienced enough for the day, with hunger creeping in, she wandered back to her hotel to collect The Park

House plans and a notebook so she could get to work. She decided to work while she ate at the pub just next door.

She found a comfortable seat at a table that provided plenty of space to lay out her plans. A bubbly, bright, young woman whose curl's seemed to bounce with every step greeted Amelia with overwhelming kindness. She introduced herself as Wendy.

Amelia surprised herself by ordering a pint from Wendy by her rec-ommendation of her favorite ale on tap. She usually never drank beer, but she thought she'd make an attempt at being a local. It occurred to her as she looked over the menu that during chemo she was always much too sick to be hungry. But today she felt like an entirely new person. For once, cancer wasn't plaguing her every second.

For a moment she thought of Kinsey when her pint arrived. She imag-ined he would have loved to be sitting with her, leaning in, and telling her wonderful folklore from the surrounding area. So, she decided to order another pint from Wendy.

"Will someone be joining you then?"

A bit shy Amelia told her, "No. It's in memory of someone. A friend."

Wendy nodded and walked away ordering another pint from the bartender.

She brought the second pint shortly after, "What would you like to order then?" She flipped her long curly hair over her shoulder and Ame-lia was so jealous of it, she could barely stand it.

"You have the prettiest hair." Amelia complimented her.

"Oh, thank you! I get my hair from my Mum. I'm a spitting image of her, I swear."

"You are so lucky." Amelia hid her jealousy well as she forced her smile.

"You've got great hair too." Wendy told her.

Amelia turned red as she touched her long wig. "Thanks." Amelia shrugged.

"What looks good to you?" She gestured at the menu.

"May I please have a burger with cheese, no pickles with chips."

"How would you like it cooked?"

"Medium please."

"And for your friend?" She nodded to the empty chair and raised an eyebrow awaiting her reply.

Amelia nodded at the empty chair and the pint that sat full in front. "He's fine."

As Wendy walked away to check on the other tables Amelia picked up her mug and picked up Kinsey's, she clinked them together and started drinking hers. Feeling eyes on her she looked over to the bartender who had been watching her. He went back to his work.

She took the plans of the Park House out from her bag and laid them out on the table and got out a pen with her notebook. As she studied the layout, she could see the master was on the second level directly above the study. There was a large dining room, sitting room and four rooms upstairs with two bathrooms. Her mind raced with all the possibilities that laid before her.

"What are you working on here?" she asked.

Amelia looked up to see Wendy peaking over at her work, "This is a home I recently inherited that I'm going to start working on."

"Now, wait just a minute." The waitress sat down across from her, "You wouldn't by any chance be the owner of The Park House," she joked.

Amelia was completely caught off guard. "How would you know?" she asked.

The waitress whispered, "I'm Charlie's girlfriend. He works for the Bonnevilles."

"Oh, my goodness. You are Charlie's girlfriend?"

"Yes!" Wendy told her excitedly.

"Your boyfriend is super sweet."

"Isn't he? I've heard so much about you then. You lucky girl. You're the town gossip."

"What do you mean?"

"Oh, yes. Everyone's been talking about you. The late Marquess' death and all. Who would inherit his estate? Is there a Christmas curse for the Bonneville family? Nottingham is a nice city but it's small, and this is, after all, a pub." She leaned in and whispered, "I hear everything."

Amelia nodded a bit annoyed. She felt like she was right back working in the salon on Rodeo Drive, ignoring the daily Hollywood gossip. Wendy could tell she was overstepping a bit and gently put her hand on her arm. "We'll be your friends, Amelia, Charlie and me. Everyone can use a friend, can't they?" Wendy smiled.

Wendy's gesture seemed earnest and put Amelia at ease. She had a trusting face and a very honest quality to her, "Thank you. I could actually really use a friend here."

"From what I hear, you and the new Marquess seemed to be quite friendly yesterday."

Amelia rolled her eyes, "I don't know what you're talking about, Wendy." She finished her pint.

Wendy confessed, "Well, I confess, I actually *saw* you two getting in his car together yesterday. You both seemed quite friendly."

Harry, the bartender, called over to Wendy, "Wendy. I need yah over here."

Wendy wouldn't budge. "I'm taking my break Harry!" With that, she took Kinsey's beer and leaned into Amelia. Amelia looked at Kinsey's beer in her hand, "What? The dead can't drink. But I can." She smiled. "So tell me your plans then."

"One day at a time. What I really need to do is hire a general contractor. I can't do anything without one."

"Well you're very lucky then aren't yah?" She took another drink from Kinsey's pint.

"How so?" Amelia asked.

"My Charlie. He's got his license," Wendy explained.

"He *does*?" Amelia was surprised.

"Yes! He put himself through school and he got his license a few months ago. Secretly he's been looking for the right opportunity to slip off but they pay so well it's hard for him to just walk away."

"He works for the Bonnevilles. There is no way I could take him away from the family."

"Oh no, Charlie would love it. His family has been working for the Bonnevilles for half a century. This is just the opportunity he needs to go out on his own." Wendy nodded encouragingly. "In fact, I'll call him right now." She took her cell phone out and Harry called back over to her.

"No cell phones at work, Wendy!" Harry yelled.

"I'm on me break Harry!" Wendy yelled back at him.

Harry threw his towel that he had been carrying to the floor, poured another pint and approached Amelia's table offering it to Wendy, "Here, would you like another then?"

"Well, thanks Harry, that's very kind of yeh." She was holding her phone up to her ear.

"Hello darling?"

Amelia mouthed the words to Harry, "I'm so sorry."

Harry stomped back to the bar mumbling under his breath.

"No, I didn't call you for *that* Charlie boy. You are naughty." She giggled and winked at Amelia.

The cook placed Amelia's burger and chips on the bar and Harry brought it over to the table.

"Thanks, Harry." Wendy winked to him while continuing her conversation with Charlie. Harry growled at her and walked back.

Amelia was so hungry she didn't care and started to eat her large chips. They tasted better than American French fries. She was grateful that she finally had her appetite back. She felt grew. The ale was relaxing her and she was excited to meet someone new.

"So I'm sitting here with Amelia. Yes! That's right, our American, Amelia."

Amelia took a giant bite of her burger. "This is so delicious."

It was as if she had never had a burger in her life.

"Yeah, she's here at the pub with me. Yes babe, she's sitting here with her big plans and all and she just told me she needs to hire a contractor. I told her you would do it."

Amelia felt dread running through her body, "I'm going to be in so much trouble with Lady Edith," she whispered.

Wendy shook her head and covered the phone, "Charlie secretly hates working for her. She's been such a mean ol' witch since the late Marquess died."

"Well, I know now Kinsey and her didn't get along," Amelia said.

"No, not the eldest son, her late husband. He burned up in that fire at the Park House. Well, your house now."

Amelia coughed out a piece of her fry onto the table in shock.

"Ew." Wendy said. She reached for a nearby napkin and offered it to her.

She took it from her and wiped up her piece of fry. Wendy continued to listen to Charlie speaking on the phone and put a finger up to Amelia signaling she needed a private moment. She left the table and walked outside to continue her conversation. Amelia watched her through the pub's window arguing, which transitioned into smiling, and then she hung up with a huge smile on her face. When she returned to the table she happily announced, "Great news! You've got yourself a General Contractor. Charlie has accepted your offer of employment."

Amelia was scared, "Wendy, I really don't think this is a good idea. Lady Edith already hates me. If I steal her employee, she will *really* hate me."

Wendy took her hand, "I can assure you with absolute certainty, that *nothing* you do will make her stop hating you. Besides, you and Charlie will be happy working together. You *will* take great care of him won't you?"

Amelia wasn't sure who she should be more scared of, Wendy or Lady Edith.

"Yes. Yes I will. If he doesn't have that much experience with this sort of job it makes me nervous. This is a huge project."

Wendy stood up and put her hand on hip, "He's got his degree doesn't he. Everybody needs a chance at something. Everybody needs a favor to have a life."

Her point came across loud and clear and Amelia was put straight in her place. She thought about her salon coworker Oliver and how he had taken the dream job without the degree she had earned. The room had gone quiet and when Amelia looked around she noticed everyone was looking over to their direction listening in. Amelia glanced down at the plans and then stood up from the table and faced her. Wendy looked like she was ready to fight, but then Amelia said, "He's got the job," and her whole demeanor changed.

Wendy screamed out loud and started jumping up and down with excitement. "Thank you so much! You won't regret it. I promise yeh." She hugged her tightly and then released her,

"Now lets have a chat. I want to know all about you." She sat down eagerly waiting.

Harry yelled over to Wendy, "Break's over, Wendy!"

Wendy didn't even look back, "I'm taking my second break then!" She smiled at Amelia and leaned in eager to hear all about her. Harry buried his face in his hands.

Amelia leaned to her and whispered, "Don't get in trouble."

"Oh, don't worry. He's my Dad." Wendy smiled and took her second pint and drank from it.

"You call your dad, Harry?"

She nodded, "That's his name."

Amelia bit her lip to keep from laughing. Wendy was bursting with energy. She had officially found her first friend in England. "Well, where do I start." Amelia began to tell her story as Wendy listened eagerly. She told her everything. Even about her awful aunt and cousin Tessa. Harry finally reached his boiling point and walked over to the table and asked politely if he could have his daughter back. Amelia was sad to see Wendy go but they exchanged phone numbers and Amelia returned to her room. She picked up her phone and called Charlie.

"This is Charlie."

"Hi, it's Amelia Levingston."

"Oh hi. Listen, I'm sorry about Wendy."

"What do you possibly have to be sorry about. She's wonderful. I just wanted to touch base with you and make sure you are okay with this?" Amelia asked.

"Honestly, this is a dream opportunity for me," Charlie whispered. "I've been waiting for the right moment and this would be incredible if you'll have me."

"Well then if you're sure," Amelia told him. "I'm so worried about what Lady Edith is going to say."

"You're worried? I'm terrified," Charlie told her between chuckles.

"Terrified," she agreed.

"Listen, I know the Park House and its grounds really well. My family worked there and I basically grew up there. Until now I thought it had all burnt to the ground so it would mean a lot to me to be able to contribute in bringing it back to life."

She felt comforted knowing that he had extensive knowledge of what the house used to be like and the grounds. This connection felt right and she knew the faster she made the decision, the faster she could get to work so she agreed, "I'll work on a contract today and perhaps later tonight you can stop by and I can make sure you agree to the terms before you say anything to her."

"Don't rush. I trust you."

"Thanks' Charlie. Talk soon."

"Thank you again Amelia." He hung up the phone. She laid back down on the bed suddenly feeling very full. Fighting back a yawn, she pulled back her covers to the bed and laid down in it.

Then her phone rang, without looking she answered, "Charlie?"

"Em, no, this is Arthur Bonneville."

She gasped and sat up, "Oh... hi Arthur."

"Were you just speaking with Charlie? Our Charlie?"

"Never mind that. How are you?"

"I'm quite well actually. How are you?"

His voice was warm and sort of *sexy*. "I'm... better. I'm doing much better today."

"I'm glad. Listen, I found you a few options for Contractors to hire."

Amelia slapped her hand to her forehead. She had completely forgot he had offered to help her. She chose her next words wisely, "Well, thank you Arthur, but you know what? Actually, I just hired someone."

"You did?" He was surprised, "That was quick. Who did you speak to?"

"Um. Let's just say, I have it covered."

"Very well then," he muttered. Amelia waited for him to say something else. Instead, a long pause grew. "Well, what are you doing for dinner then?"

"Dinner?" she asked, confused.

"Yes, Dinner."

"I actually just ate a big lunch at the pub so I'm not really sure."

"Would you like me to bring you something? I would be happy to drop something off for you."

Amelia was blown away. She wasn't sure what to say to this gesture. Something told her that it wasn't the best idea so she politely declined, "You know what? Not tonight."

He quickly asked, "How about tomorrow then?"

She blushed, "Let's chat tomorrow and we will see where we're at."

Arthur huffed, and Amelia realized he likely wasn't accustomed to rejection. "Em, well then, we'll chat later."

"Okay. Bye Arthur." She hung up the phone and bit her lip. She fell back into her pillows and began to wonder if he may have been flirting with her a bit. It felt like he had. Was he asking her *out* to dinner or just to *have* dinner. She shook her head in doubt. That would be an impossible thought. However, impossible thoughts were her favorite.

29

Lady Edith

FOR ONCE, AMELIA hadn't been plaguing Lady Edith's thoughts all day. She had spent the morning tending to her garden. She was meticulous about checking everything. Her greatest joy was spending time outdoors. It was the quiet retreat into nature, and one which her life desperately needed. She had always enjoyed being outside, ever since she was a young girl. Her English teacher had lent her a copy of *The Secret Garden* by Frances Hodgson Burnett after seeing how happily she was playing in the weeds which grew around the sandpit at school.

Today, the weather was perfect for her to enjoy her afternoon tea outside. In truth she had been avoiding all the incoming phone calls and the staff inside the house. Rosie had decided to stay a bit longer in London and she had enjoyed the quieter evenings at home.

After enjoying her tea, she returned inside the house to face the work she had waiting for her in her office. A mountain of paperwork had been growing over the past months that she could put off no longer. It was time to sort it and send it off to her accountant.

She had been such a recluse since the news of Kinsey's death and the surrounding drama of the American girl that she hadn't been returning anyone's calls. Today was the day she would reach out and reconnect to her inner circle. It was time to show her face in public, and start attending events again. The Park House was no longer in her control. Mr. Field had made it abundantly clear to her that she had *no* say in what Kinsey had arranged, and she needed to accept it, as horrible and embarrassing as the situation was.

As she began to get into a rhythm of organizing her paperwork, she was interrupted by a light knock at the office door. "Come in." She spoke gracefully.

Charlie quietly opened the door. He held his hat in his hand and took a step inside. Lady Edith wasn't at all surprised to see him, as this was part of their daily routine together. Today, he seemed different though. He had a nervous look to his face, and he was twisting his hat between his hands.

"Do you have a moment your ladyship?" he asked.

She turned her chair to face him. "Yes, of course. What can I do for you, Charlie?" she asked.

"As you know I went to school and received my general contracting license." He softly explained.

"Yes, I'm aware."

"Well, you see your ladyship, I've been offered a position doing what I love. So, unfortunately, I'm putting in my notice with you today."

Shocked, she inquired quietly, "And whom, may I ask will be your new employer?"

"I'd rather not say at this time your Ladyship. I want you to know how grateful I am to you and your family.

"Well, I won't lie. I'm entirely disappointed to see you go. I am however, grateful to you, and the work you have provided our family during your years with us. Have you found someone to replace you?"

"I do have someone in mind. My cousin Ian, your ladyship would be a fine edition. I can train him on everything before I take my leave."

"That won't be necessary. You may call him and let him know he may come to meet with me. Now if that's all." She returned to her paperwork.

Charlie burst, "I'm sorry. I really should just tell you." He said.

Her heart sunk with her shoulders, and she coldly replied, "Yes?"

"You see your ladyship; I've agreed to be the general contractor of The Park House."

Her face whitened as she pursed her lips holding her bitterness inside. Charlie started to sweat furiously.

"Do you think that's a wise decision?" she asked. The room had gotten so cold it felt like all the love in the world had been sucked out.

"I just need to tell you the truth is all. I don't want you to find out some other way." He confessed.

Taking a pen in her hand she returned to her work and turned her back to him.

"Goodbye, Mr Young."

"Your ladyship..."

"Goodbye." She sternly said warning him away from continuing their conversation any further.

Charlie retreated from her office, "Thank you again for everything."

"Oh, and Mr Young." She called after him.

With his shoulders slumped he turned to face her. "Yes, your Ladyship?"

She continued looking at her papers but refused to turn to look at him. "You need not to return to work tomorrow. I will accept your resignation effective immediately, and you may forget about Ian working here as well. We won't be needing anymore services from your family *ever* again."

"Yes, your ladyship."

Charlie let out a sigh of defeat and closed the doors behind him. Lady Edith buried her face in her hands the moment he left. Her hands turning into fists and finally slamming the desk in front of her. She stood up from her chair. Pacing and shaking, she gravitated toward a recent floral arranged vase, which she picked up and slammed to the floor.

Arthur walked in, "What is going on? Where's Charlie just ran off to?"

"This is all *your* fault!" she accused him pointing her finger to his chest, "Your father would be ashamed of you."

Arthur put his hands up in retreat, "What on earth are you talking about? I've just arrived."

"I couldn't believe you would sink so low to even consider helping that American girl. But to refer our Charlie as well? What did I ever do to you to deserve this kind of disrespect?"

"I don't know what you are accusing me of mother but I can assure you, I don't know what you are talking about."

"You expect me to believe that Amelia just woke up this morning and thought, hmmm, maybe I should offer our Charlie a job? The Charlie who's worked for our family for twelve years, and his family before him for half a century. No, you had something to do with this. I know you did. I don't even want to speak with you or look at you."

"I had nothing to do with Charlie being hired. This is the first I've heard such news. I swear on my own life."

"Lies!"

He crossed his arms. "Here we are again Mother. Life gets hard and you just shut everybody out. No second chances for anyone. You cut everybody out of your life."

"That's not fair!" She fought back.

"It's the truth.," he looked straight into her eyes and finally said what he had wanted to say for years, "It was *all* an accident. The fire was an accident."

She gasped. "You bring shame to your fathers memory making such a claim. We all knew it was Kinsey's fault. *He* is the sole reason your father is dead."

"No, *Father* is the reason he is dead." He told her.

She walked up to him and slapped him across the face. "How dare you."

As soon as she struck him she felt immediate regret, but she dare not apologize.

Arthur stared at her and shook his head in pity.

"You know what Mother? Deep down, I think you've always known that was the truth, and now it's too late."

"Too late for what?"

"Forgiveness. Too late to make things right with your own son." He turned to leave and then stopped. "And do you know what?"

"What?" she asked daring him to go farther.

"I *am* going to help Amelia finish the Park House, because it's the right thing to do, because it's what Kinsey wanted and I believe strongly, that it's what Father would have wanted as well."

He walked out of the office and Lady Edith chased after him into the hallway and toward the front entry where she stopped him after as he opened the front door.

"If you so much as put one brick back I will never speak to you again." She yelled at his back.

Arthur, still holding the door in his hand, slammed it, and returned to face her.

Lady Edith jumped in fear as he walked furiously up to her and wrapped his arms around her.

"Let go of me."

He refused as she struggled and the tears she had been fighting back started to flow from her eyes. She stopped fighting and he held her as she fell apart in his arms.

"It's time to let it go. It's time to forgive and it's time to make things right." He whispered. When he felt like it was the right time, he let go and looked into his mother's eyes.

"I don't know how." She confessed.

"Then you have to let me find the way." He turned and walked back through the front door and outside.

"Where are you going?" she called.

"I'm going to find Amelia." He called back as he walked to his car and drove away from the house.

As Lady Edith watched him from the doorway she felt eyes on her back. She turned around and saw her housekeeper in the hallway. Immediately Lady Edith resumed her status and demanded, "What are you looking at? Get back to work." She brushed her hair back and closed the doors.

30

Truth

CHARLIE AND AMELIA stood staring outside of the Park House. Charlie was rubbing the back of his head and Amelia stared down at the list they had compiled. They had talked for hours about every aspect of the house. This is what they had both trained for and now their mutual excitement was felt that they finally had the opportunity to follow their dreams. They had a plan.

Earlier, he had walked her deep into the property which had grown wild and untamed. He shared stories of being a young boy here and his father managing the grounds. Her Burberry rain boots were quickly covered in mud, and he teased her that she would need some proper boots moving forward. She agreed with him laughing at herself.

A herd of fallow deer peacefully grazed nearby, and Amelia sensed the magic that the land they walked was something truly special. Charlie shared that the Bonneville family had once had a working farm on the property. There were sheep, pigs, and chickens. Her Ladyship had managed all of the gardens. He explained that she had an incredible gift and passion for it. They made a strong plan and Charlie knew exactly who he wanted to hire for demolition of the damaged areas and how to pursue all of Amelia's wonderful ideas.

They now stood in the driveway going over their notes and looking back at the house in mutual excitement. The next huge step would be getting the permits. Just as they were wrapping up for the afternoon, the sound of a vehicle approaching on the Park House drive could be heard.

"Are you expecting anyone?" Charlie asked.

"No." Amelia answered confused as to who it could possibly be.

Once the vehicle appeared they both recognized it immediately.

"Is that?"

"It's Arthur," she said.

"What's he doing here?" he asked.

"I have no idea."

Arthur waved at them and parked his vehicle close to where they were standing. He stepped out.

"Hello, you two."

"What are you doing here?" Amelia asked.

Arthur turned a bit shy and explained, "I stopped by the hotel to check in on you and Wendy was outside the pub. She told me you and Charlie were here together, so I wanted to offer my help. Amelia, I think you hired the right person for the job."

Before Amelia could reply Charlie stepped forward and said, "Arthur, I'm really sorry about leaving your family so abruptly."

Arthur stopped him, "You don't have to explain yourself. I completely understand following your passion. My father wanted me to study Business and I studied Literature instead."

"That's wonderful." Amelia gasped.

They both looked over to Amelia who had a huge smile on her face. She looked back down at her notebook, embarrassed.

Arthur walked over to Amelia, "So, how can I help Amelia?"

She looked up to him and those eyes, those blue eyes would be the end of her.

Amelia cleared her throat, "Don't you have work?"

Arthur bashfully admitted, "I told the school I needed to take a personal leave for family reasons. I will resume in a month. Hopefully that will help you get to a more established place."

"I don't want you to have to do that for me."

Arthur smiled, "No really, I want to and it's not just for you, you see. I need to do this. I was robbed of time with my brother. I feel deeply that this will somehow, I don't know, will bring me closer to him."

"Kinsey would have really loved to hear you say that."

They stared at one another. Charlie stepped forward and interrupted their growing flirtatious tension. "We have a list."

"A list?" Arthur asked.

"Yes, a list. Show Arthur the list."

"Yes, we have a *long* list."

"Well, let me help you with this list." Arthur smirked.

"Great." Amelia smiled.

"Is anyone hungry? I am absolutely famished," Charlie announced.

"I can hear my stomach talking," Amelia agreed.

Charlie suggested, "Let's all go to the pub. Wendy's working today. My treat."

"No mine," said Arthur pleasantly. "I insist."

Charlie patted Arthur hard on the back, "Well, if *you* insist."

Amelia watched them walk toward their cars and as she started to follow them the hair raised on the back of her neck with the overwhelming feeling that they were being watched. She turned around and saw Kinsey standing in a second-floor window. She could make the shape of his bowler hat and with his cane in hand he tipped the brim of his hat and walked away from the window. She had just seen a ghost. Goosebumps filled her body as she attempted to process what she'd just witnessed.

Charlie called over to her. "Come on, Amelia, what are you waiting for?"

She searched the windows facing her but Kinsey had truly vanished. Amelia finally found the words, "I don't think you would believe it if I told you."

Charlie and Arthur exchanged curious glances.

When they got back to the cars, both men simultaneously opened their passenger doors for Amelia, then looked at each other, doing a double take.

"Oh." Arthur stopped himself.

Amelia wasn't sure what to do. "I think I'll ride back with Charlie," she called over to Arthur, who looked a bit defeated. Amelia bit her lip, trying to hide her smile. "I rode here with him and I have my bag in his car."

"Great, let's go."

Charlie started his engine. "You ready?"

She looked around, making sure she had everything with her, and gave him the thumbs up. He revved up the engine and started driving for five minutes, before turning to her with a wink. "I think someone's got a crush."

"I do not." She turned red denying the claim.

He laughed, "I wasn't talking about you."

She turned away from him and looked out the window, barely able to keep herself from smiling.

31

Fire

A WHILE LATER, Charlie, Arthur, and Amelia found themselves sitting at a table at the pub. Wendy was serving them and kissing Charlie every other minute. Their first round of drinks quickly turned into several and Charlie mustered the courage to ask the question they had been wondering about these many years. "So Arthur. What did happen?"

"What do you mean?" Arthur asked.

Charlie found Amelia's eyes and she shook her head warning him. Wendy felt the energy change, "Let me go ahead and bring another round to the table."

Amelia avoided Arthur's eyes and Charlie asked again, "Arthur, how *did* the Park House catch fire?"

"You really don't have to tell us," Amelia offered but Arthur reluctantly agreed.

Arthur stared at his glass a moment and then looked up to Amelia. "Picture this, it's Christmas night, the snow is falling outside, and Park House is freezing. We all gathered in the massive sitting room, right by

the roaring fire and the decked-out Christmas tree. After a lavish dinner and plenty of drinks, we're knee-deep in Scotch," he began, setting
the scene.

Amelia couldn't help but ask, "How old were you guys?"

Wendy brought their drinks, and Arthur took a sip before reflecting, "I was twenty-one, Rosie was just nine, and Kinsey, he was a seasoned twenty-six. He'd been doing a fantastic job working for one of my
dad's London businesses, or at least that's what my parents kept bragging about."

Wendy sat down next to Charlie, clearly invested in the story. Harry,
the bar owner, called out to Wendy, but she shot back, "I'm on break,
Harry!"

Harry grumbled, "You already took your second."

She shrugged, glancing at the two bar regulars and saying, "Harry,
it's just Niles and Ted. I think you can handle it."

Harry grunted again, and Wendy returned to the table. She gestured
to Arthur, her voice still gentle, "Please, Arthur, continue."

Charlie, being himself, looked over at Harry, shaking his head. "Your
dad can't stand me," he chuckled. Wendy kissed Charlie's cheek, and
Amelia smiled at Arthur.

"Harry loves you."

Harry let out an audible grunt and continued to work Arthur continued with a more serious tone, "So, it's getting late, and we're pretty
buzzed. Rosie couldn't keep her eyes open and said her goodnights. She
went upstairs to crash, and I poured myself another glass, settling in. I
happened to notice Kinsey, his gaze fixed on Rosie as she left. And when
she disappeared upstairs, Kinsey suddenly stood up, announcing, 'I've got
something to say.' Mother chimed in, somewhat amused: 'Oh, really?'
Kinsey always had a way of amusing her. I remember glancing over at
Father, and he had this hard, cold stare. Kinsey went on, 'Yes! I've fallen
head over heels in love and I'm getting married.' Suddenly, the room
turned icy."

Arthur's expression turned even more serious, and he took another sip from his pint. "So, my mother responded in this cold tone, 'Is that so?'" He paused, recalling the scene. "She finished her drink, stood up, and fetched another. On her way, she took father's empty glass and filled it up, too. Kinsey, with an almost taunting tone, asked, 'Well, Father, aren't you going to congratulate me?' After what felt like an eternity of silence, Father finally asked, 'And who's the lucky person, Kinsey?' Kinsey sat down, crossed his legs, and replied, 'His name is Eric. I met him in London, and he's truly magnificent.'"

My mother exchanged worried glances with Father, who retorted, 'You must be joking. That's completely out of the question.' The way he said it was cold and insulting. Kinsey's eyes welled up, and he drank from his glass, saying, 'Don't you want me to be happy? Why can't you just accept this about me?'"

Amelia couldn't contain her curiosity and interrupted, "But they knew Kinsey was gay, right?"

Arthur responded, "Of course, they knew. We all did. But in a family like ours..."

Both Wendy and Charlie nodded knowingly.

Amelia asked innocently, "What do you mean?"

"My father came from a background where, well, let's just say, our family has always had very strict rules about who's acceptable to marry. Remember, Kinsey was the first-born heir, destined to be the next Marquess and responsible for continuing the Bonneville legacy."

"That's incredibly old-fashioned," Amelia observed, looking around the table.

Charlie explained, "That's the way it is with these aristocratic families. Most people keep these things hidden. I mean, can you name one openly gay member of a royal family?"

Wendy nodded in agreement. "You're right. It's sad, but true."

Amelia then prodded, "So, what happened next, Arthur?"

Arthur continued, "So, my family started arguing among themselves.

Kinsey grew more and more upset because Father wouldn't let him speak, and he even threw his glass against the wall to get attention. Chaos ensued. Father stormed back into his study, lighting up his cigar. My mother went upstairs to check on Rosie, while I stayed back with Kinsey."

"Kinsey turned around and pointed at me, saying, 'Arthur, promise me that when you fall in love, you won't ask for permission, just fall. Take the leap.' Then he grabbed another glass and poured more Scotch, storming off to confront Father. I heard Kinsey open the door, and they started pleading with each other. Then... I heard a glass shatter. I rushed to the door to intervene, but my mother was at the top of the stairs, warning me not to go in."

"Kinsey suddenly burst out of the library, grabbed a candelabra with burning candles, and headed upstairs toward his room. Father chased after him with his cigar in hand, shaking it menacingly. There was more shouting, a door slammed, and Father appeared, confronting my mother and me."

Amelia inquired, "Did your father still have his cigar?"

Arthur's face shifted, and he leaned back, eyes widening. "I never... I never thought about that. No, he didn't."

Wendy pressed, "What happened next?"

Charlie nudged Wendy, and she asked defensively, "What?"

Charlie pointed to Arthur, who seemed distressed. Amelia reached out, took Arthur's hand, and encouraged him gently, "Go ahead, Arthur."

He pulled his hand away, grabbed his glass, took a drink, and placed it back on the table. "This time, Father turned his frustration toward Mother and me, yelling for us to go to bed. That's when we started smelling smoke. We all knew right away there was a fire in the house. My mother yelled, 'I have to get Rosie.' I didn't know what to do; I was quite tipsy by then. Father yelled for me to go to the kitchen and get water. I ran into the kitchen, and I could hear screaming upstairs. I was still grabbing a bucket of water when Father yelled down for me to get outside with my mother and Rosie, so I dropped the bucket and rushed back into the hallway. The house filled with smoke rapidly, making it unbearable to breathe. I helped my mother by picking up Rosie, and we ran outside."

Amelia commented, "That's horrifying."

"I checked the house from the outside and could see Kinsey on the rooftop, where his room was. He stumbled across it through the smoke. He managed to hang off the roof line and fall down to the ground below. My mother ran over to him, screaming, 'Where's your father?' Kinsey looked bewildered as he stood up and shouted, 'Isn't he with you?' The flames grew larger, and suddenly, the far -right corner of the house collapsed. Kinsey tried to run back inside, and I could hear the sirens approaching in the distance. My mother stopped him, saying, 'You can't go in there; it's too dangerous.' The fire department had arrived and went inside."

Charlie whispered, "So, your mother blamed Kinsey for your father's death?"

Arthur replied, "Yes, and so did Kinsey. He blamed himself entirely."

"But it's not really anyone's fault," Charlie reasoned. "I mean, it could have been your father who started the fire with his cigar, as Amelia pointed out. He could have been dropping ashes all over the hallways or carelessly dropped it somewhere."

Wendy added, "Or it could have been Kinsey with the candelabra."

Arthur shook his head, "Kinsey always blamed himself. So did my mother. But the fire never would have happened if they had just..." He hesitated, unable to utter the words.

Amelia prodded gently, "If they had just what?"

Arthur stared down at the table, unable to meet anyone's eyes. So, Amelia said it for him, "Loved him." Arthur's blue eyes met hers, and he nodded in agreement. "But don't you see Arthur, they did love him. Deep down. Your mother still does. That's why she's so angry. She's angry with herself."

"Amelia's probably right," Wendy agreed.

Arthur didn't entirely agree but didn't voice his dissent. He finished his pint and said, "That's the story, the sad truth. Let's get another round."

Wendy hurried off to get more drinks before Amelia could intervene. Charlie wiped a tear from his eye, saying, "That's just terrible luck, isn't it? I always liked Kinsey and your dad. I didn't know your dad could be such an ass, though."

Arthur nodded, "Yes, he had his moments."

Amelia suggested, "Maybe we should slow down a bit."

Charlie countered, "I say let's all get plastered. We look like we've just come from a funeral. We should just get wasted."

Wendy returned with more drinks and joined them. "Charlie's got emotions bubbling on the surface," she remarked, then kissed his cheek.

Amelia agreed and smiled at Arthur, who returned the smile. She reassured him, "I don't know why these things happen, Arthur. But thank you for sharing your story with us."

Arthur questioned, "Why? It's just terrible."

"Because now I feel like I know your mother better. I understand her much more clearly," Amelia explained.

Arthur nodded in agreement. He studied her and she felt strangely at ease with him. Amelia felt that he was beginning to trust her more as they continued to drink and reflect on his father's cigar and the unanswered questions that seemed to have haunted him over the years. It was clear to her that it would be a challenge him to find peace, knowing it might have been his father who had set it all in motion. The truth was elusive, and that seemed to trouble him at they continued drinking into the night.

Lunch had turned into dinner and dinner into a late night. Arthur and Amelia had become quite comfortable with each other and at one point he had put his hand on her leg and squeezed it. Amelia could barely keep her hands from reaching out to him, grabbing his face and kissing it. He had stepped out a few times to smoke but told her that he was trying to quit for Kinsey. Amelia was impressed he had made that decision and the night turned into laughter and a very serious darts competition.

It was near eleven when Harry told them it was time to leave but Arthur couldn't drive, neither could Charlie, and Wendy had to close. Amelia offered to call a cab and then Arthur whispered in her ear, "Let me stay with you."

Amelia turned to face him and then Charlie begged, "Amelia, can I crash on the floor?"

"Please Amelia, he's smashed and I have all these customers to attend to." Wendy begged.

"Fine." Amelia conceded. Arthur and Charlie stumbled following Amelia upstairs to her room and Charlie passed out on the floor. Arthur could barely balance himself.

"I'm so embarrassed." He slurred.

"Just lay down Arthur."

She pulled the covers back for him and he laid down on her bed. She took off his shoes and he murmured thank you as she covered him with the bedding. His eyes were closed and she thought how handsome he was laying in her bed.

After going to the restroom and brushing her teeth she knew she should keep her clothes on and looked at her wig. That would stay on tonight. There was no way she could expose herself like that yet to him. So she turned off the lights and laid on top of the covers and grabbed her nearby coat and laid it over herself. She took one last look at him and he opened his eyes and whispered, "You are truly, lovely *my* Amelia."

Before Amelia could reply he closed his eyes and fell back asleep. She reached out her hand and gently touched his hair and then with the back of her fingers she touched his bearded cheek. Then turned away from him and pulled up her coat and fell asleep dreaming of him.

32

Morning After

ARTHUR AWOKE THE next morning feeling like he'd been run over. As he groggily rubbed his eyes, he realized he was in an unfamiliar bed. "Ugh," he groaned, his head throbbing. A deep sigh from beside him drew his attention, and he turned to find Amelia sleeping on top of the covers, her long Burberry trench coat draped over her. She was in a deep slumber, her wig slightly askew.

His memory was fuzzy, but he tried to piece together how he'd ended up in Amelia's room when unfamiliar snoring interrupted his thoughts. Rolling to his side of the bed, he glanced down and spotted Charlie sleeping on a hotel pillow with a blanket hastily thrown over him. "Oh God."

A knock at the door startled them all awake. "Wake up, sleepy heads!" Wendy's familiar voice called from outside. Amelia began to stir, rolling over to Arthur's chest and draping her arm across him as if it were the most natural thing in the world. Charlie, on the other hand, stood up, stretched, and stumbled across the room, stubbing his toe on one of Amelia's suitcases in the process. "Oh shit! My toe. My bloody toe," Charlie exclaimed.

Amelia opened her eyes, realizing her arm was wrapped around Arthur. She quickly pulled it back, offering an apology, "Sorry," and adjusting her wig, pretending not to notice Arthur's presence.

Arthur exchanged a glance with Amelia and assured her, "Don't be sorry."

"Is everything alright in there?" Wendy yelled from outside the door.

Charlie opened the door to find Wendy standing there with a bag of food and a tray of coffees. "It's about time."

"Sorry, my love," Charlie apologized.

Wendy entered the room and set the food and coffees down, taking in the disheveled scene. "Well, aren't you three a mess."

Amelia and Arthur exchanged glances, then got out of bed, attempting to regain some semblance of composure. Arthur asked, "What happened last night?"

Wendy teased, "What didn't happen? Who knew Arthur Bonneville was such a stud? Right Charlie?" Charlie gasped in shock and looked at Arthur, who hastily reassured him. "I'm joking," Wendy laughed. Amelia chuckled nervously, and Wendy handed her a coffee.

"Thank you," Amelia said, accepting the coffee.

"Amelia was a saint last night and offered for you both to crash in her room," Wendy explained. "You two wouldn't stop drinking, and Harry finally had to kick you out."

"Oh God," Charlie lamented. "Your dad hates me."

"He loves you," Wendy reassured him with a wink. Charlie rushed into the bathroom, closing the door behind him, and all three could hear him getting sick. Wendy sighed, "Well, how are you two doing this morning? You both looked quite cozy."

Arthur apologized, "I'm so embarrassed. I never drink like that."

"Really? Because last night you kept bragging about how you never get drunk and were quite the professional from your days at Uni," Wendy teased.

Amelia added with a laugh, "She's right. You did."

"I'm very sorry," Arthur said, rubbing his throbbing head.

Wendy pointed to the bag of food and offered, "I brought breakfast. Harry's special— guaranteed to cure your hangovers. To take with you of course, so you boys can leave Amelia and she can have hers with some peace and quiet."

"I smell bacon," Amelia said, her eyes lighting up.

"Oh, there's plenty of bacon in there," Wendy confirmed.

From inside the bathroom, they could hear Charlie flush the toilet and wash his hands before emerging. "Did you say bacon?"

"Yes, darling. All the bacon," Wendy assured him.

Wendy pulled out her to- go boxes from the bag and separated them out on a nearby table.

As Arthur snuck into the bathroom next, and as they waited, Amelia caught Wendy's eye. Wendy leaned in closer and whispered, "Did anything happen between you two?"

"No, of course not," Amelia replied. She had no intention of sharing the truth of what had transpired, keeping it close to her heart.

"What are you two whispering about?" Charlie asked.

The sound of Arthur washing his hands signaled his return, and Wendy quickly whispered, "About Arthur and Amelia."

Charlie agreed, "Oh yeah!"

"Shhhhh," the girls warned as Arthur reappeared.

"Oh my! Is that the time? Nearly nine? Boys lets grab your food and go," Wendy instructed.

"Of course," Arthur agreed. He looked at Amelia and said, "I'll call you soon."

Amelia smiled, "I'd like that."

With a hopeful grin, Arthur closed the hotel room door. Amelia hurried into the bathroom; she'd been holding her bladder since waking up. The previous night's heavy drinking had made her quite thirsty, and she had consumed a lot of water to compensate for the four pints she'd had. It had been years since she'd drunk so much, and she had to be the responsible one once Charlie and Arthur had started competitively drinking.

Amelia finished washing up and then returned searching for her breakfast. Amelia opened the container from Wendy, and immediately located the bacon. She ate it and thought about the previous evening. Specifically six of the dreamiest words a man had ever said to her, "You are truly, lovely *my* Amelia." Those would be the words she would be repeating in her mind all day.

33

Summer

IT WAS ALREADY the second week of July. It had taken all of June to get the permits she needed in order to move forward with the plans for the Park House. Amelia was so thankful for the inheritance that Kinsey had provided, meaning there weren't any financial burdens and she could easily afford the hotel stay.

After several meetings with the Village Council, Charlie arranged for storage containers to be delivered to the house so any essentials they would need could be properly stored before renovation took place. Everything was being pulled from the house that needed restoration, from the thousands of books that would all need cleaning and the precious artwork that hung on the walls that would have to be sent off. Amelia had meticulously photographed every item that could be saved and those that were a complete loss.

Amelia was helping the workers continue their job of making sure the house was emptied out so they could commence with construction. "Be so careful with those!" Amelia yelled over to a man in a bright orange vest who was walking with two large antique vases.

"Frank!" Charlie yelled.

The man turned around with the vases in his hands, "What!?" He growled.

"If you break one of those vases you're dead." Charlie yelled at him.

Amelia put her hand over her mouth as Frank walked towards him like a charging Rhinoceros.

"What did you just say to me?" he snarled back with a terrifying walk.

"I'm just kidding mate," Charlie answered, clearly terrified as Amelia and Charlie watched Frank walk off to the storage unit they had set up near the house.

"Charlie?" Amelia said. "Just because you're the boss..."

"Doesn't mean I have to be a total shit." He finished her sentence.

"Right." Amelia patted him on the back. "It's the first day, so let's just take a breath, and try not to get anyone killed." She smiled and put her hard hat on and walked toward the house.

Charlie followed Amelia, and as they approached the front door Frank walked past them, "Sorry, Frank," Charlie yelled.

Frank growled and continued his work. Amelia walked into the Park House which was slowly beginning to reveal itself to Amelia. As everything that was salvageable was being cleared, she could see more of the original wallpaper. The rooms were opening up and she could see each space more clearly. Amelia brought out her phone and started to take photographs.

"You should start a social media page," Charlie suggested.

"I was just keeping these for myself." Amelia smiled as she took a photograph of the wallpaper in the dining room.

"This is how you build your clientele. You can get a fan base from this project and when you're finished you'll most likely be ready for your next." Charlie encouraged her.

It was a brilliant idea.

"You're right."

"Of course I'm right." Charlie joked.

Amelia looked closely at the wallpaper, "Charlie, I don't think we are going to be able to save this."

He looked at it. The smoke damage was especially horrible on one particular wall. "I know this woman in town named Celine who's an artist and she can recreate wallpaper."

"You do not." Amelia rejoiced, "You actually know a woman here in Nottingham that makes wallpaper?"

"Yes. I really do. I know everybody!" he stated proudly.

Amelia laughed, "Alright Charlie, let's get Miss Celine out here and have a chat."

Charlie tipped his hard helmet, "You leave that to me." Charlie was infectious. He always had a smile and something kind to say. It was hard to take him seriously because he was so hilarious to be around. Amelia was still amazed how things were working out. Arthur's voice broke through the noise of the busy construction, "Amelia?"

"We are in the dining room!" she called out. Arthur walked in. His blue eyes met hers. Amelia's felt butterflies as she greeted him. "Hello."

"Hello," he grinned.

Charlie waved, "Hi! Hello there." He broke their gaze. "I'm here too."

"Hello Charlie, and how are you today?" Arthur presented his hand for

Charlie to shake. Charlie shook it warmly.

"I'm very well indeed. As you can tell, we are very hard at work." Charlie said.

"You are greatly missed. My mother would never admit that to me but I can tell she misses having you around."

"Well, when you see her next, please let her know that I have thought of her," he stated, chin up.

Arthur raised his eyebrows to Amelia, "Oh?"

"That's not what I meant. What I meant to say is that I've been thinking of her fondly."

"Fondly?" Amelia teased.

"Oh bugger off." Charlie put his hand over his face in mock-embarrassment.

Amelia and Arthur laughed together and their eyes met. "I'm so happy you stopped by today."

Blushing, Arthur replied, "Well, I knew you'd be working today, so I wanted to stop by and offer some assistance. I could help you with identifying items or do some heavy lifting." He teased, flexing his arm muscle.

"Heavy lifting?" she flirted.

"The only heavy lifting Arthur is capable of is placing the complete works of Shakespeare on a top shelf," Charlie joked.

Amelia bit her lip to stop herself from laughing as Arthur exchanged a very dirty look with Charlie. "I am perfectly capable of heavy lifting," he huffed.

"Well, today is mostly just clearing everything out of the house and separating what can be restored, what to keep and what not to. We can't do much else until the permits come through. So, when these workers have pulled everything maybe you can join me at the storage containers and help identify some of the more special items your family would want to keep," she said.

"That would be really wonderful," he agreed.

Amelia pointed at the wallpaper that was peeling away, "We were just admiring the wallpaper. It was so ornate. Do you know where your mother purchased it?"

"This is actually original to the home."

"Well, it's so beautiful."

He studied it with her, amused by her admiring gaze. "My mother really loved this wallpaper as well."

"She has very good taste."

Amelia took her phone out and snuck a photograph of him touching the wall. "Did you just take a photo of me?" He teased.

Embarrassed, she admitted, "Yes. I'm saving it to your number so when you call me I have a picture of you."

"Cute." He snuck her a teasing look.

"Take a photograph of me then, Amelia," Charlie said in a high breathy voice, and posed seductively holding his chest against the wall. Amelia obliged.

"I'm sending this to Wendy," she deadpanned.

"Don't you dare." Charlie tried to grab the phone from her and Amelia sent it.

"Too late. Already sent."

Amelia gestured back to the wallpaper, "You know, Charlie told me he knows a woman in town that creates wallpaper."

Arthur wasn't surprised. "Charlie knows everybody."

"You see?" Charlie exclaimed. "I told you so, Amelia."

Amelia laughed. "I guess he does then." She put her arm around him.

"Replicating this wallpaper is a very thoughtful idea Amelia, but why wouldn't you want to design something that appeals more to your taste? Do something different, unique." Arthur studied her.

"Oh no, Kinsey left The Park House to me to bring it back to life." She nodded with conviction, "I'm going to honor his wishes and the home itself."

Amelia touched a piece of the paper that was starting to peel away and she tried to press it back. Sunlight peered in through a nearby window and shining on her pale skin. She felt Arthur staring at her. She returned his gaze and it felt right. Her throat started to feel dry and she cleared it breaking his gaze.

"Amelia, I do want to walk with you outside and go over these plans. We need you to make some decisions before we move forward." Charlie said.

Amelia took the hint, and asked Arthur: "Care to join us?"

Charlie grunted and Arthur nodded eagerly along, "I would actually."

"Only if you don't distract her, lover boy," Charlie teased.

Amelia laughed and walked ahead of the men, "I don't know what you're talking about." Arthur rolled his eyes at Charlie and elbowed him in the ribs.

Charlie whispered, "Yes, you do." He went ahead to walk with Amelia feverishly sharing the plans he held in his hand. She nodded along, glancing back at Arthur as he followed watching her. She was growing fond of him. He was handsome, and intelligent, however blissfully unaware of her hold on him.

☙ ❧

THAT NIGHT SHE officially launched an Instagram account named: @WhiteRabbitInteriorDesign

The very first photograph she shared was of the wallpaper peeling away from the wall. The caption read: "This wallpaper won't be forgotten."

34

September

TODAY WAS DEMO Day. Amelia stood staring at the Park House as the workers started their machinery for the job they had prepared months for. Through August, her account had grown to the thousands. It amazed her how many people were fascinated by the items they had found and how many gladly offered advice on restoration. It was an amazing creative outlet for Amelia, and Oliver was already texting her that he was following everything she was posting and sharing it with his coworkers. Amelia was flattered and excited for her future.

As for Arthur, she wasn't sure. He had yet to make a move. There was still no kiss, no grand gesture, no date. Yet he had kept his word and helped with the hiring process and anything Amelia asked for when it came to advice that she needed. The Bonneville family had some major connections in the town and without his help she wasn't sure that Charlie would have been able to get all the permits pulled in that short period of time.

Whenever Amelia saw him, her legs felt like they might buckle beneath her. He had an irresistibly captivating effect on her, particularly when he assisted with the library. The way he talked about books felt like a direct path to her soul, and when his big blue eyes met hers, it was nearly impossible not to lose herself in them. She was aware that he was single, as Charlie had mentioned. Surprisingly, he had never been in a long-term, serious relationship, at least that Charlie knew of. It was almost unbelievable that someone as eligible as him wasn't the dating type, but each time she encountered him, it filled Amelia with hope.

"Hey you," Arthur's voice suddenly broke through her thoughts, causing her to jump. "Sorry, did I startle you?" he chuckled.

Amelia tried to compose herself. "No, not at all," she said, attempting to appear unfazed.

"Nice hat," he commented, gesturing to her hard hat. "Looks good on you."

She smiled, grateful for the change in topic. "What are you doing here?" she asked.

"I knew today was the day, and I thought I would watch with you," he replied.

"Well, if you stay, you're going to have to wear one of these too," she teased, indicating a nearby table with hard hats.

"Very well then," he agreed, walking over to pick one up, he placed it on his head. "How do I look?"

"You would make a fine construction worker," she flirted. An excavator approached the east end of the house, raising its bucket high in the air with workers standing nearby, including Charlie. "You were just in time," she noted. The excavator began to break apart what remained of the back area and deposit it into a nearby container.

Arthur stood close to her, their hands almost touching. She could feel the proximity, and her chest tightened as butterflies fluttered in her stomach. Neither of them dared to look at the other. Just as their pinky fingers brushed, a voice came through the radio, "Amelia, we are going to bring in the Feller Buncher now to lift off these beams."

Amelia quickly grabbed her radio and replied, "Sounds great. Thanks."

"This should have happened long ago," Arthur commented, and she nervously looked at him, assuming he was referring to their relationship.

Instead, he watched with a forlorn expression as the excavator's bucket removed some of the upper floor and cleared what once was a large, cracked wall.

"This." He pointed to the wall.

"Well, it's happening now." Amelia pulled out her phone to record the process. She nervously watched the workers in action.

"Amelia. I was wondering. … " He started to ask then a large section of the back wall crumbled and she stopped recording.

She grabbed her radio, "Charlie! They need to be more careful. That wasn't supposed to happen."

"I'm on it," he said through the radio.

"Sorry, Arthur, what were you saying?" she said apologetically.

"This isn't the right time. You're clearly busy. I should get back anyway." He retreated toward his vehicle.

"Arthur?"

"I'll call you, Amelia."

Had he just attempted to ask her out? She watched as he ran off and decided that this wasn't the time to stress about it. Too much was at stake today and everyone was counting on she and Charlie to do a good job. She turned her attention back to her work and that's where it remained in the days ahead.

∗ ∗ ∗

"OH MY GOD!" Rosie screamed from her bedroom.

Lady Edith ran from the kitchen into the hallway to see what all the fuss was. "Rosie? Are you alright?"

Her housekeeper ran into the hallway as well. "Mummy! You won't even believe this!" Rosie appeared at the top of the staircase dressed in her robe and slippers with her phone in hand, and her eyes glued to it. She shook it like a mad woman as she descended the grand entry staircase toward her mother and then stuffed the phone in her mother's face. "One hundred thousand followers! Do you see this? That American has one *hundred thousand* followers on Instagram."

"What are you talking about?" Lady Edith took her phone from her as the housekeeper rolled her eyes and returned to work. She looked at Rosie's phone and recognized the Park House immediately. "What am I looking at here. What is this?"

"That girl, robbed us of our family estate and she's gloating about it all over the internet!"

"This can't be true." She stared at it for a moment and scrolled through the photos and videos of restoration Amelia had previously posted stopping at a photograph of Arthur smiling as he held a stack of old books in his hand. A sense of betrayal began to fill her and she quickly handed Rosie's phone back to her. "Call your brother right now. I want him here."

She called him as she stormed back up to her room, "Arthur, Mummy needs you home right now. I don't care if you are teaching a class this is an emergency. No, no one's hurt. It's just an emergency. I can't tell you over the phone, just get here. We need you here now!"

35

Family First

ARTHUR RAN INTO Oak Hall and quickly searched for his mother. He found her sitting at her office desk working. "What is it Mother? I came as soon as I could."

Rosie burst into the office, "He's here! Oh Arthur, it's simply awful."

"What? What is it? Did someone die?" Arthur asked.

"Kinsey did! And he just keeps embarrassing the entire family, even in his death." She screwed up her face in distress. "And... she has over one hundred thousand followers! Tell him Mother, one hundred thousand!" She held her phone out to him like it was a hand grenade and he looked at it tensely.

"This? This is what you two are so upset about?" He put a hand to his heart and slumped down in a nearby chair, taking a deep sigh of relief. "Mother, I drove here like a madman, all for this?"

"This is appalling! That American is posting all over the internet about our family and our home including our personal items. There's a photograph of a vase that was given to your father and I for our wedding from the late Her Majesty, for heaven's sake."

He started to recognize her side of the situation. He said gently: "Mother, she's an interior designer. She's trying to start a business here and she's sharing the work she's doing with an audience. That's what business-minded people do."

"You just don't see how this reflects on our family do you? I am a Marchioness. You are an unwed thirty-one-year-old Marquess, and your poor sister..."

Her voice trailed off.

Rosie crossed her arms. "What about me?"

Lady Edith stood up and gestured with her hand for Rosie to sit. "Rosie is an unwed lady, as well."

"Well, Rosie hasn't exactly made our family look wonderful either." Arthur accused her.

Rosie gasped, "What are you talking about?"

"I saw the tabloids when you were in London, smashed with that famous actress—Kit something or other. There were photographs posted with your skirt up to your elbows and giving the press the bird."

"That's not entirely true, Mummy!" She stood up and shot Arthur a wrathful glare.

"It is absolutely true!" he yelled back.

"Enough!" Lady Edith had truly had enough. She put her hand to her head and softened her voice, "Both of you have a job to do. Especially you, Arthur. You are a Marquess and you have the duty to secure our families' titles. We are swiftly becoming the laughingstock of England."

"How so?" Arthur asked.

Lady Edith rubbed her eyes with distress. "All that has transpired this past year has been circulated amongst our peers. It has not reflected well on us, or my social engagement schedule."

"Oh, I see now, this is *all* about you, Mother. God forbid the end of your social calendar."

"This is not a joke, Arthur!" she slammed her hand on the table.

Rosie gasped.

"This is bigger than us," Lady Edith continued.

"No, Mother," Arthur stood up and shook his head, "We're a dying breed." He started to take his exit.

"How dare you!" His mother yelled. He turned around and faced her.

"How dare I? How dare you."

"You show me respect young man. I didn't raise you to be just as foolish as your brother."

"I am not Kinsey." Arthur scolded her and then walked away.

"Don't walk away from your responsibilities!" she called after him.

He stopped and turned around to face her. "I'm walking toward something better." Shaking his head to himself, he turned and left.

Rosie was shocked by what had just transpired. "I can't believe he just left us."

Lady Edith sat down and then remembered what Arthur had said, "Now, what exactly was your brother saying about giving the press the bird?"

Rosie face sunk but she still managed a small smirk, "He's exaggerating." She nervously looked down at her phone.

36

Him And Her

IT HAD BEEN a long workday. Tougher than most. Just as things had started progressing the electrician warned that there would be major setbacks. If that couldn't be worse there was a delay in an order that was crucial for the exterior of the building. Charlie and Amelia struggled to keep spirits high.

Amelia was now living full time on the property. Wendy's Uncle had a camper that she was delighted to rent from him. She loved being on site although the nights were very quiet and lonely for her. Wendy was working at the pub, so Amelia offered to cook hot dogs from her charcoal grill. Charlie sat outside drinking a beer in one of Amelia's fold-up chairs when Arthur's car approached up the drive.

Arthur looked nervous as he greeted him, "Hello there, Charlie."

"Why, hello there Arthur. Whatever are you doing here?" he asked nodding in Amelia's direction.

Amelia peered through the camper's door window and she looked through caught by surprise to see Arthur standing with Charlie. Her heart skipped a beat.

"Well, I thought I might pop by and offer Amelia some dinner," he explained to Charlie.

Charlie's grinned, "That's nice. Where's the dinner, Arthur?" he teased him.

"Well, I..."

Amelia opened her door and stepped out onto the gravel, holding a plate with hot dogs and buns. "Hello Arthur. What a nice surprise." She set the tray down on the table near the grill.

He smiled at her.

"Hello Amelia," he shyly greeted her.

"Arthur here was just telling me he came to offer you some dinner. I think he means to take you on a date," Charlie teased.

Amelia's face felt flush. "Well, it was a long day of work for Charlie and Wendy is working late. So I thought I would grill dinner for us tonight. Plus, I needed some company. It gets very quiet here at night."

Arthur nodded, looking wistful. "Well, I don't want to intrude."

"No, we would love for you to stay, wouldn't we Charlie?"

Charlie nodded, pulling out a chair and offering it to him, "Have a seat, your Lordship."

Before Arthur sat he offered to Amelia: "Do you need any help with those?"

"Oh no, I can handle hot dogs." Amelia smiled, "If you want to though, will you go inside the camper and grab us some more beers from the fridge."

Arthur walked inside her camper and Charlie hopped up from his chair.

"Why don't I handle these, Amelia. You go help Arthur find what he needs," he teased.

Amelia grinned and stepped back into her camper. She found Arthur holding up a photograph of mother and of herself.

"Sorry, I didn't mean to spy or anything." He looked apologetic as he gently placed the frame back where he found it.

"That's my mother. She died in a car accident when I was ten. I grew up living with my aunt and cousin." She took the beers from his hands and popped off the bottle caps one at a time.

"This must have been a very difficult move here for you. To leave your family behind."

She surprised him with her reply. "Not at all. They aren't good people."

"Oh?"

"Anyway, let's not talk about them."

"I very much like what you've done with the space. I was admiring your book collection."

He pointed above her small table that had a lined upper wall filled with all her books.

"Yes, books are my great love." She grinned. "I couldn't bring them all with me when I moved, so I brought my mother's collection and my other personal favorites."

"You've made it quite homey in here."

"It's functional," she laughed. "I have a working shower so I will take that as a win. All though the generator is kind of iffy."

"Oh?"

"It's pretty old."

Amelia grabbed the beers out of her small fridge.

"Here, let me help."

He took the beers from her and followed her outside.

✑✑ ✑✑

"MMMMMMMMM," CHARLIE SAID with his mouth full of hot dog bun. "I love them." He burped.

"You're disgusting!" Arthur told him.

"I can't believe you ate four hot dogs," Amelia laughed. "Wendy is going to be very upset with you tonight."

"How's that?" Charlie asked with a confused grin on his face.

"Because hot dog's make you..." She stopped herself. Arthur and Charlie tried not to laugh as they exchanged knowing glances with each other.

"You know," she smirked.

They eagerly waited for what she would say next, trying to stop themselves from laughing. "No, we don't know," Charlie insisted.

"Oh come on, don't make me say it." Amelia rolled her eyes and took another sip of her beer.

"Go on," Charlie chuckled. "Say it."

Amelia was blushing red and finally uttered the words thoughtfully, "Break... wind?" she laughed. They both burst out laughing with her.

Charlie agreed, "I agree. Wendy won't be very happy with me *tonight*. However, she is going to be very happy on Christmas Eve."

"Oh? Why's that?" Arthur asked.

"I bought her a ring." he proudly hinted.

Amelia asked, "Are you going to?"

"Yes. I'm going to propose." Charlie grinned proudly ear to ear.

"Oh, that's amazing Charlie!" Amelia stood up and hugged him. "I'm so happy for you both."

Arthur stood up and gave him a quick hug and pat on his back as well. "That's wonderful mate. Congratulations. She's going to be very happy."

They all sat back down and drank their beers. Arthur looked over to Amelia and gave her a warm and loving smile. Perhaps it was her beer that gave her the courage, but she finally asked what she had been wondering all these months, "How come you don't have a girlfriend Arthur?"

Charlie's eyebrow raised and he bit his lip eager to hear Arthur's reply. Arthur thought a moment and then flirtatiously answered, "I just hadn't found the right girl yet, I suppose."

"But you do date. Don't you," Charlie nagged.

"Yes, I date. Of course I date."

Amelia frowned at that answer and looked away. He quickly corrected himself, "What I mean to say it that I've dated. I'm just not *currently* seeing anyone."

"Did you hear that Amelia? Arthur isn't seeing anyone." Charlie teased.

She returned a hard stare at him, "You're so funny, Charlie. You should be a comedian." Avoiding eye contact with Arthur she looked down at her phone. "Oh man, I forgot to charge my phone again. It just died."

"You never charge your bloody mobile!" Charlie scolded her as she stood up from her chair and ran off inside her camper to plug it in. "I swear that woman's mobile is always dead." Arthur looked back over his shoulder watching the camper door close behind her. Charlie made sure Amelia was still inside the camper and then quickly turned to Arthur and whispered,

"Seriously mate. What are you waiting for? She likes you."

"It's complicated," Arthur explained.

"Well 'un-complicate' it, then. Amelia's amazing. If I didn't have Wendy, I would have already swept Amelia off her feet," Charlie told him.

"It has nothing to do with me." Arthur lowered his head in frustration.

Charlie could tell Amelia was about to return and quickly said, "It has *everything* to do with you!"

Amelia opened the camper door and announced, "It's getting late and we have an early day tomorrow. The electrician is arriving at seven," she explained.

Arthur stood up from his chair, a hint of embarrassment on his face. "No need to explain. We will leave you in peace."

Amelia walked toward Arthur, crossing her arms. "I'm glad you stopped by tonight."

"I am too. Well, I better be off," he replied and bowed.

Confused and a little embarrassed, Amelia looked over to Charlie, who was struggling to contain his laughter. "Goodbye then."

Arthur quickly made his way back to his car, shaking his head. Charlie glanced at Amelia, shrugged his shoulders, and called out, "Bye, Amelia!" as he hurried to catch up with Arthur. Leaning over to Arthur, he whispered, "Did you just bow?"

Arthur, still perplexed, asked, "Why did I just bow?"

Charlie slapped him on the back and ran off to his own car, waving goodbye before driving away.

Amelia watched Arthur sitting in his car and waited for him to look at her. When he finally did, she smiled, and in response, he smiled back. Then...she slowly curtsied. She knew this might charm him. He jumped out of his car and her heart raced as he approached her.

"I don't know why I bowed," he admitted, slightly flustered.

Nervously, she took a step back. "I thought it was sort of gallant," she giggled.

He chuckled. "Would you go on a date with me?" he asked.

Without hesitation, she replied, "Yes."

It was that simple, so easy.

"Perfect," and he walked back to his car and drove away.

Amelia was the happiest she had ever felt.

37

Sherwood Forest

AMELIA PULLED HER Burberry sweater over her t-shirt and admired herself in the mirror. She had been saving this sweater for a special day, and it seemed like that day had finally arrived. Today, Arthur was taking her on a date, and she wanted to look her best. The cold weather had settled in, and she needed to keep warm. Amelia and Arthur's schedule had been tricky all month long. It wasn't until the first week of October that they both finally had a full day free.

Her hair had grown long enough that she didn't need to wear a wig, but she still lacked the confidence to show her short hair. So, today, she wore her favorite long blonde wig and a cute white snow hat she found while vintage shopping with Wendy. She slipped into some comfortable tennis shoes, took one last look in the mirror, and felt satisfied. She knew she looked good, and she wanted Arthur to notice her.

Outside her camper, she heard the approaching sound of Arthur's car on the gravel. With a quick glance in the mirror, she decided to apply some lipstick. She wanted her lips to stand out, and she felt a rush of butterflies in her stomach at the thought of seeing him. Amelia couldn't deny her attraction to him. Each night when she lay in bed, she thought back to the morning they had woken up together in the hotel. There was something undeniable between them. However, she couldn't help but be held back by thoughts of his family. Her own family wasn't perfect either, and she had deliberately put distance between herself and them. Despite this, her aunt and cousin had not reached out to her since she had moved to Nottingham. It hurt, although she tried not to let it show.

As Arthur stepped out of his car, Amelia watched him from her camper window. She quickly grabbed her purse, and when he opened the door and stepped outside, she joined him. "Hey, you," Arthur greeted her, taking her left arm with his hand and pulling her close, planting a gentle kiss on her cheek. The unexpected kiss startled her, causing her to stumble back slightly. He held onto her arm to steady her. "Are you alright?" he asked.

Amelia felt her cheeks flush with embarrassment, but she managed to reply, "Yes, I'm fine."

Shyly, she asked, "So, where are you taking me?"

"You need a coat," he pointed out.

"Oh, alright," she agreed, and they both stepped into her camper as she retrieved her Burberry trench coat. Inside, she noticed that it was a little colder.

"Is your heat working?" Arthur inquired.

"Yes, the generator outside sometimes gets a little lazy," she joked. "But it's fine. I mostly need the electricity."

"It gets very cold here, especially at night in the winter," Arthur remarked, concerned.

"Have you still not bought a winter coat?"

"I will, I promise. Don't worry; I have a sweater on. I'll be fine," she assured him.

He started the car, turned on the heat, and they were off on their date. "It's going to be just over a half-hour drive," he told her.

"Where on earth are we going?" Amelia asked, puzzled.

"It's a surprise," Arthur replied with a mischievous smile.

As they peacefully enjoyed the drive, he played some music, and they discussed the books they were currently reading. Their shared passion for literature drew them closer together, making Amelia feel safe and comfortable in his presence. She realized she had never been on a real date before. Sure, she had attended high school parties and dances with friends, but she had never felt a genuine connection with someone until now. Each time Arthur looked at her with his piercing blue eyes, she felt a deep sense of comfort and attraction.

Amelia couldn't help feeling a bit guilty that she hadn't explored the areas outside of Nottingham since her arrival. Her focus had been entirely on The Park House, and any errands she ran with Charlie or Wendy were usually within the city limits. Learning to drive and getting a license were tasks on her to-do list, but she hadn't found the time for them. The drive passed quickly, and as they turned off the road and entered a village, Amelia read a sign that said "Edwinstowe."

"We have entered the gateway to Sherwood Forest," Arthur announced with a smile.

"Sherwood Forest?" Amelia exclaimed with excitement.

"Yes, The Sherwood Forest," Arthur confirmed. "This village is where we'll have our lunch. Right now, I'm taking you to the visitor's center."

"Why? Because I'm a tourist?" she teased.

Arthur parked the car in the visitor's center parking lot and turned to her. "No, because you live here now, and it's time for you to get to know your home." He grinned, his eyes sparkling with a hint of flirtation.

The sparks between them were undeniable, and Amelia felt herself falling for him even more. They entered the visitor's center together, greeted by warm, heated air. Arthur suggested using the restroom before they continued, and Amelia obliged. As she exited the restroom, she explored the gift shop filled with books, games, medieval costumes, and even swords that reflected the era of Robin Hood.

Arthur's voice caught her attention from behind, "I'm just going to order at the cafe for us. Tea?"

"Yes, thank you. I'll be just a minute," she replied with a giggle.

Amused, Amelia couldn't resist buying a Robin Hood hat and quickly paid for it, secretly stashing it inside her coat. She made her way to Arthur as he waited for their teas.

"Did you see anything you liked?" he asked.

"Oh, yes," she grinned. Arthur handed her a cup of tea.

"These will keep us warm on the trail," he remarked.

Amelia was curious. "The trail, huh? This isn't some sort of huge hike or something, is it? I'm not exactly a trained outdoorswoman if you haven't noticed."

"Don't tell me you've never been hiking before?" Arthur asked, surprised.

"Once, through Griffith Park back in high school. We hiked up near the Hollywood sign," she admitted.

"The Hollywood sign? My God, you are quite the city girl, aren't you?" he teased.

"Why, yes, yes, I am," she said with pride. "But I'm open to new experiences."

Arthur led her along the quiet trail. He was right; there were very few people around, and aside from the occasional breeze rustling through the trees, it was peaceful and silent.

"It's so quiet," Amelia whispered.

"In the summer, it's quite busy here with tourists, so we've always come here in the off season. I love it here," Arthur explained.

"We?" Amelia inquired; her curiosity piqued.

"Well, when I was younger, my father would take me and my brother, and when Rosie was old enough, she joined us. This was something we did quite often. But now, it's just me," he said, his voice tinged with nostalgia.

"And me. I'm here now," Amelia flirted.

Arthur nodded, smiling warmly at her. "Yes, you're here now."

Taking a sip of her tea, Amelia confessed, "You're right about the tea. It's helping."

But as they continued their walk, the cold wind suddenly picked up, and Arthur noticed that she was shivering. Concerned, he asked, "Are you still cold?"

"I think my blood is thinner than yours," she joked.

He stopped and reached into his backpack, pulling out a blanket. "You brought us a blanket?" Amelia asked in surprise.

"Yes, of course," he replied, draping the blanket over her shoulders. "Is that better?"

"Yes, thank you," she said, grateful for his thoughtfulness.

"It's been unseasonably cold this October."

"Oh?"

"Yes. It feels like everything is changing."

"Yes, it does."

They walked a while more and then with nervous excitement he said, "Here it is."

They both gazed at The Major Oak, standing majestically in an area fenced off to the public. It was the largest oak tree she had ever seen, and its presence felt otherworldly, like something out of a fairy tale.

"This is The Major Oak. It's somewhere between eight hundred to eleven hundred years old," Arthur explained.

"You're kidding," Amelia gasped.

"The legend has it that Robin Hood and his men would use this mighty tree for shelter," Arthur said with a smile.

Amelia was awestruck to be standing at a place where Robin Hood might have once stood. It was everything she had ever dreamed of and more. The boyish grin on Arthur's face as he looked at the tree only added to the enchantment.

"So, this is Arthur Bonneville's favorite place in the world," she said, her eyes fixed on the majestic oak.

"This is my favorite place in the world," he confirmed.

"How many girls have you brought here?" she teased.

His eyes lit up, "You're the first Amelia."

She felt the blood raise to her cheeks, and she turned away shyly. After spending some time admiring the tree, Arthur reached into his jacket and pulled out a small, wrapped package. He handed it to her, and she felt her heart race with anticipation.

"What's this?" she asked.

"It's a surprise," Arthur replied with a wink.

Amelia carefully unwrapped the package, revealing an older book with the title "Robin Hood" on the binding. Her mouth dropped open in astonishment.

"It's from my personal collection. It was written in eighteen fifty-five by Stephen Percy,"

Arthur explained. "I thought you might like it."

Amelia opened the book and saw that it was indeed "Robin Hood and His Merry Foresters" by Stephen Percy, just as he had said. She hugged the book close to her heart.

"The key to my heart," she said. "Although, I'm a bit surprised, "I would have imagined that if you were to gift me a book, it would have been about King Arthur."

"Oh, heavens no," Arthur replied emphatically.

As they both gazed at the tree and the wind picked up again, this time giving Arthur the chills, Amelia pleaded, "Let's stay a few more minutes."

She took his hand in her as if it was something they had done a thousand times before this perfect moment.

"Of course, Amelia," he agreed, and they stood hand in hand, falling in love with each other amidst the tranquility of The Major Oak and the beauty of Sherwood Forest.

38

Romance

IT WAS A short drive to a nearby restaurant named The Royal Oak. Amelia pointed to the sign with a smile and said, "I can tell there's a common theme to this first date."

Arthur grinned. "Yes, very much so." He parked his car.

As they stepped out of the car, Amelia reached into her coat and pulled out the Robin Hood hat she had bought at the visitor's center. She handed it to Arthur. "I also have a gift for you."

He accepted the hat and couldn't help but laugh. "Shall I wear this inside?"

Amelia teased, "I really think you should." However, as they approached the restaurant, she stopped him. "You don't have to keep wearing that, Arthur."

"Why not?" he said, a hint of playfulness in his eyes. "I think I look quite good in it." He offered his arm, and Amelia took it willingly.

When they reached the front door of The Royal Oak, he took off the hat, and she let out a sigh of relief. "Oh, good. I really thought you might be serious for a moment," she giggled. He put the hat in his pocket, and they entered the warm and cozy restaurant. They were quickly welcomed by a hostess and shown to their table near a crackling fireplace. The restaurant had bookshelves filled with books, and Amelia spotted a decorative brass rabbit on its side, seemingly watching them. She smiled at the rabbit, feeling as if Kinsey was always close by.

The hostess handed them menus, and Amelia was grateful to find that she had a healthy appetite. Arthur asked Amelia, "Is it to early for wine?"

"It's never too early," she assured him with a grin.

They were both looking at their menus as their waitress approached them.

"Welcome I'm Stacy, may I start you with something to drink or are you ready to order?"

"Everything here is good, I promise," he replied with a wink. "How about we both have burgers?"

"Oh yes the burgers are great." Stacy nodded in agreement.

Amelia nodded. "That sounds great to me."

"We will have two burgers, medium, chips, and a bottle of your best Pinot Noir," Arthur told the waitress when she came to take their order.

"Excellent," Stacy said before moving on to other tables.

As they waited for their food, Arthur leaned over and took Amelia's hand, rubbing his thumb gently along her palm. Their eyes locked onto each other, and Amelia felt a deep connection between them. She noticed two elegantly dressed women at a nearby table, roughly Lady Edith's age, staring in their direction. Arthur noticed them too and seemed to recognize them.

He released Amelia's hand and explained, "The woman to my left, that's Lady Evelyn Hampton, and her friend Ms. Kathryn Archer, is on the city council. In fact, she was involved in the approval of your planning for the Park House."

Amelia was surprised. "I should go and thank her, shouldn't I?"

Arthur quickly pushed her back down into her seat. "No, you really shouldn't."

"Why not?" Amelia asked, puzzled.

He whispered, "Because she wasn't going to approve any of it. It took quite a bit of convincing of the other members to get their approval. She's very close with my mother, and it was all a bit of a headache."

Amelia had no idea, and she leaned back in her chair, absorbing this revelation. She couldn't believe that Arthur had helped secure the approval for the Park House project.

He whispered again, "Charlie reached out, and I stepped in to help convince them."

Amelia was touched by his gesture and felt a surge of gratitude. "I don't know what to say, Arthur."

"You don't have to say anything," he replied, reaching for his wine glass and gesturing for her to do the same. "A toast."

"To what?" she asked, her tone flirtatious.

"To you," he said with a warm smile, squeezing her hand. "You are truly lovely, my Amelia."

Amelia felt a rush of emotions, hearing those words again, the same words that had lingered in her memory since that night at the hotel.

"Say that again."

"What? How lovely you are?"

"No, the other part."

He leaned in and whispered, "My Amelia."

She wanted to hold onto this perfect moment, but the disapproving looks from the two women sitting behind them were impossible to ignore. She sensed their judgment, and it made her uneasy.

"We're getting some very disapproving looks from across the room," Amelia remarked, taking a sip of her wine and setting the glass back on the table.

Arthur turned to glance at the women, and they quickly averted their eyes, looking ashamed.

"Well, I approve," Arthur said, his hand back in hers. "And that's what matters." Their eyes locked once more, and in that moment, Amelia knew that this was real. He wasn't ashamed of her; in fact, he seemed entirely at ease. She felt a warmth and connection with him that she had never experienced before. They were linked, and Amelia knew she was his.

⚬⚬⚬

LATER THAT EARLY evening, when Arthur had returned her to her camper at The Park House, Amelia felt a mix of nervousness and hope. Their hands were intertwined as they drove up the long driveway, and occasionally, he'd glance at her with an intensity that made her heart race. She was sad the date had come to an end, but she held onto hope that there would be more to come.

When they parked the car, Arthur showed his gentlemanly side by offering his hand to help her out. As they walked towards her camper, Amelia couldn't help but feel nervous about what might happen next. She carried her purse and the book he had given her, and when they reached her door, she turned to face him, her legs feeling weak. She mustered the courage to speak.

"Thank you for today. It was perfect," she said, grinning.

"It *was* perfect," he replied, his finger tracing the lining of her coat. He moved closer to her, and her heart raced as their faces drew nearer. This was the moment she had been anticipating, their first kiss. Just as their lips were about to meet, Arthur's phone rang, and they both paused. He quickly apologized and looked down at his phone, revealing it was his mother calling.

Amelia felt a mix of embarrassment and disappointment. "Oh, okay," she stammered.

Arthur took the call, holding his phone to his chest to silence it. Before he spoke into the phone, he leaned in and kissed Amelia on the cheek, whispering, "Get inside, it's freezing out here."

Amelia was left standing by her camper door, watching as he walked back to his car to take the call. She felt hurt and confused. Was his mother really so controlling that she could interrupt a moment like this? Doubt crept in, and she began to question the future of their relationship.

Once inside her camper, she felt a growing sense of unease. She watched as his car's lights disappeared up the driveway, and a sick feeling churned in her stomach. She had already faced judgment from strangers at the restaurant, and now this interference from his mother made her question whether their relationship could continue.

⁂

LYING IN BED, she considered reaching out with a goodnight text, but fear held her back. The silence was suffocating, and she couldn't shake her restless thoughts. Eventually, she drifted off to sleep, where dreams of Arthur filled her night, offering a brief escape from her worries.

39

Let It Be

AMELIA'S FRUSTRATION WITH herself grew as she navigated the chilly Nottingham weather without a proper winter coat. She hugged herself tightly within her Burberry trench coat, realizing that Arthur would likely be displeased with her lack of preparation. Their last date had gone well, but since then, their communication had grown colder, leaving her feeling dejected.

One day, while a window specialist worked on restoring a historic window frame, the Beatles' "Let It Be" filled the air. The song had been resonating with her for days, beckoning her to St. Mary's church. The medieval architecture had always intrigued her during her time in Nottingham, but she had never stepped inside the massive church until now. It had been nearly a year since she last attended a church service, but something about St. Mary's called to her.

Upon entering, she was greeted by the unusual sight of a lion and a unicorn, symbols that piqued her curiosity. She found a seat towards the back, focusing more on the grandeur of the architecture than the congregation filing in. The service that followed, led by the reverend, was truly inspiring. The reading from First Samuel, verse sixteen, resonated deeply with her, reminding her of the grace that had guided her through life's trials.

As the service concluded, Amelia felt a renewed sense of self and wholeness. The church's age-old beauty had a personal touch, making her regret her long absence from religious gatherings. She resolved to make this a regular part of her life, a grounding force in her new Nottingham home.

The gilded ten angels that seemed to float above her on the ceiling smiled back at her. A person sat down beside her and she realized quickly it was the Reverend.

"Hello dear." He greeted her warmly.

"Hello, Reverend. I'm Amelia Levingston."

Amelia offered her hand to him and he shook it. "Welcome to St. Mary's Amelia, where are you visiting us from?"

"I'm originally from California but I just recently moved here."

"Oh how wonderful. I hope you will be visiting us more."

"I certainly will. I really enjoyed the service today."

"Well thank you. I'm so glad you did."

She smiled looking back up at the angels. He looked to where she was looking up. "The church is really amazing. And those angels are lovely." She studied them as they shined brilliantly in gold.

He looked up to the angels and explained, "Aren't they? You know, for over one hundred and seventy years no one noticed them."

"What do you mean?" She asked.

"It's true. They just blended into the ceiling. All ten of them sat silently in the dark watching over us, secretly smiling through our worship. We just recently had them all gilded in gold and now everyone can see them."

"That's incredible." She was fascinated by his story. "To think they were hiding in plain site like that."

"Isn't that just like people. They can be hiding in plain site, and all it takes is one person to notice them so they can truly shine." He stood up and took another look at the angels and then back to her. "Looking forward to seeing you again, Amelia wasn't it?"

"Yes, Amelia Levingston. Thank you."

As she admired the angels one last time before leaving, she noticed Lady Edith standing at the church's entrance, glaring at her. Surprised, Amelia raised her hand in greeting. Lady Edith approached.

"Did you follow me here?"

Caught off guard by her allegation, Amelia retreated and replied, "No, of course not."

"Good."

She turned to walk away and Amelia pursued her. "Lady Edith, wait."

"What?" she demanded.

"I just wanted to say I'm sorry that I've made a bad impression on you."

"Is that all you have to say?"

"No, that's not all. I hope that somehow, by some miracle," gesturing to their surroundings, "You might take some time to get to know me better. Perhaps we might get along."

Her face twisted and she took a step toward her, "Are you dating my son?"

Hesitant, she thought a moment and answered, "No."

Her eyes narrowed, "You shouldn't lie, especially in church."

"I'm not lying to you. We had a date, but we aren't dating one another."

"Let's keep it that way." She hissed and turned to walk away once more.

"But, why?"

"Do you really need to know why? Do you really not see it?

"I'm not sure what you mean?"

She turned to face her one final time, which she made clear by her affluent turn and force that she spoke for the last time. "Do you see where you are standing you foolish, ignorant child? Look around you. My family's blood is here, this is our land. You have no place in it. You will never be enough for my son. You are nothing but a pathetic American who won the lottery and you will never be anything more. Our world will never welcome your kind."

Amelia felt gutted. It took a moment for her to collect herself before she could follow Lady Edith out of the church entry. She watched as Lady Edith entered the all-to-familiar car for Arthur had been waiting for her. Her stomach turned as she quickly shut her car door and ordered Arthur to drive away. He noticed Amelia and as he was about to say hello his mother screamed at him to move, and they left Amelia heartbroken and abandoned outside the church.

Feeling helpless and alone, Amelia wandered aimlessly through the cold streets, cursing herself for not buying a warmer coat. Eventually, she found refuge in a restaurant, where she sat at the bar to warm up and gather her thoughts. Her appetite was nonexistent, and she ordered a glass of wine to numb the pain.

Amelia's phone buzzed with calls from Arthur, but she ignored them, opting to drown her sorrows in her glass. She felt embarrassed and was too nervous to hear what he had to say. After a couple of drinks on an empty stomach, she realized she needed a taxi back. The bartender called one for her, and she gratefully accepted.

During the taxi ride, her thoughts shifted between the hurtful encounter with Lady Edith and memories of her difficult past with her aunt and cousin. Determined not to let bitterness rule her life, she sent a heartfelt message to her relatives, expressing gratitude for their past support and wishing them well.

The taxi returned her to The Park House, and as she thought of Lady Edith, she decided to rise above the resentment and earn Lady Edith's respect through actions rather than words. Amelia was resolved to be kind, honor her true nature, and live her life to the fullest in Nottingham.

After paying the taxi driver, she stepped outside and was greeted by something cold touching her nose—snow, her very first experience of it. Overjoyed, she held out her hands to catch the snowflakes, twirling in delight like a child. Nottingham's winters, with their enchanting snowfall, were now hers to experience.

Amelia returned to her camper, curled up with a good book, and watched the snowfall through her windows. Suddenly she heard and then watched Arthur's car approach. She quickly collected herself and then met him at the door.

"Why haven't you been answering my calls?" Arthur asked.

The blood rushed to her face. She felt sick. "My phone's dead," she lied.

He slowly approached her inside and Amelia took a step back. Confused he asked, "What's happened? I thought we were in a good place?"

She folded her arms, "Your mother put me in my place."

His face softened, "What did she say to you Amelia?"

Amelia bit her lip. "Maybe, we should take some time apart. So we know, for sure, this is what we want."

He looked hurt. She couldn't believe she had just said those words to him. She didn't feel that way at all. She just wanted to jump into his arms and kiss him.

"Why are you pushing me away?"

She stared into his blue eyes and all she wanted to say was, *she was afraid. Terrified of love. Terrified of trusting him with her heart.*

After patiently waiting for an answer Arthur retreated. "Fine. I'll give you space."

Amelia watched him return to his car and knew she had hurt him. She retreated to her bed and pulled the covers over her face in regret and fear.

40

Christmas

WINTER HAD DRAPED The Park House in a pristine blanket of snow, and Amelia had been deafened by the silence of no Arthur in her life. He had honored her request for space, and she hated every moment of it.

Since their last encounter, Amelia had felt a heaviness in her heart, which was taking a toll on her overall well-being. She was grappling with lower energy levels but channeled all her strength into overseeing the house's renovation. November and December had proven challenging for the workers, with unpredictable weather hindering progress. Despite the hardships, Amelia diligently chronicled the restoration process on Instagram, where her followers had now surpassed one million. She anticipated lucrative offers once the house was complete and dreamed of restoring more historic homes.

The workers had Christmas Eve and Christmas Day off to spend with their families. Charlie and Wendy insisted she join them, but she resisted the temptation. She knew that Charlie was going to propose and didn't want to get in the way of their joyful celebrations. Besides, she relished the solitude of her camper and imagined the festive scenes that would soon unfold within the restored house—twinkling Christmas lights, laughter, and the aroma of holiday feasts. She envisioned roaring fires in the fireplaces and the joyful merriment of the season. It would also mark one year since Kinsey's passing, a friend she missed dearly but who had profoundly influenced her.

Over the past months, Amelia had secretly formulated a plan with Mr Field. She intended to return the Park House to its rightful owners, an idea that she harbored each day as she worked on the house. Handing Lady Edith the keys and witnessing her reaction was a vision that brought her both satisfaction and hope. Her mother's teachings had instilled in her the importance of doing the right thing, and she was determined to honor those values.

On a chilly Christmas Eve morning, Amelia awoke feeling a bit achy but decided to take a stroll around the snow-covered house. The picturesque scene inspired her to capture moments for her Instagram. As she walked, she marveled at the idea of a warm, festive Christmas inside The Park House. Her thoughts drifted to Kinsey, her dear friend who had brought blessings into her life.

After an hour walk in the cold, her aching body demanded warmth, and she retreated to her camper. She felt a sore throat coming on and knew she needed rest. The previous night had been spent bidding on an antique bed frame at an auction and scrolling through paint samples.

As darkness fell around 6 PM, the snow began to fall once more. Amelia watched from her camper with a cup of tea in hand, charging her phone. Suddenly, the power went out, plunging her into darkness. Panic gripped her momentarily, and she realized she needed to check the generator outside. Bracing herself against the biting cold, she ventured out, using a flashlight to navigate.

However, her limited knowledge of the generator's workings left her feeling helpless.

Returning to the camper, Amelia contemplated whom to call for help. She ruled out interrupting Charlie's proposal to Wendy and reluctantly decided to call Arthur. Just as it started ringing, her phone died, leaving her in complete darkness.

Frustration and anxiety grew as the snowstorm intensified. She knew she had to conserve heat, so she huddled inside the camper, hoping that her absence the following day would prompt the workers to check on her. As the night wore on, her anxiety heightened, but she clung to the hope that dawn would bring not only light but a solution to her predicament. Amelia layered herself in warm clothing and sought refuge in her bed, hoping it would be enough to endure the long, cold night ahead.

THE FOLLOWING MORNING, Amelia was greeted by the glistening sun filtering through the ice-covered windows of her camper. The air inside was frigid, and her breath formed visible puffs in the cold. She felt feverous and was fighting a cough.

The pressing need to use the bathroom forced her to confront the discomfort of an icy toilet seat. When she attempted to wash her hands, no water flowed from the tap. The freezing temperatures had caused the water lines to freeze, leaving her without running water. It was a dire situation, and she felt a growing sense of urgency. Putting on her boots and layering up as much as possible, Amelia opened the camper door.

To her astonishment, she was greeted by a herd of Fallow deer that had surrounded her camper during the night. They regarded her with surprise, and she raised her hands to reassure them. The deer scattered gracefully through the deep snow as she took a step outside, sinking into over a foot of snow. She had apparently slept through a blizzard. The biting cold wind cut through her, making her shiver.

Returning to the camper, she added an extra pair of gloves and ensured she had her phone and charging cord. With a heavy chest and an increasingly sore throat, she coughed as she trudged through the deep snow. She recognized the telltale signs—she was coming down with a cold.

Amelia painstakingly made her way to the back of the house. Upon entering she flipped a light switch and there was no power to be found. The blizzard had evidently cut all power. Outside, she made her way toward a makeshift shed that sheltered several generators the workers had been using due to the lack of electricity in the house. Approaching the first generator, she tried unsuccessfully to start it, feeling a wave of helplessness wash over her.

Realizing she had to make a decision, she assessed her options. It was still early, and there might be people traveling on the nearby main road. Her best chance was to reach the road and flag down help. As she began the arduous trek, her regret of not pursuing a driving license and relying on the use of taxies and rides with hired help and friends alike was making her angrier by the minute. Snowflakes were starting to fall and in a moment of frustration, the enchantment she had previously felt for snow turned into bitter resentment. With her hands raised to the sky, she voiced her exasperation, "Really?" The thought of enduring another night like the last was terrifying, and she knew she had no choice but to press on. Her energy was waning, and she felt feverish, yet she slowly pushed forward toward the main road.

✦✦✦

AMELIA COULDN'T HELP but think that venturing out had been a terrible idea. Nearly half an hour had passed, and exhaustion was setting in. The thick snow was unforgiving, and her attire—just rubber boots and socks—offered little protection. As the snowfall continued steadily, she clutched her crossed arms in an attempt to stay warm, but she felt her body growing colder by the minute, especially her feet.

Then disaster struck. Her right foot snagged a hidden branch buried beneath the snow, causing her to trip and fall face-first into the cold ground. The shock of pain radiating from her right ankle was excruciating. Although it didn't feel broken, it was undeniably injured. She gazed around, and her thoughts turned bleak. Is this how it ends? After surviving cancer and embarking on a new life in Europe as a wealthy woman, would she meet her demise in the snow, alone and frozen? Who would discover her lifeless body?

Suddenly, movement caught her eye. In the nearby woods, something smaller darted through the snow, and then a white rabbit emerged, perched on a stump. Amelia couldn't believe her eyes. The rabbit sat there, its nose twitching, and its blue eyes fixed on her. Could this be a dream? The throbbing pain in her ankle reminded her that it wasn't. She stared at the rabbit in amazement, and then it hopped through the snow toward the main road, as if beckoning her to follow. She felt the presence of Kinsey, as if he were guiding her, urging her to heed the sign.

With renewed determination, she pushed aside her fears and told herself, "No, I won't meet my end like this!" The white rabbit eventually disappeared back into the woods, but Amelia followed its trail with a hobbling gait. Her hope began to outweigh her trembling despair.

Finally, she reached the main road, and as exhaustion washed over her, she felt a glimmer of hope amidst the cold. Using a branch she found near the gate as a makeshift cane, she pressed on. Her fingers were numb, and she knew she had to find help. The road was close now, and she pushed through the pain. When she finally reached the road, she collapsed from both exhaustion and the cold. However, there were no cars in sight. It was Christmas Day, and everyone was likely with their families. She regretted her decision to leave the warmth of the camper.

As her body grew colder and wetter from slush kicked up by previous passing cars, she tried to stand but failed. Her ankle throbbed with pain, and she realized she was stuck. Exhaustion, cold, and despair had taken over. She lay back in the soft snow, which strangely felt like a gentle pillow.

Apart from the throbbing in her foot, she could hardly feel anything.

She gazed up at the low-hanging clouds and closed her eyes as snowflakes settled on her face, their gentle touch a soothing embrace.

Resigned to her fate, she made peace with the idea of being buried alive in the snow, her body discovered when spring melted away the icy shroud. She closed her eyes, surrendering to the numbing cold and fatigue, when the distant sound of a car horn pierced the air. She turned her head to see a familiar vehicle approaching, slowing down, and stopping. She recognized the voice and the piercing blue eyes of the person who rushed toward her.

"My God! Amelia?" he exclaimed.

He tried to lift her, and she managed to whisper, "It's you."

She closed her eyes again.

41

Back To The Light

WHEN AMELIA TRIED to open her eyes, the brightness of the room was blinding. She could hear muffled voices and the faint beeping of a monitor. Her voice was hoarse as she inquired about the sounds.

"What is that?" she asked, her voice barely above a whisper. She felt disoriented, her head heavy.

A doctor and Arthur entered the room. Arthur rushed to her side, relief evident in his eyes.

"Thank God you're alright," he exclaimed.

Amelia reached up to feel her head and noticed she was wearing a snow hat. She had trouble keeping her eyes open against the blinding light.

"I need some water," she croaked, her throat dry. A nurse entered the room, and the doctor instructed her to fetch some water for Amelia.

"You're a very lucky woman, Miss Levingston," the doctor said as he examined her. "If Mr. Bonneville hadn't found you, you would have frozen to death."

Amelia's eyes struggled to adjust to the light. She realized she was in a hospital bed, and her left index finger was connected to a monitor.

"Is she going to be alright?" Arthur asked, taking her left hand gently.

Amelia felt the throbbing pain in her right ankle intensify, but it was hard for her to keep her eyes open.

"It's so bright," she muttered.

"What on earth were you thinking?" Arthur shook his head with a mix of relief and anger.

Amelia coughed weakly.

"My chest feels so heavy."

"You have walking pneumonia," the doctor explained.

Amelia's confusion grew. "What?"

"We've given you a heavy dose of antibiotics. You also have a severely sprained ankle," the doctor elaborated.

Amelia began to feel the aching pain radiating from her right foot, but she was too exhausted to complain.

The nurse brought her water, and the ice-cold liquid provided relief for her sore throat.

Arthur's worry-filled eyes never left her.

But when the doctor and nurse left the room to give them privacy, Arthur's concern turned into stern questioning.

"What were you thinking, Amelia?" he asked.

Amelia tried to explain, her voice raspy and weak. "The power went out. My phone was dead, so I couldn't call for help. I tried to turn on the generators the workers were using to charge my phone, but I couldn't get them to work. I didn't know what to do, so I walked to the road to find help."

Arthur contemplated her explanation for a moment. "What if I hadn't found you?"

"But you did find me," she said softly, looking at him with gratitude. "Thank you, Arthur, for finding me."

She sighed, her eyes growing heavy as she laid her head back on the pillow. Her body felt drained, and she was drenched in sweat.

"I'll be fine," she assured him. "I'm just so tired."

"You're not fine. You have a fever," Arthur replied, his worry palpable.

The nurse returned, and Arthur requested her to check Amelia's temperature. After a quick reading, the nurse reported, "Thirty-eight point three degrees Celsius. That's a bit higher than we want to see. I'll inform the doctor."

Arthur sat down in a nearby chair, concern etched on his face. His hands trembled, and Amelia couldn't help but wonder if he had refrained from stepping out for a cigarette for a while.

"What's that in Fahrenheit?" she asked.

He thought for a moment and replied, "About one hundred and one."

Amelia tried to sit up slightly and asked him to raise the bed, which he did. As she settled back, she hesitated before saying, "You should go home, Arthur. You don't need to stay here with me."

He looked conflicted for a moment. "And leave you here alone? Absolutely not. The nurse wasn't even aware you had a fever."

Amelia pondered this unusual situation for a moment before speaking, "I mean. If you want to stay... then stay."

He squinted in thought and watched the nurse and doctor conversing in the hallway. "I think I'll stay for a while. Make sure you have what you need," he decided.

"Okay," Amelia agreed softly, closing her eyes.

She fell back asleep, comforted by Arthur's presence.

A few hours later, Amelia woke up in her hospital room, half-expecting to see Arthur by her side. However, he was nowhere to be found. The nurse checked on her and delivered some good news.

"Your fever has broken. All your vitals are normal. You needed the rest," the nurse whispered to her.

Amelia nodded weakly and replied, "My ankle is throbbing."

"I'll get you some pain meds for that, dear," the nurse assured her.

Amelia asked, "When do you think I'll be able to leave?"

The nurse considered it for a moment. "Tomorrow, I should think."

Amelia felt relieved. "That's good to hear."

"Do you want something to eat?"

"Actually, yes. I'm quite hungry," Amelia admitted.

"I'll order you some lunch then," the nurse said before leaving the room.

Amelia waited, hoping Arthur would return, but he remained absent. She couldn't help but feel a pang of disappointment.

A different doctor entered her room and asked, "Are you taking visitors, or should I send them away?"

Amelia hesitated for a moment before replying, "Sure."

To her surprise, Wendy and Charlie burst into the room. Wendy was carrying a bouquet of balloons, and Charlie had a bouquet of flowers in his hand. Wendy was the first to speak, her relief evident.

"Oh my Lord, Amelia! I seriously was freaking out," Wendy exclaimed.

Charlie, emotional and relieved, approached her, struggling to hold back tears. "Are you alright?"

Wendy hugged her tightly, and Charlie asked, "Can I hug you too, please?"

Amelia chuckled softly, "Of course, Charlie. Just don't cry, okay?"

Charlie stepped back, wiping away his tears with a tissue, and hugged Wendy. Wendy patted his back, offering him comfort.

"She looks good. She's going to be fine, right?" Charlie asked, still teary-eyed.

Amelia assured them, "I'm going to be fine. It was just a stupid accident. My power was out, and my cell phone was dead..."

"You have got to keep that bloody mobile charged," Wendy chided gently. "But please, continue."

Amelia explained the sequence of events, emphasizing that she had started feeling sick that morning even before she ventured outside.

"You could have died," Wendy remarked with a worried expression.

Amelia smiled weakly, replying, "But I didn't."

Charlie chimed in, "Thank God Arthur found you in time."

Amelia thought about Arthur's absence. "Wait, where's Arthur?"

"He left to give you some space," Wendy replied. "He's been incredibly worried about you. He's a complete mess."

Amelia felt a mix of emotions but chose to focus on Wendy's engagement ring instead.

"Your ring!" Amelia exclaimed, reaching for Wendy's hand to get a closer look.

Wendy proudly displayed her beautiful engagement ring. Charlie, overwhelmed with emotion again, had to leave the room. Amelia and Wendy shared a laugh at his reaction. Wendy took a seat next to Amelia's bed.

"How are you feeling, my love? You alright?" Wendy inquired.

Amelia's eyes drifted back to Wendy's ring as she replied, "I'm so happy for you both. I truly am."

Wendy glanced at her own ring and back at Amelia. "I'm really happy."

As Wendy prepared to leave, she mentioned that Arthur had fixed everything for Amelia's trailer at The Park House.

Amelia was taken aback. "Oh wow. Okay."

Wendy raised an eyebrow, her tone playful. "You know, Amelia, I think he has feelings for you."

Charlie chimed in, "Oh, he's madly in love with her."

Amelia tried to deny it, saying, "He's not in love with me. We had one perfect date and then I messed it all up."

Wendy teased her, "Give it another chance. You should keep him around, Amelia.

Amelia shook her head with a smile. "I'm just glad he found me in time."

"What if he wouldn't have found you? I can't even imagine." Charlie began to get upset and quickly exited to the hallway.

Wendy and Amelia chuckled together. "We love you, Amelia." Wendy leaned over and kissed her hat.

Amelia reassured her, "I'm going to be fine, I promise. The nurse said I'm most likely out of here in the morning."

Wendy was relieved to hear that. She had to leave for work but assured Amelia that Charlie would stay to take care of her.

The nurse reentered the room and asked, "Is that crying man alright? He was making quite a scene in our hallway. I almost asked him to leave."

Amelia chuckled and replied, "He'll be fine."

42

He Loves Me

THE NEXT DAY, as the nurse had predicted, Amelia was discharged from the hospital with a prescription for pneumonia and her foot in a boot. She was feeling much better, although frustrated about the prospect of being in the boot for six weeks. Charlie arrived to pick her up, but she felt hurt and confused about Arthur's absence. He had been there for her one moment and then disappeared, which seemed to be his typical behavior.

As they approached The Park House, Amelia noticed that the road had been freshly plowed. The workers were busy, and the lights of her trailer were on. Outside, she saw a brand new, massive fire pit with four chairs around it. Charlie remarked, "Someone's been hard at work."

Amelia agreed, saying, "I can see that."

Charlie helped her out of the car, and she marveled at all the work Arthur had done. Some of the workers waved at her, and she greeted them with a smile and a wave. Charlie offered his arm, which she initially declined, but he insisted, telling her, "Just take my arm, girl. Honestly, haven't you ever had any help in your life?"

Amelia admitted, "No, I haven't."

Charlie responded with a warm smile, "Well, you do now." She felt an overwhelming sense of love and support from Charlie and Wendy, her chosen family.

Upon entering her trailer, Amelia couldn't believe her eyes. The entire trailer was perfectly cleaned, and her bed had all new bedding with a stack of warm blankets nearby. A large box from Burberry sat on her bed, wrapped in a bow. She opened it to find a giant winter coat inside and couldn't help but giggle. Her trailer was filled with surprises, including a stack of new interior design magazines, two new lanterns, and flashlights. There were also three phone chargers, including a portable one. A beautiful bouquet of flowers waited for her, accompanied by a note.

Amelia picked up the note and read it aloud to Charlie. It simply said, "Here are more than enough chargers for your mobile. - Arthur"

Charlie found the note to be lacking in humor and remarked, "What a knobhead."

Amelia corrected him with a smile, "That's not at all what it says, Charlie. It says he's in love with me." Charlie was confused, as he had read the note differently. "Trust me, that's exactly what it says." She assured him.

She looked around her trailer, smiling at all the thoughtful gestures Arthur had made.

Charlie, finally understanding, nodded and said, "Oh, I see."

Amelia decided to lay down for a bit, and Charlie suggested checking her temperature.

After Charlie left, Amelia went to bed and thought about Arthur. Her phone buzzed, and she hoped it was a message from him. However, it turned out to be a message from her former coworker Oliver.

"Hey girl. I have awesome news. I've been showing my boss your Instagram, and she was blown away. She was so impressed by the work you've been doing; she wants to speak with you."

Amelia's heart raced with excitement. She replied, "That's amazing, Oliver. I would love to."

Oliver responded, "Great. I'll give her your info. Sending you California sunshine!"

Amelia grinned at the message and replied, "Sending you England snow."

43

The Painting

AMELIA FELT MUCH stronger the following day. The sound of hand saws outside her trailer had woken her up, and she decided to take a long, refreshing shower. Afterward, she put on some comfortable pajamas, wrapped a towel around her short, curly hair, and donned her boot to make herself some morning coffee. Just as she picked up the pot, there was a knock at the door, and she hoped it might be Arthur. To her delight, it was Wendy, carrying more food than seemed humanly possible.

"Harry made you breakfast, lunch, and dinner," Wendy announced, her arms laden with bags of delicious meals.

"Come in!" Amelia greeted her warmly, pulling Wendy into a hug.

Wendy looked around the trailer and commented, "It's so cute in here." She deposited her bag of food on the small table next to the flowers.

"Want some coffee?" Amelia offered.

"Yes, please."

Amelia poured her a cup, and they settled at the table together. Wendy noticed the pile of phone chargers and quipped, "Um, do you need another charger?"

"Arthur," Amelia replied with a smile as she took a sip of her coffee.

"How are you feeling, love? How's the ankle?" Wendy inquired. "You look really good."

Amelia, sitting across from her, sipped her coffee thoughtfully. "Good. My ankle doesn't hurt as much, but it's swollen. I don't think it likes this boot. I feel okay otherwise, thanks to some heavy antibiotics."

Wendy noticed the scar on Amelia's chest from her port and asked about it. Amelia recognized the shift in energy but reassured her, "Wendy, it's fine. I'm really fine." She then noticed Wendy's gaze on the towel wrapped around her head. "So, what's going on under there, eh?"

"Oh. It's still growing back."

Wendy's expression was confident and encouraging as she said, "Let's see it then, go on."

Amelia removed the towel, revealing her drying, curly, short hair. Wendy smiled, "Oh wow. Your hair is so curly. I love it."

Amelia felt a bit self-conscious about her short hair and touched it, saying, "It's so short. It's growing back so slowly. Before chemo my hair grew so fast and now..."

Wendy stood up, gently feeling Amelia's hair and expressing admiration, "Yes but I love it. It's very pretty. Embrace it."

Amelia still felt a bit uncertain about her hair and reached for a hat. Wendy frowned at her, saying, "You know you don't have to cover it up, love. You are beautiful."

Amelia smirked, "Actually, I do because it's freezing outside."

Wendy understood Amelia's hesitation and encouraged her, "You know what I'm saying. You don't have to wear your wigs anymore. Be proud of who you are and what you've been through. Rock that short hair."

Amelia sighed, "I'm just not there yet."

Wendy assured her, "Well, whenever you're ready. You are gorgeous, darling!"

Amelia was touched by Wendy's support and sat back down. Wendy excitedly shared her plans for the day, saying, "I get to spend the day with you today. We can rest up here. I'll paint your nails. We could watch YouTube and eat all this yummy food." She pointed to the stack of meals.

Amelia was delighted to have Wendy's company and asked, "You do?"

"Yes! We can have a girls' day," Wendy confirmed.

Amelia smiled, feeling grateful for her friend's presence. "Actually, there is something you could do for me," she said, her eyes lighting up with an idea.

AN HOUR LATER Wendy stood filming with Amelia's phone as she explained to her viewers the events that had transpired over Christmas and why she was stuck in a boot. She even took the time with one of the construction crew to film a tutorial of restarting a generator. She explained the importance of this knowledge and how it can save lives. Afterward she showed the newly renovated kitchen area.

"This is really a unique space. We wanted to increase the light to the original kitchen and so we decided to add this huge window over the sink. The new owner can enjoy this beautiful view." Wendy smiled along and used her camera to show Amelia's followers the vast tree line of snow-covered fields. Amelia continued, "Isn't it so peaceful here?"

Wendy stopped recording and asked, "What do you mean the new owner?"

"Well, the house doesn't really belong to me does it?"

Before they could continue Charlie burst into the kitchen. "Girls, you have got to see this."

Amelia and Wendy followed Charlie to the sitting room of the house.

"We were starting to sand down these floors and Fred noticed a loose board in the corner by the fireplace."

"Film this Wendy." Amelia urged. Wendy started to record as Amelia followed Charlie over to where Fred was waiting.

"Go ahead, Fred. Show her."

Fred nervously looked at the camera and swiped his hair back and put on a very announcer voice for the audience. "As you can see friends, I noticed a loose floorboard here and I studied it. There was a hole and I lifted the board up and look."

Amelia looked inside the hidden space under the board. Inside there was a medium sized rectangular parcel covered in a dirty cloth. Amelia gently removed the object.

"Woah." Wendy exhaled continuing to film.

Amelia revealed an original oil painting of The Park House. Just as it was when it had first been finished.

"That is incredible." Charlie said.

Amelia held it up so Wendy could capture the painting she was holding. "I believe The Park House wants us all to know that it's ready to be brought back to its former glory. Look how absolutely beautiful it is. What a precious, precious gift. Thank you, Fred for finding this."

"I was just doing my job." He winked at the camera and everyone giggled as Wendy ended the recording.

Amelia held the painting staring at it, "I have to wonder if the Bonneville's knew about this?"

Arthur's voice interrupted, "Knew about what?"

There he was. Standing under the entryway of the sitting room.

"Arthur." Amelia grinned from ear to ear.

"Hello Amelia."

She stared at him lovingly. "Hello Arthur."

He put on a frown, "Shouldn't you be resting?"

"I'm feeling much better today."

Amelia's heart raced and could feel Fred, Charlie, and Wendy watching the two of them as if they were attending the finale at Wimbledon. Arthur slowly closed the space between them staring deeply into Amelia's eyes and finally broke contact to look down at what she was holding. "What do you have there?"

"Look at what Fred found."

Arthur gently took it from her. "Wherever did you find this?"

"So you haven't seen this before?"

"No. I haven't seen this. It's wonderful."

He met her eyes. Charlie and Wendy both sensed romantic tension brewing and so Charlie announced, "Okay Fred. Great work mate. Let's get back to sanding these floors. Wendy let's just... em... go somewhere else."

Amelia took the painting back from Arthur and placed it gently on the fireplace mantle. "Follow me Arthur. There is something I want to show you."

Arthur followed Amelia as she hobbled in her boot slowly toward the kitchen. "You really need to get off that foot, Amelia."

"I just want to show you something and then I promise to go put my foot up."

She took his hand and he helped her walk toward the kitchen. She proudly showed the work in the kitchen space and the new window. He praised her work, "That is wonderful." They both stared out at the view together still holding hands. Amelia looked up to him and softly kissed him on his lips. He was stunned.

"What was that for?"

"Because I wanted to."

Then there, basking in the glow of the window they kissed each other. The warm light of the window bathed over them as if to celebrate their connection. Their lips parted, and they shared an intimate moment, foreheads pressed together.

The unexpected entrance of a worker carrying a large box, caused them to step apart.

The worker grunted, "Oh sorry. Excuse me."

Amelia bit her lip slightly embarrassed. "Don't worry about it."

The worker's presence reminded them of the painting they had found earlier. Arthur suggested, "That painting that was found, you should bring that to my mother."

Amelia considered his suggestion. "I don't think that's a good idea."

"Why not? It could be a sort of... peace offering."

"I'll think about it." she sighed.

The idea of facing Lady Edith again made her slightly ill. She sensed his uneasiness and leaned into him, and he put his arm around her.

"I was so scared I lost you," he said.

"You didn't."

They stood together, gazing at the newly refurbished kitchen, imagining the future of The Park House. It was more than just a building; it was a place filled with history and potential, much like their own lives.

As they continued to talk about their plans for the house, the workers went about their tasks, bringing new life to the old estate. The Park House had more surprises in store for them, and Amelia and Arthur were ready to embrace whatever challenges and joys lay ahead.

44

Peace Offering

AMELIA SAT IN Arthur's car nervously holding the wrapped painting in her lap as he approached Oak Hall's driveway. She pulled down the passenger mirror to check her lipstick once more and Arthur sensed her nervousness. "You look lovely."

"I'm having second thoughts. I don't know if this is really the best idea Arthur. You mother doesn't seem to like surprises."

He parked the car in front of the grand residence and turned off the engine. He turned to face her and assured her, "I promise not to leave your side."

"You promise?"

"I give you my word."

He stepped out of his car and opened her door offering his hand gallantly as she stepped out searching for balance with her boot. She stared up at the daunting building and started to feel sick. She walked with him carrying the painting and he helped her up toward the front door and opened it for her.

Lady Edith's voice echoed down the hall.

"Arthur darling? Is that you?"

Rosie appeared at the top of the staircase and stopped at the sight of Amelia. "What is *she* doing here?"

"I brought Amelia as my guest for dinner tonight."

Amelia trembled and forced a smile at the sight of Lady Edith. She stood immaculately dressed with a cold stare. Amelia forced a smile. "Hello, your Ladyship."

"That's out of the question. She is not welcome in this house."

Rosie was a little surprised by the coldness in her mother's voice. She was feeling slightly embarrassed. Arthur pled, "Mother, Amelia has brought you something."

"Your ladyship, I brought you this."

"Take that back to wherever it came from and leave this house at once."

Arthur warned his mother, "Mother, please."

"Did your recent near-death experience give you amnesia or do you not recall our conversation at St. Mary's? You have no place here Miss Levingston. Now leave and take that back with you."

Amelia looked upward to see Rosie slowly descended the staircase observing the situation that was unfolding. Amelia looked to Arthur for help but he just stood confused and silence. Heartbroken, Amelia made a decision. She abandoned this terrible idea and placed the package on a nearby table and retreated as quickly as she could back to Arthur's car. Her foot hurt with every step but the heartache was worse.

Meanwhile, Arthur stood torn apart. His mother retreated to the kitchen in victory. Rosie followed Arthur as he burst through the kitchen door.

"You should be ashamed of yourself, mother."

The chef glanced up at Arthur from checking the temperature of his roasted chicken. Lady Edith encouraged the chef, "Carry on Chef. Arthur, I don't know how many more times I need to say this to you, but she is not welcome in this house."

"I love her."

"No you don't"

He slammed his hand on the table and the chef uncomfortably continued his work around them.

"I'm in love with her."

Lady Edith swallowed in fear and continued to keep face, "Honestly Arthur, you don't really love her."

"I do."

Her body shifted and then she spoke candidly, "Well, this isn't going to work. So let me put this into terms that you will understand. Choose her or us.

Arthur was sickened by what his mother had just told him. Rosie who had been standing near the doorway listening, burst in and pled for her brother, "Mother. Don't ask him to choose."

"Stay out of this, Rosie."

"I can't stay out of this because it has everything to do with *me*. You cut Kinsey out of my life and now you would willingly cut Arthur out now too? You can't do this to me again."

"I can and I will! Arthur you need to choose. Is family more important to you? Or your American."

The chef shook his head and shut the oven door and left the kitchen. Arthur watched him leave. Vulnerably he said, "You can't honestly ask me to decide that. This is totally unfair."

"You will be completely cut off from me and Rosie. I refuse to associate with this girl for one more moment of my life. She has stolen so much from us and now she wants to steal you. I won't have it." The countess stood her ground steadfast with her conviction.

Arthur looked to Rosie and she begged him with her eyes and voice, "Please Arthur. You can't leave me." Arthur's heart was breaking.

"I came here with Amelia tonight so you both could see what I see in her. She is wonderful in every way. She's caring and selfless. Something I'm not sure you will ever see Mother, as you have proven to be the opposite in nature these past ten years."

"Decide now."

Rosie grabbed onto Arthur's arm and begged, "Please Arthur. You can't leave your family. You can't leave us."

Arthur felt torn apart. He was being robbed by the joy that Amelia had brought to his life and he knew if he wasn't a role of Rosie's life, she would break. She was fragile like Kinsey. He had to stay for Rosie. Sadness and rage filled his heart. He gave Rosie a hug and whispered, "I couldn't leave you."

Lady Edith's face was filled with a victorious smile. "Now then, go drive her back to where she came from and then come back quickly. We don't want cold chicken for dinner."

Arthur faced his mother by the same face of her son when he knew his father had died. He was truly shattered. The light of his face had gone dark and she realized she had made a horrid mistake. But before she could utter another word he fled.

"Arthur!" Rosie called after him. Angrily shouted at her mother, "I hope you know what you've done. You can't just shut people out all the time. You are ruining us!"

Rosie ran toward her room.

"Where are you going?"

"I'm not hungry anymore."

She ran upstairs and slammed her door. Lady Edith followed and stopped when she noticed the wrapped package. Her curiosity overtook her and she picked it up noticing the great care Amelia had taken to wrap it. She slowly unwrapped it and inside she could tell it was some sort of artwork that had protective plastic around it with a card. The card read.

Dear Lady Edith,

Recently we found this painting hidden under the floorboards. I want you to know I am taking the greatest care to restore your home. You see, The Park House never belonged to me, your son has simply let me borrow its keys because he knew I would have the courage to open its doors. My hope is that soon the house will reflect the love that this artist was able to capture in this beautiful painting. I feel that same love every time I get the privilege to step foot inside the house. I am forever grateful for this life changing journey that your late son Henry gifted to me. For a son's love is a reflection of his own mother's.

- Amelia Levingston

Retreating to a nearby chair she read the letter again and held it to her heart. She had made a mistake. This was never about Amelia. She wasn't angry at her. She was angry with herself and what she was become. The past ten years she had grown bitter and angry. The sound of Arthur's car driving off made her wonder if it was too late.

Lady Edith, realizing the gravity of her actions, decided it was time for change. As she looked upstairs towards Rosie's room, determination filled her. She knew she needed to begin by mending her relationship with her daughter.

Quietly, she ascended the staircase and approached Rosie's room. She could hear faint sobs coming from inside. Gently, she knocked on the door and called, "Rosie, may I come in, my dear?"

There was a moment of silence before Rosie replied, her voice trembling, "I don't want to talk right now, Mother."

Lady Edith felt a pang of guilt and regret but remained patient. She responded, "I understand, but I'd like to apologize and make amends. Please, can we talk?"

There was a hesitant pause, and then Rosie finally said, "Alright, Mother, come in."

She entered Rosie's room, where her daughter sat on the edge of her bed, her eyes red from crying. The room was filled with mementos of Rosie's childhood, photographs, and cherished belongings.

With a deep breath she shared, "Rosie, I want to start by saying I'm truly sorry for my behavior earlier. I let my anger and fear cloud my judgment, and I hurt you and Arthur in the process. That was never my intention."

Rosie looked up at her mother, her eyes still filled with tears. "Mother, why can't you accept Amelia? Arthur clearly loves her, and she's a good person. She makes him happy."

Lady Edith sighed deeply, her resolve to change growing stronger. "You're right, my dear. I've been so consumed by my own pain and fears that I've let it affect those around me. I see now that I need to open my heart and let people in, especially if they bring happiness to the ones I love."

Rosie's tears began to subside as she listened to her mother's words. "Mother, I want you to be a part of our lives, but I can't stand by and watch you drive Arthur away. He deserves to be happy."

She nodded, her eyes misty. "I promise, Rosie, that I will try my best to change. I don't want to lose Arthur or you."

Rosie reached out and took her mother's hand, a glimmer of hope in her eyes. "I want to believe you, Mother. But it will take time and actions, not just words."

Taking Rosie's hand she squeezed it gently. "I understand, my dear. Actions speak louder than words, and I'm ready to prove it."

They shared a moment of understanding and forgiveness, a small but significant step toward healing their fractured relationship. Lady Edith knew that change would be challenging, but she was willing to make the effort for the sake of her family.

45

He Loves Me Not

THE DRIVE BACK to The Park House was silent. Amelia was so hurt she was fighting back tears and internally begging Arthur to drive faster. She just wanted to get back to her camper and lock the door so she could let it all out with a good cry. She stared out her window not daring to look at him. She was so disappointed in him. He had convinced her to bring the painting as a peace offering and instead that deep trust she had given him had been broken. He didn't fight for her. His silence was deafening. Once again Amelia was caught fighting for herself.

When they arrived at the driveway Amelia urged him to stop at the gate.

"What? No. I'll drive you back home." Arthur told her.

"Stop here at the gate!" She yelled at him and he braked. She couldn't get out of the car fast enough and started to stumble walking up the drive in anger and sadness.

"Amelia, get back in the car. Don't be stupid. You have a sprained ankle." He yelled at her as she walked down the road.

"Stupid?!" She turned and faced him crushed, "I was so stupid to love you."

Arthur stood there, staring at her silently. She wanted more than anything for him to run to her and hold her confessing his love for her but he didn't. Amelia refused to wait any longer, "Go home Arthur." Tears began to roll down her cheeks.

"No. Get back in the car." Arthur plead with her. He walked back to his car and sat inside. He watched the woman he loved slowly walking away from him. Car lights approached. It was Charlie.

"What in God's name are you doing Amelia. Get in the car." Charlie told her. Amelia grateful for his arrival sat in the passenger seat crying.

Charlie got out of his car and walked up to Arthur and hit his hand on his car. "You were going to make her walk on that foot? What the hell is wrong with you!"

Arthur stepped out, "No, mate. That's not what's happening."

"Get back in the car, Charlie." Amelia yelled out.

"What's wrong with you?" Charlie scolded him angrily and returned to find Amelia burying her face in her hands. Arthur drove past them and turned his car around and back up the road and away from them.

"What happened? Are you alright, Amelia?"

"No, I'm not alright."

"Did he hurt you?"

"I don't want to talk about it, Charlie. Can you take me to the camper?"

"Just tell me if he hurt you."

"He didn't hurt me." Tears streaming, "He broke my heart."

Charlie hugged her and let her cry, he let her cry until she couldn't cry anymore. He then drove her to her camper.

Wiping away the tears from her eyes she explained what happened.

"Who cares what she thinks, Amelia."

Defeated, Amelia stepped out of the car. "Arthur does."

"Amelia, he loves you, he truly does."

"Not enough. Thank you for taking me home."

She shut the camper door and waited for Charlie to drive away. When he finally did, Amelia stepped back outside into the cold to get some fresh air. She was startled by the reappearance of the white rabbit but couldn't ignore the feeling that it was a message from Kinsey. She felt a sense of purpose was over he as she followed the rabbit's lead and began to walk toward the entrance of The Park House.

As she approached the grand old mansion, she reflected on the recent events. The pain of Arthur's silence still stung, but she knew she couldn't let it consume her. Kinsey's message, whether real or a figment of her imagination, reminded her that she had a mission to fulfill.

Amelia reached the entrance of The Park House and hesitated for a moment before pushing open the heavy wooden doors. She stepped inside, the creaking of the door echoing through the empty halls. The house was dimly lit, and shadows danced along the walls, giving it an eerie atmosphere.

Amelia made a promise to herself and to Kinsey that she would not let the pain of recent events define her. She would continue to restore The Park House, not for Lady Edith or anyone else but for herself, for Kinsey's memory, and for the love she had for Arthur.

With newfound resolve, she knew that the journey ahead would be challenging, but she was ready to face it with courage and love in her heart. The shadows that had threatened to consume her were pushed back by the light of her determination and the memory of her dear friend.

46

January

IN LATE JANUARY, the Park House was a hive of activity as workers bustled about. Over the past weeks, every nook and cranny of the home had been lovingly tended to with dedication and honesty. Amelia was the key to keeping the crew content. She had earned the respect and affection of everyone she worked alongside. She took the time to get to know each person by name and ensured they felt recognized and valued for their hard work.

To Amelia, Charlie was more than just an employee; she genuinely cared for him as if he were a brother she never had. Wendy and Charlie had become like family to her, and they spent most of their time together. In fact, Amelia had even hired Charlie's brother, Peter, as her full-time assistant. Peter would chauffeur her and assist with any tasks she needed help with, and they had grown very close. Especially after Arthur had essentially disappeared from their lives.

She still deeply loved Arthur and worked hard to conceal her broken heart. She felt proud of herself as each day, she felt that she was demonstrating her talent further, upholding the integrity of the original home while infusing it with her unique creative flair and modern touches. This even included a substantial extension to the back of the house, designed as a solarium. Her ideas were all falling seamlessly into place.

Amelia's popularity on Instagram was soaring, with her account now boasting two million followers. She had become so renowned that they often had to turn away curious locals who unexpectedly visited the house. The entire town buzzed about her and the way she had engaged many local businesses to showcase their specialties.

Amelia played a crucial role by capturing people's stories, showcasing their passions in antiquities, lace making, curtain drapery, carpentry, and more. She had truly achieved something extraordinary while staying true to herself and respecting the Bonneville family's privacy and her future plans.

However, after her fallout with Arthur, she was strongly considering a tempting offer in Los Angeles though Oliver. Amelia was torn between making a new life in England and her lingering heartbreak, unsure if she could stay. Every day, she hoped for a message, a call, or even a glimpse of him from afar, but there was nothing. It was as if he had vanished.

This day seemed like any other as she entered the home. Workers were busy installing the kitchen sink and countertops. A box containing the hardware she had chosen caught her eye. She knelt down, took out one of the brass pull handles, and examined it. A smile crossed her face as she held it up against one of the nearby drawers, confirming her choice. Just as she was about to return it to the box, she heard a familiar voice at the door.

"Amelia?"

Her heart skipped a beat as Charlie suddenly appeared from another room, peering in and whispering, "Arthur's here."

Amelia swiftly concealed herself behind a doorway, acknowledging Charlie's presence with a nod. Charlie, in a hushed tone, offered, "Want me to handle him?"

Feeling embarrassed by her own actions, she shook her head, declining his offer.

"Amelia?" Arthur called out for her once more. She could sense his approach as he made his way through the house toward her. Taking a deep breath, Amelia gathered her courage and stepped out to greet him. He halted in his tracks upon seeing her, extending two cups as peace offerings. "I brought you some tea," he said.

Taken aback she stared at the paper cups in his hand and asked, "Tea?"

Charlie positioned himself behind Amelia, adopting a protective stance. "Arthur," he said, greeting him with an air of guarded suspicion. "What are you doing here?" Charlie inquired.

"Charlie, it's okay. Arthur, let's step outside," she instructed him. Arthur followed her slowly, taking in the transformed surroundings. "Wow, it's changed so much. It's really coming along," he remarked, awed by the progress of the house.

Amelia replied with a touch of dry humor, "Well, offer enough money, and people tend to work swiftly, don't they?"

Arthur found a nearby table to set the tea down and followed her outside the entryway. As they stepped outdoors Arthur reached for her hand. She recoiled in shock, yanking her hand away. She demanded an explanation, her frustration evident: "What are you doing here? You abandoned me."

"I know..." he tried to interrupt her.

"I don't understand you at all. We haven't spoken in weeks and you just show up here with...tea?" She crossed her arms and stepped away from him.

As he stood in front of her, her heart pounded in her chest, and she felt it all over again. She was still madly in love with him but hated him so much. Such horrible conflicting feelings rushed through her, she wanted to hit him. He took a step toward her and she took another step back.

"Amelia, I'm so sorry. Truly, I am. I was put into an impossible position, and I didn't know what to do. I wanted so badly to call you but every time I picked up my phone..." Arthur confessed.

"What are you talking about?" she asked.

"I did love you Amelia." He said and her face sunk hearing his words. He quickly corrected himself, "I do. I do still...love you."

Before they could continue a familiar car approached them. Peter stepped out appearing with a lunch delivery in his hands and announced, "I have lunch." Upon recognizing Arthur, he added, "Oh Lord Bonneville."

Surprised and slightly embarrassed, Arthur greeted him, saying, "Hello Peter. It's been a long time."

Amelia turned to Peter, knowing that he was aware of everything that had transpired between her and Arthur.

"Um, I'll just go find my brother," Peter decided, and he turned around and walked back outside. Coworkers nearby were taking attention to the conversation that Amelia and Arthur were having. They were drawing an audience quickly.

Amelia placed her hands on her face in exasperation and then gestured for Arthur to follow her back into the house.

"Where are we going?" Arthur asked.

"Some place where we can have some privacy," she explained through her frustration.

Arthur followed Amelia into the Park House, apprehensive about what she might say next. He reached and touched her back, "Amelia, stop."

She turned and leaned her back against the wall whispering, "What is there to say, Arthur? You love me? But you don't love me enough."

"That's not true," Arthur protested.

Charlie and Peter were in the hallway listening in. Amelia grumbled and grabbed Arthur's hand pulling him into a nearby bathroom. She closed the door behind her and collected her thoughts as he waited patiently.

"Then why? Why won't you fight for me?" Amelia demanded.

"Are you sure you want to have this conversation in the loo?"

Amelia bit her lip looking at their surroundings. She realized quickly it wasn't the best choice of room, however she folded her arms to issue a clear warning to him that he needed to reply.

"I needed some time for myself to sort things through."

"I haven't heard a single word from you."

"I've never felt this way for anyone before, and my mother told me... I had to choose," he explained.

"Choose what?" Amelia inquired.

"Between my family and you," he confessed.

Amelia was stunned, feeling as if the wind had been knocked out of her. She realized the impossible position he had been placed in. However, anger welled up in her toward him and his family. "So, you chose your family."

"I ran, actually. After that night, I haven't spoken to mother since. I've spoken to Rosie but not to my mother. I'm still angry at everything, to be quite frank, even you," he replied honestly.

"Me? What did I ever do to you?" Amelia challenged.

"No, not at you. That's not what I mean. What I meant to say is that I was angry at Kinsey because he left us all in such a mess, and you..." he hesitated.

"I'm a mess?" she questioned.

"No. Well, yes... in a way," he nervously laughed while she stood there, arms crossed in anger. "That's not what I meant to say. My God, I've never been so tongue-tied in all my life."

Taking a step forward, he approached her cautiously. She allowed him to close the gap between them.

"Amelia, I just took some time for myself to understand my true feelings. With everything that happened between us, and with the circumstances of the house and my family, I needed to know."

"Know what?" she asked, her curiosity piqued.

He took another deliberate step toward her. "If the feelings I had for you were real."

"And?" She waited as he took the final step to stand right in front of her. Gently, he unfolded her hands and held them dearly, his eyes downcast with shame.

"I do," he whispered.

Her heart raced as she felt his hands in hers. She prodded further, "Do what?" She leaned her forehead against his, their hands and fingers intertwined. "I want to hear you say it," she whispered.

"I love you, Amelia," he looked into her eyes, sincerity reflecting in his gaze.

She loved him too, but she wasn't ready to confess it just yet. She held her words tightly.

"What about your mother?" she asked.

"She'll just have to accept us." Although he spoke with conviction, a hint of fear lingered in his words. He whispered in her ear, "These past weeks have been agony. I can't live another day without you."

Just as he leaned in to kiss her, she stopped him and said, "I want to show you something."

She opened the bathroom door and she took his hand. Arthur and Amelia watched Charlie and Peter scatter down the hallway.

"Where are we going?" Arthur asked.

"I want to show you something." Amelia explained. She lead him down the hallway to his father's study.

47

Forever

AMELIA STOOD IN front of the study's doors. Arthur kept his eyes on hers. She smiled mischievously. "This is the first completed room in the Park House," she proudly shared.

She pushed the office doors open and he followed her into the room, taking in the emotions it evoked. Slowly, he walked around, admiring the work she had done, while she closed the freshly painted doors behind him. The room exuded a rich winter green, and he was struck by the beauty she had transformed it into. It was better than it had ever been.

The new wallpaper was whimsical, adorned with oak trees that mirrored the property's landscape. Rich brass sconces illuminated the empty bookcases, and his father's desk had been meticulously cleaned and returned to its original position. What truly took his breath away was the newly installed enormous stained-glass window, which had replaced the original smaller one that had been there since the house was built.

"Wow," he uttered as he approached the window, studying the artwork. It depicted The White Rabbit from Lewis Carroll's 'Alice in Wonderland,' on a grand scale. The colorful light streamed through the glass, casting a rainbow of colors throughout the library. The rabbit was adorned with Kinsey's favorite bowler hat and held Kinsey's famous lion-head cane. The White Rabbit stood leaning against the cane, clutching his gold pocket watch attached to his waistcoat, beneath a large tree with a mysterious, dark entry hole. It was a masterpiece.

"This is unbelievable, Amelia," he told her, smiling as he turned to face her.

Amelia stared into his eyes and her heart pounded in her chest. She knew what she had always know. She didn't just love him; he was the one. She was his, and he was hers. The way he gazed back at her. Her heart was beating so fast she had to look away and returned her attention to their surroundings.

"So, do you like it?" she teased, walking toward Kinsey's cane, which leaned against the large fireplace. She paused to lovingly touch the brass lion head on his cane. "Kinsey would have loved it."

Arthur approached her and placed his hand on her lower back. She felt his touch and turned to face him. "He would be very proud of what you've done," he said, touching a strand of her hair. She was nervous and blushed. Arthur paused and asked politely, "Why don't you ever show me your real hair?"

Amelia was surprised and turned red. She broke away from him and muttered, "I'm not sure if it's long enough yet." She truly felt torn about it, almost sick.

Arthur reassured her, "Amelia, you are the most beautiful woman I've ever seen."

Amelia looked back at him, feeling the depth of her love for him. He was the ending and the beginning of it all. She did something she had never felt ready to do and removed her wig, revealing a curly, beautiful mess of near shoulder-length hair. Refusing to look at him in fear, she anxiously fussed with her real hair using her hands to fix it as best she could. He walked toward her, and she felt his fingers under her chin. He gently lifted it, and her eyes welled with tears when she met his gaze. She knew she would only ever look into his eyes for the rest of her life.

"You are the most beautiful woman I've ever seen, Amelia Levingston," he repeated.

This time, those words cut deep into her soul, and she kissed him passionately. They embraced each other with fervor, moving across the library to the desk. He picked her up and placed her on it. She could feel his longing for her. However, their passionate moment was interrupted by a knock at the door. Arthur and Amelia stopped themselves to hear Charlie's voice on the other side, "Is everything alright in there?"

Amelia's legs were still wrapped around Arthur's, and they both looked at each other, laughing. Amelia called out, "Everything is good Charlie."

They continued kissing passionately, and on the other side of the door, they could hear Charlie starting to cry tears of joy. Arthur and Amelia stopped to listen, and Arthur asked, "Is he crying?"

On the other side of the door, Charlie yelled out, "I'm just so happy for you."

Arthur and Amelia could tell their passion would have to wait. They reluctantly let go of each other, collecting themselves. "It's okay, Charlie; you can come in now," Arthur said.

Charlie opened the door, wiping the tears from his eyes. "I am so happy!" He ran over to them both and gave them a huge hug. Arthur was surprised, and Amelia just held him.

"We know, Charlie," she said.

Charlie let go, composed himself, then pointed his finger at Arthur, "But if you ever, EVER, break Amelia's heart again, I will bury you on the property somewhere no one will find you. I mean it. I have a cement truck that's one phone call away."

Amelia was shocked, and Arthur pretended to take him seriously. "That's fair, mate."

Arthur extended his hand, and Charlie took it, and they shook.

"Amelia, I have good news. They just finished installing the flooring in the solarium,"

Charlie said excitedly. "You both have to see it. It's perfect."

Arthur followed Amelia and Charlie into the new solarium that Amelia had designed, he was awestruck by her creation. The space was vast and unique in every way. The glass and ironwork were impressive, and the floor was checkered with limestone. It was a sight to behold. Large iron potholders had been installed in the stone masonry above the arched entryway.

Arthur loved it. "This is fantastic.".

"It's a work of art, Amelia," Charlie added.

Amelia studied the work, examining the tiles throughout. Then she noticed the large copper sink in the corner of the room. "Oh, I see they finally installed the sink."

"Yes, and the water is working," Charlie said with a grin. "You're kidding," Amelia replied.

"Did I forget to tell you?" Charlie smiled at Arthur and joked, "The Park House is coming alive once more."

As Amelia tested the faucet, turning the copper handle and seeing the water flow, she held her scarred hand underneath. "This is perfect," she said, looking to Arthur, who watched her with admiration. All her hard work was making this dream a reality. She turned the handle and smiled thinking about Lady Edith. "She's going to love this," Amelia whispered to herself.

"Who?" Arthur asked, confused.

"Your mother, of course," Amelia explained.

Arthur was puzzled, "What are you talking about?"

"I built all of this for her because she loves to garden. I could tell it was her passion just by visiting her home. So I thought, this way, she could enjoy it year-round," Amelia said.

"But I'm confused; this is your home," Arthur pointed out.

"This was never my home," she clarified. "This is your family's home. I'm just here to put everything back together for you. It's all been taken care of. When the Park House is finished, I'm giving the keys back to your mother."

"You don't have to do this, Amelia. You can live here. Kinsey left this house for you," Arthur insisted, walking toward her and wrapping his arms around her.

She looked up at him and said, "I've taken care of everything. Well, I should say a very overpaid Mr. Field took care of everything."

Arthur seemed lost. "Wait, then what? You wouldn't go back to America?"

Charlie gasped and choked up, "You can't leave us!"

"No crying, Charlie," she warned him with her finger, and Charlie stopped.

Amelia thought for a moment. "Before today, with you here now, I was considering leaving England. I have a great job offer back in Los Angeles."

Arthur started to pull away from her, and she pulled him back. "But I've reconsidered."

Charlie exclaimed, "Oh, thank God. I was about to lose my mind."

Arthur took her hands and stared into her eyes. "Amelia, The Park House does belong to you. Kinsey made his choice."

"Why can't you see? This is your home. This is where your family and the generations before you made their memories and should continue to do so. I trust Kinsey knew I would make the right decision," she explained.

"Well, then there is only one thing we can do about this," Arthur told her.

"What would that be?" she asked.

"You shall have to come live with me," he said with a smile.

She kissed him on the lips and then whispered in his ear, "I'll think about it." She smiled and walked away.

He ran after her like a schoolboy. "You'll think about it?"

"Yes, I'll think about it," she teased. He wrapped his arms around her from behind and picked her up, carrying her.

"Well then, let's go think about it together in your camper," he said.

She laughed. "Arthur, put me down."

"Never," he said and kissed her on the lips again. In her heart, she knew she would be staying with him always.

48

Follow

LATE JUNE. LADY Edith was outside her home walking through what she had planted that spring and enjoying the new growth. Her peaceful moment was interrupted by a familiar soft voice, saying "Hello Mother."

Stunned, she turned around to find Arthur standing next to Rosie. "Arthur." she gasped.

Rosie held onto her brother's arm tightly, "Mummy, Arthur has something he needs to tell you."

Lady Edith was so happy to see her son again she couldn't care what he would say to her. She ran to him and hugged him. Arthur was shocked. Lady Edith reached her arm out to Rosie and held her tightly as well. She wiped her tears and stepped back to look at him. "I'm so sorry," she said in a half-whisper. "I've missed you so much. These months have been agony for me."

Arthur was relieved. He knew she meant it. "It was wrong of me to ask you to choose."

"It was wrong because I want you to know. I would have chosen her," he answered honestly.

"I wouldn't have blamed you. My behavior has been appalling and I'm deeply ashamed of myself," she confessed.

"Why didn't you try to talk to me?" he asked. "Months, of waiting. You are by far the most stubborn woman I have ever known."

"I know darling. But I am your mother, and I know you well. I knew when you were ready, you would come talk to me. So let's have it then."

"You have to stop pushing people away when you don't get what you want, Mother." He had practiced these words in his head many times and to finally say them felt like a burden had been lifted.

She nodded in agreement and reached out to hug him again. This time he took a step back from her and he waited for her to answer.

"I know my son. I've behaved badly. But I'm willing to make changes if you would give me a second chance."

Arthur looked over to his sister Rosie who smiled and nodded along. Arthur opened his arms to his mother and she warmly hugged him with a great sigh of relief.

Rosie joined into the family hug. "We have to all be there for one another. We're all we have."

"We will be. That's a promise." Lady Edith agreed, then kissed both her children on their cheeks.

"Now I want both of you to go get dressed. I have a surprise for you." Arthur smiled. "A surprise? Really?" She clapped with joy.

"What sort of surprise?" his mother asked.

"You'll see," he told her.

⁂

MR FIELD, AMELIA, and Charlie stood outside the Park House. It was finally finished. All that remained was the landscaping. She had long garden beds dug surrounding the house and filled with fresh soil so Lady Edith could choose what plants she wanted and enjoy the freedom of that process. Amelia had felt strongly that it wasn't her place to decide what should be outside the home.

Amelia put a hand on Charlie's shoulder and said, "Well done, Charlie."

"Well done, Amelia."

"Well done both of you and in a year no less. That's quite remarkable. I'm so impressed by the work you did here, Amelia. The remaining funds as promised will be wired to your account first thing tomorrow."

"Thank you. Mr Field, and again thank you so much for helping me arrange all these final details for The Park House."

"Well, you will be billed for that." He raised his eyebrow and they both laughed.

"You know Amelia, after looking at the work you did here perhaps you can come to my house in London and help me give my house a much-needed face lift."

"I would love that Mr Field. However, my partner Charlie and I have a full schedule for this year."

Charlie nodded in agreement and took out a business card and handed it over to him.

"White Rabbit Interior Design. Call us." He proudly winked and put his arm around Amelia. The sound of the approaching car overwhelmed both Charlie and Amelia's nerves. They were here.

"Okay this is it. I'll be waiting in my car." Charlie hugged her, "It's going to go great."

He gave her two thumbs up and ran off to his car and waited in the driver's seat.

Mr Field looked over to Amelia and said, "You're sure you want to do this, Amelia?"

"I'm sure." She smiled and he shook his head at her decision. Amelia took a deep breath in and let it out. Her nervousness grew as Arthur's car slowly approached them. She refused to show her worry and collected herself. This was the moment she had been waiting for.

49

Let There Be Peace

LADY EDITH SAT next to Arthur in the front seat with a blind fold on. Rosie sat in the back with a blind fold on as well. He parked and stepped out and opened their doors. Arthur led them both to the front of the Park House. "Where are we Arthur? Can you take this silly thing off me, please?"

"Not yet," he said as he walked them up to Amelia. "Hold out your hand, Mother."

Lady Edith held out her hand and Amelia took her hand and placed the keys to the house in them. She felt the keys and took off her handkerchief and saw Amelia and quickly realized exactly where they were. "Oh my goodness," she said.

"It's just as I remember." Rosie said in amazement. "I was so little but I remember it so well."

"It's just the way it was. How, how did you ever manage this?" Lady Edith couldn't find the words. She was overwhelmed and then looked back to Amelia confused, "I don't understand. Why are we here?"

"These keys are yours. I'm giving The Park house back to you. Thank you for letting me borrow it for a little while."

"What?!" Rosie asked confused.

Lady Edith studied Mr Field confused. "What is Mr Field doing here?"

"He's here to help me," Amelia said.

He nodded, holding the paperwork for the home in his arms and taking out a pen. "Just sign here your Ladyship, and the rest I will take care of this week." He offered the pen and paperwork to sign and her hand shook as she took the pen from him.

"What are you saying?" Lady Edith was confused and looked over at her son who was nodding and smiling, "What is she saying?"

Amelia took a step forward and looked into her eyes and warmly explained, "Lady Edith, I never was going to take this place from you. It belongs to your family. It always has."

"But, I've been so terrible." Lady Edith shamefully admitted.

"The thing is, I love your son. I loved *both* your sons, and that great love is enough for me to forgive everything between us. So please, just sign, so we can move forward to the next chapter of our lives."

"Sign here, your Ladyship," Mr Field showed her again.

"Are you absolutely sure?" she asked.

"I'm sure." Amelia looked to Arthur and smiled at him with all the love in her heart.

Lady Edith signed the document.

"Thank you, Lady Edith. We will be in touch," Mr Field said.

Amelia smiled at the three of them and walked up to Arthur and kissed him on the cheek and started walking toward Charlie who was waiting nervously in his car.

"Well wait, where are you going?" Arthur asked.

"Charlie's giving me a ride back to the village. I truly hope you like what I've done, Lady Edith." Amelia winked at Arthur then ran to Charlie's car and they quickly drove away.

Mr Field followed them out. The three of them stood surprised. Arthur hadn't anticipated Amelia leaving. But he realized she was just giving his mother some space. *As if I couldn't love Amelia any more fiercely*, he thought. Arthur turned to face his mother who stood in shock staring at the keys in her hand and back at the house.

"Did she really just leave?" Lady Edith asked.

"You seem to have that affect on people." Rosie joked.

Arthur laughed with her. "Come along Mother. It's time for you to see the house. Rosie took her mother's arm and they followed Arthur.

"This is crazy! She is just giving us back the house?" Rosie asked.

"Yes," Arthur said.

Lady Edith shook her head. "Why? Why would she do something like that? After how cruel I've been."

Arthur thought for a moment and smiled, "Because as she said, she loved our Kinsey."

He held his arm out to his mother. She took it and followed him to the door. Rosie started clapping her hands in excitement as Lady Edith opened it.

Walking inside The Park House was like walking into a mirror image of what she had held so dear those many years before. Straight off to the left as she entered, she noticed the canvas of "Son of Man" with Kinsey's hat hung on the wall next to it. Tears filled her eyes as she walked toward it, touching it.

"Look around you, Mother. Is it just as you remembered?" Arthur asked.

"It's so much more," Lady Edith whispered as she stared down the hallway. The integrity of the house was just as it was but she quickly realized Amelia had replaced nearly all of the furniture and many of the fixtures. She had left her own influence or touch on each room with such a careful eye. A splash of paint color or a unique new wallpaper.

They wandered the house slowly, taking in every detail. Amelia's love was evident everywhere. Before she entered the study, Lady Edith stopped for a moment and paused with a sad look on her face, "You know? This was the last place I ever saw your father alive." She spoke in a whisper.

"I know." Arthur took her hand and they entered the room together. She looked around the study and couldn't believe the changes Amelia had made. When she saw the huge stained glass with the White Rabbit she put her hand to the mouth and started shaking with laughter. Tears filled her eyes and she shook her head amazed as the rainbow of light filled the space all around her.

Rosie shook her head and laughed, "That's a bit odd, isn't it?"

Lady Edith's tears streamed down her face. "No. No. It's perfect."

She sat down at her late husband's desk and placed her hand on top of it, "She kept this."

"Of course. She kept everything she possibly could."

"I'm, honestly speechless."

"That's a rare moment." Rosie giggled.

Arthur held out his hand, offering it to her, "There's one more surprise."

"I'm not sure how much more I can possibly take darling."

"Trust me. You will love this." He smiled and she took his hand and followed him through the large, beautiful kitchen.

"I love the tile she chose." Rosie said.

"The wallpaper is heaven." Lady Edith stopped at the window that looked over the property. "Look at this window she added. It's wonderful." She followed him to a section of the house that was new to her. "Wait, what's this? This wasn't here."

He stopped at the door and before he opened it he said, "Amelia thought you needed this." He opened the door that lead out the into the huge solarium. Amelia had filled the solarium with beautiful antique pots and a few plants here and there. Lady Edith walked on the tile floors and looked at the beautiful light. A large potting table stood in a corner with beautiful big chairs. There was a wrought iron shelf filled with gardening books that ranged from antique to the newest releases. Lady Edith walked over to the copper sink and turned it on. She took a moment as she turned the water back off and looked back at Arthur. "You know Arthur. I could never have dreamt up something so beautiful."

"You love it don't you?" he said.

"I can't believe she did all this," Rosie said. "She truly did a magnificent job. It feels like home, but somehow it doesn't. It feels like the next chapter of this home doesn't it, Mother?"

"Rosie is right you know, Arthur. It feels like home but I'm not entirely sure it's mine."

"Well of course it is. You heard Amelia and Mr. Field made it so. She wants you to have it."

"She did the most beautiful job, Arthur." She looked around the room and then back to her son and walked up to him and put her hand on his cheek and said, "But I can't honestly see myself living here again. Rosie, could you? Someday?"

Rosie thought a moment and looked around the room, "I think I prefer London. Sorry Mum. I mean, I would come back to holiday with you. I'll always love this place. There are good memories of father here, and of Kinsey. But we've all moved on haven't we?"

Lady Edith nodded in agreement. She looked at all the unopened bags of soil Amelia had placed for her and smiled at them, then turned around and looked to Arthur.

"She's right you know. I loved this place. I love what she has done and I am in awe of her grace. But I've started a new life and I'm finally ready to move on."

Arthur got upset, "But look at what she's done. What do you plan to do? You can't honestly sell the place."

Lady Edith placed her hands on his shoulders and said, "Darling, the Park House doesn't belong to me."

"Well, of course it does. Amelia's given you back the keys."

"No darling, that's not what I mean. The Park House belongs to you. Those keys never belonged to me. You are the son and heir to this land, and this home is yours again." She handed him back the keys. He looked at them in his hand. "You can do with it whatever you like." She smiled and winked at him.

His face changed suddenly. Lady Edith continued to smile. She knew his face all too well. He had the face of a man in love. "Are you sure?" he asked.

"You have my blessing. Now go to *her* my darling boy."

He hugged his mother and then ran off with the keys. Rosie sat down on the marble bench and began to look around the room at all the work Amelia had done. Her mother sat down beside her and sighed, and Rosie put her hand on her mother's back, "You did the right thing, Mummy." Rosie laid her head on her mother's shoulder.

Lady Edith leaned her head onto hers. "I know." She then had a worried thought, "I just thought of something."

"What's that?" Rosie asked.

"Arthur drove us here."

"Yes?"

"He just drove off, didn't he?" Lady Edith sighed.

"Bollocks," Rosie said.

"You do have your phone don't you?" Lady Edith asked. "Of course you do, you always have your phone."

Rosie stood up, searching her pockets. Lady Edith's eyes became larger with worry until Rosie found her phone triumphantly, "Oh my God, I was about to lose my shit."

"Rosie!" Lady Edith scolded her.

"Sorry Mummy. But I was. Actually, I do need to take a wee. I'm off to use the loo. I'll call for a ride after." Rosie ran off into the house.

Lady Edith laughed and looked around the solarium and smiled. She felt at peace. For the first time in eleven years. She finally felt at peace.

50

Ever After

SIX YEARS HAD passed and Amelia held hands with Arthur as they walked down the wooded pathway back to their home, the Park House. It was early summer and the sun was glistening through the shade of the tall trees that swayed playfully in the wind above them. Just up ahead they were watching their beautiful four-year-old, brown-haired boy wander the path in curiosity. Amelia and Arthur were taking in the beautiful weather that day, and it felt like heavenly skies had opened up just for them. The day was as near to perfect as it could possibly be. Their son stopped after picking up a stick and turned back to look at his parents with a big smile.

"Mummy, I'm hungry!" he said.

"Okay, darling. Let's go have some lunch." Amelia smiled.

Arthur squeezed her hand and they continued walking. As they rounded the corner of the pathway the view of their home appeared. It was a beautiful sight to behold. The flowers were all blooming and they could see Lady Edith in the front pruning their roses.

"Oh, what's she doing now?" Arthur murmured.

Amelia laughed, "Your mother has been obsessing about those roses for weeks. I swear."

"Nana!" Their son had spotted her and excitedly ran toward her. Lady Edith set her sheers down and took her gardening gloves off, opening her arms wide with a smile on her face.

"Kinsey darling!" she yelled back to him. Little Kinsey ran to her loving embrace and she picked him up and squeezed him.

"Do you want to eat lunch?" he asked her very proud of himself.

"Well that would be wonderful, darling. I am absolutely famished," she told him squeezing him again and kissing him on his cheeks.

Amelia and Arthur smiled at the two of them. The roses she had pruned were beautiful, and they all leaned in to smell their sweet aroma. "These are gorgeous Edith." Amelia welcomed the scent.

"Thank you darling. I thought you would love them." Lady Edith admired all of the landscaping that she had helped to shape. "It truly is starting to look like Wonderland again isn't it?"

Amelia's stomach flipped, "What did you say?" she asked.

Lady Edith looked at Amelia and said again, "It's starting to look like Wonderland. Like the Queen's rose garden you see? When Kinsey was a little boy, well about Little Kinsey's age here, we would play outside and I would play Alice and Kinsey would play the mischievous White Rabbit and I would chase him all around the garden."

"I want to be chased Nana." Kinsey told her with a mischievous grin.

"Oh, do you now?" Then Lady Edith started chasing Kinsey around and caught him tickling him into infectious giggling.

"More Nana! More," Kinsey pleaded.

"No one loves tickles more than you." She laughed with him.

Arthur smiled and looked at Amelia. She gazed into his blue eyes, just as he said those words she had been longing to hear: "I love you, Amelia."

Amelia kissed him and said, "I love you too, Arthur."

Kinsey pointed to his Mum and Dad and said smiling, "Kisses."

Lady Edith kissed Kinsey on his cheek, "Here's a kiss for you darling."

He giggled.

Amelia asked, "Where should we have lunch then? Should I fix something here?"

He suggested, "How about the pub?"

Lady Edith, "Oh no, not that place again."

Kinsey said, "I want to see Auntie Wendy. Please Nana?"

Lady Edith caved. "How can I ever say no to you?"

"Perhaps we should call Charlie and ask if he will join us as well," Arthur suggested.

It was decided. They all walked back into the house and took off their outdoor boots.

"Now go wash up your hands, Kinsey. Take Nana with you," Arthur said.

Kinsey and Lady Edith walked hand in hand. Arthur followed them inside. "I'll just go fetch the keys then."

Amelia smiled lovingly at her family who were spreading through the house. Over to her left at the hanging canvas that had always remained just as Kinsey had wanted. She stood there staring at it thinking fondly of Kinsey. His bowler hat hung on the nail Amelia had hammered the last day of renovation. She touched it lovingly as she passed by and walked into the rest of her life.

THE END

KACIE FOOS lives in Chattanooga, Tennessee with her husband Mike, daughter Frankie, their two dogs Loki and Love, and a white rabbit named Easter. She grew up in the Pacific Northwest, in a magical little city called Spokane, Washington. At an early age she took an interest in acting, which blossomed into a career in Hollywood. She graduated from AMDA LA, but also studied film at UCLA, Shakespeare at RADA in London, and even lived in Paris, France studying French literature. While living in Hollywood, she developed a passion for writing for theater and the screen. This blossomed into a dream of writing novels, The Park House is the first of many stories to come. To learn more, visit www.kaciefoos.com.